"Now, Retief," Snart said stonily, "I can see you're a practical fellow. You know how to get things done, and when to keep the old nostrils out of something which you'll just get 'em packed full of lint. So why don't you just buzz off like a smart guy which he knows next time the sneaker may be on the other pedal extremity, hah?"

"This little installation interests me," Retief said as if Snart had not spoken, indicating a large but inconspicuously mounted lever beneath the main panel, secured open with a loop of wire and a large blob of black sealing compound.

Snart uttered a humorless chuckle. "Just test it out, chum, and maybe, just before the last brain cell vaporizes, it'll dawn on you that a Bogan go-boat's not so easy to hijack."

"A black seal means lethal category in Bogan usage," Retief mused. "That's a security classification. So what's so secret about a lever—especially one that gets vaporized as soon as any unauthorized personnel mess with it?" And he threw the big lever.

D0036647

Other Baen Books
by Keith Laumer

The Return of Retief
Retief and the Pangalactic Pageant of Pulchritude
Retief in the Ruins
Retief and the Warlords
Retief of the CDT
Retief's War
Retief: Envoy to New Worlds
Retief: Emissary to the Stars
Retief: Diplomat at Arms

Rogue Bolo
A Plague of Demons
Dinosaur Beach
The Star Treasure
Time Trap
The Ultimax Man
Earthblood (*with Rosel George Brown*)

KEITH LAUMER

IS THERE A DIPLOMAT IN THE HOUSE?

RETIEF TO THE RESCUE

BAEN BOOKS

RETIEF TO THE RESCUE

This is a work of fiction. All the characters and events portrayed in this book are fictional, and any resemblance to real people or incidents is purely coincidental.

Copyright © 1983 by Keith Laumer

All rights reserved, including the right to reproduce this book or portions thereof in any form.

A Baen Book

Baen Publishing Enterprises
260 Fifth Avenue
New York, N.Y. 10001

First Baen printing, January 1988

ISBN: 0-671-65376-8

Cover art by Craig Farley

Printed in the United States of America

Distributed by
SIMON & SCHUSTER
1230 Avenue of the Americas
New York, N.Y. 10020

THIS BOOK IS DEDICATED TO
DON McCANN,
WHO CAME TO THE RESCUE

CHAPTER ONE

A TIMEWORN AND USE-BATTERED landing craft bearing
the white and purple insignia of the Ten Planet Line
descended creakily into the dense yellow fog shrouding
the surface of the planet Furtheron. Under the rattle of
the elderly boat's turbos, a dull rumble, as of heavy
artillery far below, was almost inaudible. At the open
debarcation hatch two figures stood, one a tall, broad-
shouldered Terran, the other a squat but mightily mus-
cled native of the desert world Jaq, carefully dressed in
the soiled and ill-fitting whites of the TPL, his cranial
spines unfiled, an expression of disapproval on his leathery sense-organ cluster. He ducked back with a yelp as
a gigantic boulder, hurled upward from below and rotating lazily, passed close by the hatch before disappearing in the smog.

"Groints! Didja see that one?" he gasped in a shocked
tone. "I seen smaller mountains than that one with
snow on top of 'em," he complained. "These boys play
rougher all the time." He shifted the grips of his

1

tentacular members on the heavy grab bars by the hatch and set himself to resist the buffeting. "You better go below, Mr. Retief," he ordered curtly. "I ain't even sure *I* can hang on to my space legs or equivalent this time. Seems like they're shooting at us on purpose this trip; usually it's just the wild shots we gotta look out for."

Beside him, Jame Retief, Terran Foreign Service Officer of Class Two, Consul General of Career in the Terran Consular Service, and First Secretary of Embassy of Terra in the *Corps Diplomatique Terrestrienne*, on emergency detail to the Terran-sponsored Interplanetary Tribunal for the Curtailment of Hostilities convening at Furtheron, nodded, scanning the much-cracked and little-patched tarmac below, now visible through occasional rents in the wind-whipped fog.

"Smells like old-fashioned black powder," he commented. The captain-cum-cargo officer poked a bloodshot bloof organ past Retief's gold-braided CDT shoulder board to assess the blovial aspects of the scene below.

"Looks like yer gonna hafta change yer plans, mister," he suggested indifferently. "I heard there was some kinda armistice in the works, but from the looks o' that shrapnel flying around down there, they still got the war going full blast."

"Good thing, too," Retief assented. "Without the occasional war to stamp out, peace-making as we know it would soon become a dying art."

"Yeah," the cargo officer conceded. "I can see a guy's got to be careful about what he knocks these day. Like it usta be safe to frown on rape and vandalism and like that, but now we know it's just some guys' mode of expression of legitimate grievances and all, like it says in the handbook."

His further comments were cut off by a sudden clattering suggestive of a roller skate in a spin dryer, emanating from the baggage delivery hopper into which the faded carpetbag of Retief's lone fellow passenger had just disappeared. Its owner, a spindle-legged Groaci in modish solar topi and ankle-patch sneakers, at variance with his shabby traditional hip cloak and tarnished greaves, uttered a breathy complaint:

"To protest, Mr. Fronik-of-the-Thousand-Alibis-Endlessly-Repeated, this cavalier handling of the official luggage of a Groacian dignitary! To insist that you take steps at once to clean the malfunction, ere I venture to entrust the remainder of my personal effects to the maw of this barbaric device?"

"Take it easy, Fliss," Fronik replied wearily. "Like it says in the fine print on yer ticket, you hold Ten Planet—*and* its personnel—harmless in the event of any loss or damage of articles, and all that jazz; we had the slickest shysters in the Arm work out the wording. Tough E-pores, pal—but you can maybe pick up a new spine-file and all at the motions counter inside the terminal."

"To have no need of spine files, fellow!" Fliss objected. "But my priceless kiki-stones, my albums of early Terry porno-cubes—my Rockamorran ceremonial head bladders—all, it seems, are now pulverized in the primitive gears of your baleful apparatus." He tilted three of his five stalked eyes accusingly at the baggage conveyor.

"Primitive, nothing!" the captain demurred. "That there's a genuine Groaci copy of a Japanese version of a late-model Motorola matter transmitter, which I admit the maintenance contract is a few runs behind. Leastways you don't have to worry none, Retief," Fronik reassured the Terran. "*Your* trunk wouldn't fit the hopper anyways." He glanced up as two hulking TPL porters shuffled, grunting, into view, bowed under Retief's regulation CDT-issue trunk, junior grades, for the use of. They paused and dumped the big box heavily.

"I think maybe I sprained a ulterior metacostal or something," one of the shaggy green Hondu porters muttered, casting a baleful glance at both his chief and Retief.

"And what, George, is the immediate effect of such an injury?" Captain Fronik inquired stonily.

"Well, it occasions a abrupt disinclination to any activity which might tend to fatigue one," George quoted promptly. "Right, Chauncey?" He glanced at his colleague for confirmation.

"You bet, Georgie," was the prompt reply. "Spikking which, I feel a little pain in the metacostal area my own self." Thus reminded, he fingered a hard-to-reach spot on his side. "That means you got to carry on alone, George, bum joint or no, in case I get the same thing, too."

"Fat chance," George stated, eyeing the CDT trunk glumly, "Not broody likely I'll take and heft that thing solo, not without a dock crane to help out, anyways."

"Well, I guess that's it, Retief," Fronik said briskly. "If my boys don't wanna touch yer baggage, it looks like it stays put—and you too, which yer not likely to be getting off anyways, I guess, in the middle of a bombardment."

"On the other hand," Retief pointed out, "this not being a pleasure trip, Ambassador Pouncetrifle will expect me to report on time, shellfire or no. So run out the down ramp and I'll be saying goodbye, fellows, and keep that breathless charm, just the way you look tonight." He stepped to the trunk, grasped both handles, bent his knees, and with a surge lifted the bulky box to his shoulder; as soon as the narrow foot ramp had extruded and locked, he strolled down it into the murk at the bottom.

2

Retief eased the trunk down on the broken pavement and took a deep breath of the sulphurous local air, enjoying the sensation of being again under an open sky, even a baleful yellow one. It had been a long voyage out to the frontier world dubbed Furtheron by its earliest Terran explorers, but known as Ynnezadoog to its autochthones, a wormlike people, one of whom was at the moment looking Retief over idly, while picking its extremely un-annelidish fangs with a nine-inch dirk.

The TPL porter, who had followed Retief down to await a tip, looked around without visible approval. "By the way, Mister," he said in a tone of rebuke, "I guess you don't know us baggage smashers got a strong union. I work outa Local 97683 myself, and when the chief gets outa the lockup, he's gonna take a dim view of guys which they take it upon theirselfs to do our work." He eyed Retief's trunk sourly. Then, sidling behind it as one taking shelter, and with a glance at the bystanding local, he commented, "Reckon this here feller is one o' them Furtheronians, which I hear they got no use for foreigners."

"Too right, Jack," the alien assured Retief, undulating his elongated torso, which seemed to extend back for a surprising distance before being lost to sight in the smog. "You must be one o' them Terry troublemakers I hear are tryna get us Crawlies to stop shooting back at the lousy Creepies, which they got a light-sensitive pore on our territory. What's wrong, pal, not enough trouble back home, you gotta come looking for it out her in the sticks?"

"Something like that," Retief agreed. "It's called diplomacy."

"Yeah," the local grunted. "Well, if anybody asks you

did you go through Immigration and Customs, tell 'em Inspector Lum Glook give ya the nod."

"Oh, Retief," a reedy voice cried through the fog. "There you are; I see Mr. Glook has you well in hand." An undersized Terran with a pale, narrow face under floppy CDT regulation foul-weather headgear emerged into view and hurried up to clasp Retief's hand warmly.

"Actually, I *am* glad to see you, Retief," the new-comer said, a bit out of breath. "Things are terrible here. Sorry to greet you alone, but five minutes ago, Chairman Ambassador Pouncetrifle finally left with the rest of the staff; said you'd never be able to debark in the midst of this smog, not to mention the medium-heavy bombardment. But I just thought I'd scout about a bit, just in case, and here you are! I have an Embassy car and driver."

Retief expressed his appreciation of his old colleague's confidence, and they ducked as something passed over-head with a shrill whistling sound.

"Where'd he go?" Retief asked, noting the abrupt absence of the local inspector.

"Oh, don't bother with bribing Glook," Magnan said in a low tone as the local reappeared from the murk, muttering. "He's on annual retainer," Magnan explained.

"Yeah, but—" Glook and the Hondu porter said as one. Retief placed a worn hundred-cee coin in each proffered palm. Glook pocketed his with a deft motion, but the porter eyed his coin dolefully. "Geeze, a lousy hunnert cees—" he began, ducking too late as Glook plucked the brass disc from his hand with a limber tentacle and whicked it away.

"You and me could get along, chum," Glook commented to Retief. "Maybe you ain't like the rest of them Terry cheapskates. Ta." He rippled again and was gone in the haze.

"What impudence!" Magnan commented as soon as Glook was out of earshot. "And to think that after we of

ITCH have come all this way to assist these barbarians in their aspirations to the halcyon joys of peace, they show us no more consideration than one would so many nosy parkers." He shied each time a large rock impacted nearby, ignoring those smaller than baseballs.

"What's the war all about?" Retief asked.

"Well, as to that," Magnan temporized, "it isn't exactly clear; that is, all we've been able to determine so far is that the Hither Furtheronians lay claim to the territory of the Nether Furtheronians, which they insist comprises the interior of the planet, it being hollow, they say—and the Nether Furtheronians appear to covet the surface, now occupied by the Hither Furtheronians."

"Sounds complicated," Retief commented. "Is the planet really hollow?"

"Of course not, Retief. That's merely a silly superstition the Furtheronians use as an excuse for never coming to grips with their elusive enemy and thus ending this fratricidal conflict. Clearly the idea of a hollow planet, Pellucidar-style, is geological nonsense."

"Yeah," George still standing hopefully by, put in, "but the word below decks is these lousy Creepies and Crawlies *like* to shoot at each other, which I guess it's about the only fun they get."

"Mind your tongue, fellow!" Magnan rebuked the union member sharply. "The use of racial epithets is not only déclassé in the extreme but is the object of a special Corps program aimed at its suppression."

"Chauncey says it too," George muttered defensively. "Well, hang loose, gents; I still got that little five-eyed sapsucker to contend with." He retired up the gangplank, still muttering.

3

Assuming an expression (r-762-d) appropriate to one about to confide inside dope to a colleague, Magnan lowered his voice and edged closer to Retief.

"We're faced with a grave situation here on Furtheron, Retief," he said. "After a full week in residence—you're the last of the Terran delegation to arrive—the Ambassador has yet to manage an appointment with His Excellency the Foreign Minister to present his credentials—either as Chief of the Terran Mission or as Chairman of the Tribunal. This, as you see, leaves us in a curious position, diplomatic immunitywise—" He broke off with a yelp as a low-flying aircraft of primitive design loomed from the fog, its machine guns twinkling, hosing a stream of tracers about the two diplomats. The noisy craft waggled its scarlet-painted wings and banked away, to be lost in the fog.

"What cheek!" Magnan sniffed as the buzz of the aircraft's engine faded.

"Nobody's diplomatically immune to being strafed, or mashed by a cannon ball," Retief commented, "so don't feel too bad about our lack of documentation. The fanciest Exequatur wouldn't help now. Let's get under cover."

"By the way," Magnan said, "these antique pursuit craft have been imported just recently under a loophole in the Arms Covenant that permits museum exhibits."

As they moved off toward the dim glow of the lights of the terminal building, another missile crashed down nearby, showering them with stinging chips. Retief dug a sliver from the side of his neck and examined it thoughtfully.

"How long has this war been underway, Mr. Magnan?" he inquired.

"It was apparently in full course at the time of the

initial survey, some ten years ago," Magnan replied glumly.

"Who's winning?" Retief asked.

"Oh, you mean the Good Guys or the Bad Guys—in this case the Crawlies and the Creepies respectively, our official sympathies lying with the former, formally rejoicing in the sobriquet 'Hither Furtheronians.' The Nether Furtheronians, it appears, are the aggressors, and as such deserve to be pacified in the most vigorous fashion."

"In that case, why haven't we called in a detachment of Peace Enforcers?" Retief pursued the point.

"Alas, our Groacian colleague, Ambassador Nith, pulls considerable weight on the Tribunal, and he's dead set against it."

"No clues to what started the fighting?" Retief asked.

"It's a traditional mutual antipathy, it seems," Magnan replied in a tone of disapproval. "Each side claims the other's real estate. Rather odd—but then so is everything else on this benighted planet. Do you know," he went on indignantly, "the populace is kept in complete ignorance of the *casus belli*, the plan of campaign, and even the specific war aims—but then they're no more ill-informed than the Ministry of War itself, or so it appears from the brief interview which Colonel Otherday wangled yesterday with a Third Assistant Deputy War Minister. Small wonder there appears to be minimal progress in the suppression of hostilities."

4

As they reached the covered walk leading into the passenger lounge, it collapsed under the impact of a slab of concrete dislodged from above. Skirting the debris, they entered through a gaping hole blasted in the wall by an earlier hit.

"No enemy troops in sight," Retief commented, scanning the cavernous lounge, unfurnished and war-torn, where only a feeble glare panel over a lunch-information-ticket counter suggested the presence of life. "It's strange these Nether Furtheronians don't follow up all this artillery preparation; they seem to have driven our side from the field completely."

"Oh, the Crawlie troops never come out in the bombardment, and we *never* see any enemy troops," Magnan supplied. "The Creepies are much too cagy for that. And anyway, since the bombardment never lets up, if they sent troops in now, they'd be shelling their own forces."

"Has it occurred to you, Mr. Magnan," Retief asked as they took stools at the bar, "that their artillery is remarkably primitive?" At that moment a sizable missile crashed through the roof to bury itself in the scarred and littered floor.

Resuming the stool from which he had leaped at the impact, Magnan commented: "Nonetheless, it appears quite sufficiently effective."

"All they have, it seems," Retief went on, "is mortars—though in a remarkable range of calibers, I concede—firing stone cannon balls."

"We should be grateful for small mercies," Magnan sniffed, "rather than questioning them. Why, if that one"—he eyed the boulder half-buried among the tiles a few yards distant—"had been armed with even an old-fashioned HE warhead, we'd have been atomized."

"Still, with modern heavy weapons available from any one of a thousand enterprising munitions peddlers in this end of the Arm, you'd think they'd have been signed up for a few batteries of annihilator cannon before now."

"Possibly," Magnan suggested, "even the Nether Furtheronians, barbaric though they are, stop short at annihilating their own planet."

"It ain't that, stranger," put in a fanged head which had abruptly risen on a long neck from behind the counter. "It's just we already got a lot o' boulders and stuff laying around for free, so why not get some use out of 'em?" The intruder yawned, affording the Terrans a glimpse of an impressive depth of scarlet-lined and needle-toothed maw. His mop of coiling pink head tendrils was only partly confined under a greasy white toque.

"Anyways," he went on, "us Creepies are expecting a off-planet aid deal any day now; see, we got a like ancestral tradition for first-class haggling. We're playing off the Bogans against the Fustians, and the Hoogans against the Slunchans, and all. We'll whittle 'em down to size. Then you'll see some first-class action around here, insteada all this gravel flying around." The Nether Furtheronian flicked out the yard-long crimson rope that was its tongue, and whisked in a small, low-flying lifeform. Magnan watched in fascination as the peristaltic ripple passed down the long neck and out of sight.

"By the way, Thull Dud is the handle," the native volunteered, and extended a flat, calloused three-fingered hand at the end of a remarkably long and flexible arm. Magnan grasped the member gingerly, twitched and dropped it.

"I'm Magnan, First Secretary of Embassy of Terra, detailed as Recording Secretary to ITCH," he said tonelessly. "Delighted to know you, Mr. Dud. This is my colleague, Mr. Retief."

"Sure, just call me Thull. All you Terries look alike, so don't get upset if I don't get the handles right every time. I don't stock no Terry chow, but what about a nice plate of garg whilst you're here?" Without awaiting assent, the local deftly dealt out two square plates with chipped corners, each heaped with a glutinous grayish-brown mass. Magnan neatly segued his involuntary shud-

der of disgust into a delighted quiver and looked about
brightly, as if for eating utensils, while the counterman
moved on to Retief.

"It's admirable, Mr. Dud," Magnan chirped, "that
you've stayed on at your post in spite of the bombardment."

"Naw, I got a job to do, Mister Uh. No sweat.
Anyways, the counter here was put in a null spot on
purpose, so we're OK as long as we stay put."

"I'm surprised the entire site isn't covered yards
deep in spent missiles," Magnan commented. "If, as
I'm told, this barrage has been continuous for some
years, one would think—"

"Yeah," Dud cut in, "but there's like holes in the
ground and all them rocks keeps falling in so she stays
pretty clear. The ground kind of slopes down toward
the holes—'craters,' I hear they're called by you
Terries—so after a while the rocks all roll in." Having
clarified this point, Dud poised his ladle over Retief's
plate.

"None for me, thanks," Retief said. "I ate last year."

"Don't blame you, pal," Thull said philosophically.
"Just between us, I think maybe the garg worms held
this batch in their breakdown pouches a little *too* long—
and then it maybe went the wrong way. Some o' these
here like gowermetts and all, they like their garg ripe,
but I'll stick with the fresh stuff, you know, when it's
still got some undigested narf-bug heads showing. Less
bowkay, maybe, but a more interesting texture, you
might say. How about some fancy imported berp-nuts
instead?"

"Garg," Magnan said, poking at his plate with the
single-pronged fork Thull had provided. "I just remembered, I'm due at the ITCH banquet tonight, right after
the dedication, so I'd best not spoil my appetite."

"Too right, Jack," Thull agreed. "They say a plate of

real ripe garg can spoil it permanent if you're not used to it."

"By the way," Magnan said brightly, "wasn't that a slip of the tongue just now, when you referred to yourself as a 'Creepy'? The Creepies are the enemy, I believe. That is to say, the Nether Furtheronians are the faction we hope soon to pacify."

"Nope, no slip," Thull rebutted promptly. "I'm a spy. Don't let on I told you."

"You mean to stand, or sit, or lie—"

"'Lay here,' you mean, Mr. Magnan," the intelligence operative supplied. "Did I get the handle right? Sure I do. Maybe you noticed us Furtheronians keep our troops out o' sight. But we do our spying in public— get to see a lot more that way."

"Sensible," Magnan conceded. "And inasmuch as you've been so candid, perhaps you'd care to confide further—since we're neutral peacemakers and impartial non-combatants. First, where is the main Creepy attack to be made, and, most urgently, when?"

"Nope," Thull cut him off. "I don't spy on headquarters, you know; I just scout the Crawlies. And the only plan they got is to keep their heads down until it's their turn to do the shooting."

"How is it we see no troops in the field?" Magnan demanded. "A soldierless war—ridiculous!"

"Oh, us Creepies got plenty troops," the spy reassured the diplomat, "only, like I said, we got this quaint native custom, like, where the armored battalions do the sneaky number, whilst us spies work right out in the open, pretty near. But I better get back to work, fellows, before old Lum pokes his snoot in."

"Old Lum has already poked his snoot in," Glook's bass voice spoke up near at hand. Then his fanged visage appeared, dangling from a beam far above, his eye stems deployed, his neck attenuated to a mere rope by the long stretch. "Say, that's nice aged garg you boys are having," the inspector exclaimed. "Dud, you been holding out on me—said you didn't have any of the good stuff, only that green garg not a week in the pouch. Better gimme a plate o' that."

"Certainly, Inspector," the attendant agreed, and deftly switched Magnan's plate for a clean one.

Glook's face shrank upward as he retracted his neck, to reappear a moment later draped over the adjacent stool. He at once dipped three fingers into his garg and thrust it deep into his maw; after a momentary pause, he gulped. Then, with a glance at Magnan's bare plate, he said, "I got to hand it to you, Master Mignan; for a foreigner you put away a mean plate o' garg—and I mean RIPE. *I* even had a little trouble getting it past the old tonsils." He gazed at the slightly built diplomat admiringly. "Any guy that can get with the old spirit o' the tribal traditions that way, just to cement relations, is OK." He returned without enthusiasm to his lunch.

"If I didn't know better," he commented, "I'd be wondering if I was supposed to eat this, or if I already did. Why couldn't our ancestors of come up with something like, say, hot dogs, or *Chateaubriand avec pommes frites*, or *ka-swe*, or worm-and-olive salad, or some o' them other swell eats you Terries got?"

He gave Magnan a confidential look. "Frankly, your Terry chow is one item I got to hand it to you Terries for: them jellybeans you stock at the commissary are the real stuff."

"Why, how would *you* know, Mr. Glook?" Magnan inquired in a shocked tone. "After all, commissary stores are afforded duty-free entry on the basis that they're exclusive for the use of Mission personnel."

"Well, you know, Ben, them boys works the stockroom don't get paid a whole lot—so they got a like right to conduct a little like cladestine traffic in exotic items, which even that way they barely hack it, what with inflation and all."

"Disgraceful!" Magnan sniffed. "Why, as GSO, I personally selected those locals, gave them top wages, trained them—"

"That's where you blew it, Ben. Never trust a Crawlie farther than you can stretch him, as the saying used to go before you Terries got on us about racial bias, and all."

"But—*you're* a Crawlie!" Magnan protested. "How can you castigate your own people in that fashion?"

"Easy," Glook reassured him. "It's what you call common knowledge."

"That's *quite* beside the point," Magnan said coldly. "The most resented racial jibes are those based on the truth."

"So how's the peacemaking coming along?" Glook dodged aside as fragments from a close impact whistled past. "Or maybe I shun't ask."

"More o' that fine aged garg, Inspector?" Thull Dud proposed, his brimming ladle poised over the clean-scraped plate, Glook having deftly dumped his first helping in the cuspidor while the chef's back was turned. He declined seconds. The ladle shifted to drip glutinously on Magnan's plate.

"More for you, sir?" Thull inquired as he heaped Magnan's plate with what looked like a mixture of used motor oil and tapioca. Instead of replying, Magnan beckoned the counterman to draw close for a whispered conference.

"You seem on curiously friendly terms with a member of the enemy camp," he stated suspiciously. Thull nodded matter-of-factly.

"Old Lum ain't a bad fellow," he replied loudly, at which the inspector leaned closer.

". . . not that he ain't above tryna eavesdrop—and him without a license, too." With this, Thull turned away and began polishing an unglazed clay cup.

"As for you, Inspector"—Magnan turned his attention to the official now idly bobbing his head in time to a wheezy Furtheronian version of the Cow-Cow Boogie emanating from the jukebox beside him, the discordant jangles and twangs barely audible above the rattle of gravel on the roof—"I'm surprised at you: an official of your government fraternizing so blatantly with an enemy national!"

"Why, Dudsy and me are old pals," Glook replied. "You wun't expect me to snub him just because he happens to be on the other side o' the fence, I hope. Us Crawlies ain't like that."

"But his country is at war with yours," Magnan insisted. "They're bombarding you at the moment!"

"Dudsy ain't doing no bombing," Glook protested. "He's layin' right over there behind the counter, loyally featherbedding, like always."

"Still," Magnan persisted, "he *does* represent a hostile power. I should think you'd clap him in irons at once, as a precautionary measure."

"Then we'd hafta be supplying *him* with his daily garg 'steada the other way around."

"But at any moment he might turn on you. Why, he admits he's a spy."

"Sure, he's patriotic—a trait which ya gotta admire a fellow for it, right? He's just doing his job, like me—and you too, I guess, even if I never did quite figger out what your angle is."

"We diplomats have no 'angle,' " Magnan replied coldly. "We are here in the interest of peace, selflessly striving to end the horrors of war for all Furtheronians, Hither and Nether alike."

"Cool," Glook conceded. "So why are ya tryna stir up bad vascular fluid between me and a boyhood chum?"

"Crudely put," Magnan rebuked the laybeing. "These matters are perhaps too subtle for the unprepared mind."

"Well said, Ben." A breathy voice came from behind the Terran. "To be like old times, once again to be associated with you—but not too much like them, to hope,"

Magnan whirled. "Why, if it isn't Fliss, Cultural Attaché at Adobe when last we met, as I recall," he caroled, rising to extend a hand. "Welcome to Furtheron, and pay no heed to these boulders crashing through the roof—merely a quaint native custom, it appears."

"To have risen in the ranks since last we met, Ben; to now rejoice in the title of Chief Lackey in Subordination to His Excellency Nith, Ambassador Extraordinary and Minister Plenipotentiary of the Groacian Autonomy to this benighted plague spot."

"Impressive, Fliss," Magnan said, giving an extra squeeze to the cold, flabby manipulative member of the alien diplomat. "But are you *quite* sure it's a promotion? By the way, I myself am now Deputy Counselor for Trivial Affairs."

Fliss executed a dizzying interweaving of his five stalked eyes, which Magnan at once recognized as the Groaci equivalent of a 402-d (Emphatic Reassurance, with Only a Hint of Rebuke at the Veiled Impertinence of the Question). "A coveted post indeed, Ben," the Groaci confirmed, "and one which will place me in a position of close interpersonal relationship to His Excellency."

Magnan shuddered. "You might at least have accorded me your 'a,' Fliss," he said in mild rebuke. "After all, the only difference is you leave out the negative nuance—and how was *I* to know?"

"No matter." Fliss dismissed the matter, placing his worn flight bag on the adjacent stool. "More to the point," he went on, "just what is the situation we of ITCH are confronting here on this dismal world?"

"Why, as to that," Magnan replied, "it appears that we must deal not with a brutal invasion from a neighboring planet, but with a fratricidal civil war between two factions of the local dominant species, one of which joyously inhabits the pristine surface of Furtheron, while the aggressor skulks below, in the hollow interior, a gloomy place, no doubt, thus explaining their vicious nature (no offense, Mr. Dud) as well as their elusiveness. In fact, it is precisely this geographic distribution which appears to the the bone of contention in the present dispute. Each side claims the other's territory, maintaining that it alone is their ancestral homeland, from which they've been driven by the iniquitous enemy. The tides of battle never progress, it seems, but merely surge back and forth. Thus we not only find ourselves perpetually in the midst of an invasion, but are forced to maintain great ideological flexibility, as to the focus of our neutrality, in consonance with the momentary reality of geopolitik. To date no actual enemy forces have so much as been seen, making it awkward to negotiate therewith."

" 'Enemy,' Ben?" Fliss queried. "We of the Committee haven't taken sides, one hopes."

"It's just that they keep shelling the Embassy of Terra, along with the port here, and the Groacian Mission as well, I presume, day and night. It seems just the teentsiest bit inimical; I suppose after a time one tends to lose one's objectivity."

"A tendency to which one must never yield, Ben," the Groaci said severely. "Sweet impartiality must be our unfailing policy." He ducked as fragments of a missile whistled above his head. "Of course," he amended, "if one were to determine the precise identity of the miscreants who hurl large stones at newly arrived diplomats, a trifle of severity might perhaps not be amiss." In his start of alarm, Fliss had inadvertently nudged his grubby carpetbag, which fell from the stool with a complicated metallic clatter, its' clasps falling open. Dozens of tiny brassy cylinders rolled from its interior and spread across the chipped floor. Hastily Fliss gathered them up, all but a few half hidden in a shallow cavity behind Retief's stool post. Retief stopped quickly to gather those, and after a close scrutiny of one he dropped half a dozen in his pocket and handed the others to Fliss, who accepted them grumpily. Fliss snapped the container shut and replaced it beside him. "My pills,," he explained tersely.

"I'm glad to see you managed to extricate your hand baggage from Fronik's infernal machine," Retief said.

"By no means, Retief!" Fliss objected. "The confounded apparatus broke down completely at last, and expelled this lone item. *All* of my hold baggage, plus my *entire* wardrobe, is gone. To weep for treasured possessions, never more to be seen." He wiped a grain of lachrymal exudation from one eye stem.

"By the way, Ben, just what is the essential ethnic difference between the two factions?" the Groaci inquired casually.

"Oh, the usual," Magnan replied. "The Hither Furtheronians are natural democrats, the sodium chloride of the planet, nature's noblemen, while their iniquitous opponents are moral lepers, conscienceless rogues, enemies of peace and order, aggressors, miscreants of the worst stripe."

"Shocking, Ben," Fliss commented. "Still, we must retain our utter impartiality."

"Of course," Magnan agreed. "Why, candidly, I've always had a sneaking admiration for a throughgoing scoundrel. In fact, some of my best friends—"

"Enough, Ben." Fliss cut off Magnan's flow of flexible ideology. "I must be off, to report in. I'll see you later on when ITCH convenes."

"Retief!" Magnan gasped suddenly. "There's a special staff meeting scheduled before the dedication. We too must away at once!"

"To see that one thing at least is clear," Fliss commented as both he and the Terrans descended from their stools, while yet another glassy boulder impacted nearby. "These confounded folk have no idea of the proper way to conduct a war. Good evening." Fliss set off jauntily as Retief and Magnan went in search of their waiting car, which they found at last, parked in an obscure alley where Fred, the driver, had hastily camouflaged it with rubble. It was the work of a moment to excavate it, and after a brief drive through the least obstructed streets, the staff car drew up before the shell-pocked façade of the Embassy of Terra. Choosing a moment between impacts, the diplomats gained the relative security of its cavernous foyer, at once took the lift to the third floor, and hurried to the conference room in the chancery wing.

5

Magnan pushed open the heavy oak door and ducked as a rain of plaster chips clattered down from the ceiling. The chandelier, a baroque construction of Yalcan glasswork, danced on its chain and fell with a crash on the center of the polished greenwood table. Across the room, drapes fluttered at the glassless windows which rattled in their frames in resonance with the distant *crump-crump!* of gunfire.

"Ben, you're ten minutes late for the staff meeting!" a voice said from somewhere. Magnan stooped, glanced under the table. A huddle of eyes stared back.

"Ah, there you are, Mr. Ambassador, gentlemen," Magnan greeted the Chief of Mission and his staff. "Sorry to be tardy, but there was a brisk little aerial dogfight going on just over the Zoological Gardens. The Crawlies are putting up a hot resistance to the Creepies' thrust this time."

"And you perhaps paused to hazard a wager on the outcome?" Ambassador Pouncetrifle snapped. "Your mission, sir, after meeting that fellow Whats-His-Name, was to deliver a sharp rebuke to the Foreign Office regarding the latest violations of the Embassy! What have you to report?"

"The Foreign Minister sends his regrets," Magnan improvised. "He was just packing up to leave. It looks as though the Creepies will be reoccupying the capital about breakfast time.

"What, again? Just as I'm on the verge of reestablishing a working rapport with His Hither Excellency?"

"Oh, but you have a dandy rapport with His Nether Excellency, too." The voice of Counselor of Embassy Clutchplate sounded from a position well to the rear. "Remember, you were just about to get him to agree to a limited provisional preliminary symbolic partial cease-fire covering left-handed bloop guns of calibre .25 and below!"

"I'm well aware of the status of the peace talks!" Pouncetrifle cut him off. The peppery diplomat emerged, rose, and dusted the knees of his pink-and-green-striped satin knee breeches, regulation early afternoon semi-informal dress for top-three-graders of the *Corps Diplomatique Terrestrienne* on duty on prenuclear worlds.

"Well, I suppose we must make the best of it." He glared at his advisers as they followed his lead, ranging themselves at the table around the shattered remains of the chandelier as the chatter and rumble of gunfire continued outside. "Gentlemen, in the few weeks since this Mission was accredited here on Furtheron, we've seen the capital change hands four times. Under such conditions the shrewdest diplomacy is powerless to bring to fruition our schemes for the pacification of the system. Nevertheless, today's despatch from Sector indicates that unless observable results are produced prior to the upcoming visit of the Inspectors, a drastic reassessment of personnel requirements may result—and I'm sure you know what that means!"

"Ummm. We'll all be fired." Magnan brightened at the thought. "Unless, perhaps, Your Excellency points out that after all, as Chief of Mission, you're the one"—he paused as he noted the expression of the Pouncetrifle features—"the one who suffered most," he finished weakly.

"I need not remind you," the Ambassador bored on relentlessly, "that alibis fail to impress visiting inspection teams! Results, gentlemen! Those are what count! Now, what proposals do I hear for new approaches to the problem of ending this fratricidal war which even now—"

The ambassadorial tones were drowned by the deep-throated snarl of a rapidly approaching internal combustion engine. Glancing out the window, Retief saw a bright green twin-winged aircraft coming in from the northwest at treetop level, outlined against the disk of the planet's nearest moon. The late-afternoon sun glinted from the craft's polished wooden propeller blades; its cowl-mounted machine guns sparkled as they hosed a stream of tracers into the street below.

"Take cover!" the Military Attaché barked, diving for a favorable position under the table. At the last instant, the fighter plane banked sharply up, executed a flashy slow roll, and shot out of sight behind the chipped tile dome of the Temple of Erudition across the park.

"This is too much!" Pouncetrifle shrilled from his position behind the bullet-riddled filing cabinet. "That was an open, overt attack on the chancery! A flagrant violation of interplanetary law!"

"Actually, I think he was after a Creepy armored column in the park," Retief said. "All we got was the overkill."

"Inasmuch as you happen to be standing up, Mr. Retief," Pouncetrifle called, "I'll thank you to put a call through on the hotline to Lib Glip at the Secretariat.

I'll lodge a protest that will make his cranial cilia stand on end!"

Retief pressed buttons on the compact CDT-issue field rig which had been installed to link the Embassy to the local governmental offices. Behind him, Ambassador Pouncetrifle addressed the staff:

"Now, while it's necessary to impress on the Premier the impropriety of shooting up a Terran mission, we must hold some measure of ire in reserve for future atrocities. I think we'll play the scene using a modified Formula Nine image: Kindly Indulgence tinged with Latent Firmness, which may at any moment crystallize into Reluctant Admonition, with appropriate overtones of Gracious Condescension."

"How would you feel about a dash of Potential Impatience, with maybe just a touch of Appropriate Reprisals?"the Military Attaché suggested.

"We don't want to antagonize anyone with premature saber rattling, Colonel." Pouncetrifle frowned a rebuke.

"Hmmm." Magnan pulled at his lower lip. "A masterful approach as you've outlined it, Mr. Ambassador. But I wonder if we mightn't add just the tiniest hint of Agonizing Reappraisal?"

Pouncetrifle nodded approvingly. "Yes—an element of the traditional might be quite in order if we don't overdo it, thereby eliciting obstructionist backlash."

A moment later the screen before Retief cleared to reveal a figure lolling in an easy chair, carelessly draped in an irridescent Bromo Seltzer-blue tunic, open over an exposed framework of leather-looking ribs from which gaily bejeweled medals dangled in rows. From the gold-braided collar, around which a leather strap was slung supporting a pair of heavy Japanese-made binoculars, the stout neck extended, adorned along its length with varicolored patches representing auditory, olfactory, and radar organs, as well as a number of other senses the nature of which was still unclear to Terran physiologists. At the tip of the stem, a trio of heavy-lidded eyes stared piercingly at the diplomats. The pale-purple hair was cropped in a severe military cut.

"Creepies in the Premier's office!" someone muttered.

"General Barf!" Pouncetrifle exclaimed. "But I was calling the Premier! How—what—"

"Evening, Ajax," the general said briskly. "I made it a point to seize the Secretariat first, this trip." He brought his vocalizing organ up on the end of its tentacle to place it near the audio pickup. "I've been meaning to give you a ring, but I'll be damned if I could remember how to operate this thing."

"General," Pouncetrifle cut in sharply. "I've grown accustomed to a certain amount of glass breakage during these, ah, readjustment periods, but—"

"I warned you against flimsy construction," the general countered. "And I assure you, I'm always careful to keep that sort of thing to a minimum. After all, there's no telling who'll be using the facilities next, eh?"

"—but this is an entirely new category of outrage!" Pouncetrifle bored on. "I've just been bombed and strafed by one of your aircraft! The scoundrel practically flew into the room! It's a miracle I survived!"

"Now, Ajax, you know there are no such things as miracles." The Nether Furtheronian officer chuckled easily. "No doubt there's a perfectly natural explanation of your survival, even if it does seem a bit unreasonable at first glance."

"This is no time to haggle over metaphysics!" Pouncetrifle shook a finger at the screen. "I demand an immediate apology, plus assurances that nothing of the sort will occur again until after my transfer!"

"Sorry, Ajax," the general said calmly. "I'm afraid I can't guarantee that a few wild rounds won't be coming your way during the course of the night. This isn't a mere commando operation this time; now that I've secured

my beachhead, I'm ready to launch my full-scale Spring
Offensive for the recovery of our glorious homeland.
Jump-off will be approximately eight hours from now;
so if you'd care to synchronize chronometers—"

"An all-out offensive? Aimed at this area?"

"You have a fantastically quick grasp of tactics," Barf
said admiringly. "I intend to occupy the entire North-
Central Massif first, after which I'll roll up the Crawlie
Divisions like carpets, in all directions!"

"But—my chancery is situated squarely in the center
of the capital! You'll be carrying your assault directly
across the Embassy grounds!"

"Well, Ajax, I seem to recall it was you who selected
the site of your quarters—"

"I asked for neutral ground!" Pouncetrifle shrilled.
"Now it appears I was assigned the most fought-over
patch on the planet!"

"What could be more neutral than no man's land?"
General Barf inquired in a reasonable tone.

"Gracious," Magnan whispered to Retief, "Barf sounds
as though he may be harboring some devious motiva-
tion behind that open countenance."

"Maybe he has a few techniques of his own," Retief
suggested. "This might be his version of the Number
Twenty-three Leashed Power gambit, with a side order
of Imminent Spontaneous Rioting."

"Heavens, do you suppose . . . ? But he hasn't had
time to learn the finer nuances; he's only been in the
business for a matter of weeks."

"Perhaps it's just a natural aptitude for diplomacy," a
Second Secretary put in. "Not to be confused with
criminal insanity, of course."

"That's possible; I've observed the intuitive fashion in
which he distinguishes the bonded whiskey at cocktail
parties."

". . . immediate cessation of hostilities!" the Ambassador was declaring. "Now, I have a new formula, based

on the battle lines of the tenth day of the third week of the Moon of Limitless Imbibing, as modified by the truce team's proposals of the second week of the Moon of Ceaseless Complaining, updated in accordance with Corps Portocol Number 746358-b, as amended—"

"That's thoughtful of you, Ajax." Barf held up a tactile member in a restraining gesture. "But as it happens, inasmuch as this will be the final campaign of the War for Liberation of the Homeland, further peace making efforts become nugatory."

"I seem to recall reading in the files of similar predictions at the time of the Fall Campaign, the Prewinter offensive, the Winter Counteroffensive, the Postwinter Anschluss, and the Prespring Push," Pouncetrifle retorted. "Why don't you reconsider, General, before incurring a new crop of needless casualties?"

"Hardly needless, Ajax; I need a few casualties to sharpen up discipline. And in any case, this time things will be different. I'm using a new technique of saturation leaflet bombing followed by intensive victory parades, guaranteed to crumble all resistance. If you'll just sit tight—"

"Sit tight, and have the building blown down about my ears?" Pouncetrifle cut in. "I'm leaving for the provinces at once— "

"I think that would be unwise, Ajax, with conditions so unsettled. Better stay where you are. In fact you may consider that an order, under the provisions of martial law. If this seems a trifle harsh, remember, it's all in a good cause. And now I have to be moving along, Hector. I have a new custom-build VIP-model armored car with air and music that I'm dying to test drive. Ta-ta." The screen blanked abruptly.

"Nope," someone muttered. "They don't stand on end—his cranial cilia, I mean."

"This is fantastic!" the Ambassador stared around at his staff for any insubordinate disagreement with his assessment of the situation. "In the past," he grated, "the opposing armies have at least made a pretense of respecting diplomatic privilege; now they're openly proposing to make us the center of a massive combined land, sea, and air strike!"

"Don't forget subterranean," Colonel Otherday put in. "Confounded blighters live underground, you know."

"We'll have to contact Lib Glip at once," the Political Officer said urgently. "Perhaps we can convince him that the capital should be declared an open city!"

"Sound notion, Oscar," the Ambassador agreed. He mopped at his forehead with a large monogrammed tissue, and handed a slip of paper to Retief. "Here's the emergency number for the Government-in-Exile," he said. "Keep trying until you reach him."

Half a minute later the circular visage of the Crawlie Foreign Minister appeared on the screen, against a background of the broken glass of passing shopfronts seen through a car window. Two bright black eyes peered through a tangle of thick tendrils not unlike a tangerine-dyed oil mop capped by a leather Lindy cap with green-tinted goggles.

"Hi, fellows," the Futheronian chief greeted the Terrans airily. "Sorry to break our lunch date, Pouncetrifle, but you know how foreign affairs are: 'Here today and gone to dinner,' as the saying goes, I think. But never mind that. What I really called you about was—"

"It was I who called *you!*" the Ambassador broke in. "See here, Lib Glip; a highly placed confidential source has advised me that the capital is about to become the objective of an all-out Creepy assault. Now I think it only fair that your people should relinquish the city peaceably, so as to avoid a possible interplanetary incident—"

"Oh, that big-mouth Barf has been at you again, eh? Well, relax, fellows; everything's going to be OK. I have a surprise in store for those bums."

"You've decided to propose a unilateral cease-fire?" Pouncetrifle blurted. "A munificent gesture—"

"Are you kidding, Pouncetrifle? Show the purple glimp feather while those usurpers are still occupying our hallowed soil?" The Hither Furtheronian leaned into the screen. "I'll let you in on a little secret: The retreat is just a diversionary measure to suck Barf into overextending his lines. As soon as he's poured all his available reinforcements into this dry run—whammo! I hit him with a nifty hidden-ball play around left end and regain the cradle of the Crawlie race and end the war once and for all! By the way," he went on, "what does 'hallowed' mean? Anything like poisoned?"

"I happen to be directly in the path of your proposed dry run!" Pouncetrifle keened. "I remind you, sir, this compound is neither Hither nor Nether Furtheronian soil, but Terran!" A patch of plaster fell with a clatter as if to emphasize the point.

"Oh, we won't actually bombard the chancery itself—at least not intentionally—unless, that is, Barf's troops try to use it as a sanctuary. I suggest you go down into the subbasement; some of you may come through with hardly a scratch."

"Wait! We'll evacuate! I hereby call upon you for safe-conduct—"

"Sorry; I'll be too busy checking out on the controls of my new hand-tooled pursuit craft to arrange transport to the South Pole just now. However, after the offensive—"

"You'll be manning a fighter?"

"Yes indeed! A beaut. Everything in it but a flush john. I'm personally handling the portfolio of Defense Minister in the War Cabinet, you know. And a leader's place is with his troops at the front. Maybe not actually *at* the front," he amended, "but in the general area, you know."

"Isn't that a little dangerous?"

"Not if my G-2 reports are on the ball. Besides, I *said* this was an all-out effort."

"But that's what you said the last time, when you were learning how to operate that rolled-and-pleated-leather-upholstered tank you accepted as a gift from the Bogan people!"

"Nosed and Frenched, too," Oscar contributed.

"True—but this time it will be all-out all-out. And now I must scoot or I'll have to flip my own prop. You won't hear from me again until after the victory, since I'm imposing total communications silence now for the duration plus two hours. That's so I can attend the Victory Banquet. Ciao." The alien broke the connection.

"Great galloping galaxies," Pouncetrifle breathed fervently as he sank into a plaster-dusted chair. "This is catastrophic! The Embassy will be be devastated, and we'll be buried in the rubble."

6

There was a discreet tap at the conference room door; it opened and an apologetic junior officer peered in. "Ah . . . Mr. Ambassador, a person is here, demanding to see you at once. I've explained to him—"

"Step aside, buster," a deep voice growled. A short, thickset man in wrinkled blues thrust through the door.

"I've got an Operational Instanteous Utter Top Secret despatch for somebody." He stared around at the startled diplomats. "Who's in charge here?"

"I am," Pouncetrifle barked. "These are my staff, Captain. What's this despatch all about?"

"Beats me. I'm Merchant Service. Some Navy brass hailed me and asked me to convoy it in. Said it was important." He extracted a pink emergency message from a pouch and passed it across to Pouncetrifle.

"Captain, perhaps you're unaware that I have two emergencies and a crisis on my hands already!" Pouncetrifle looked at the envelope indignantly.

The sailor glanced around the room. "From the looks of this place, I'd say you had a problem, all right, mister," he agreed. "I run into a few fireworks myself on the way in here. Looks like Chinese New Year out there."

"What's the nature of the new emergency?" Magnan craned to read the paper in Pouncetrifle's hand.

"Gentlemen, this is the end," Pouncetrifle said hollowly, looking up from the message form. "They'll be here first thing in the morning."

"You mean the Creepies?" someone inquired.

"Worse than that, Chester! The Inspectors!"

"My, just in time to catch the action," Magnan said.

"Don't sound so complacent, you imbecile!" Pouncetrifle yelped. "That will be the last straw! An inspection team, here to assess the effectiveness of my pacification efforts, will be treated to the sight of a full-scale battle raging about my very doorstep!"

"Maybe we could tell them it's just the local Rock Festival— "

"Silence!" Pouncetrifle screeched. "Time is running out, sir! Unless we find a solution before dawn all our careers will be in ignominy."

"If you don't mind sharing space with a cargo of condemned Abalonian gluefish eggs, you can come with me," the merchantman offered over a renewed rumble of artillery. "It will only be for a couple of months, until I touch down at Adobe. I hear they've got a borax mining camp there; you can work out your board until the spring barge convoy shows up."

"Thank you," Pouncetrifle said coldly. "I shall keep your offer in mind."

"Don't wait too long. I'm leaving as soon as I've off-loaded."

"All right, gentlemen," the Ambassador said in an ominous tone as the captain departed in search of coffee. "I'm ordering the entire staff to the cellars for the duration of the crisis. No one is to attempt to leave the building, of course. We must observe Barf's curfew. We'll be burning the midnight flourescents tonight— and if by sunrise we haven't evolved a brilliant scheme for ending the war, you may all compose suitable letters of resignation—those of you who survive!"

"But, sir," the Cultural Attaché quavered. "What about my dedication—*your* dedication, that is, sir—the Yankee Stadium-type sports arena? The ceremonies are all set for about an hour from now!"

"As to that, Morris," the great man responded gravely, "of course I had no intention of imploying that *I* would skulk here in safety—ah, relative safety, that is to say," he conceded as another near-miss shook the building, raising a fresh dust cloud. "No, gentlemen," he went on as one patiently over-coming stubborn resistance, "to boycott the occasion would hardly tend to enhance the Terran image of that invulnerable majesty which rises above trifling inconvenience."

". . . by golly, sir!"

". . . show these upstarts!"

". . . *some* guts, eh, fellows?"

When the chorus of stunned admiration had faded, Pouncetrifle swept grandly from the room, leaving a parting command floating in the dusty air behind him: "We depart instanter, no time now to dress. Rendezvous in the garage in ten—make that five—minutes."

CHAPTER TWO

STOPPING BY HIS NEWLY ASSIGNED OFFICE, Retief encountered a local clerk-typist, just donning a floppy beret dyed a sour orange as an expression of his political alignment.

"Hi, sir," he greeted the diplomat glumly. "You must be the new man, Mr. Retief. Dil Snop's the handle. I was just leaving. I guess you know the Creepies are back in town."

"So it appears. How about a stirrup cup before you go?"

"Sure; they won't have the streets cordoned off for a while yet."

The clerk parked his bulging briefcase and accepted a three-finger shot of black Bacchus brandy, which he carefully poured into a pocket like a miniature marsupial's pouch.

He heaved a sigh. "Say, Mr. Retief, when that Creepy incompetent Kark shows up, tell him not to mess with the files. I've just gotten them straightened out from the last time."

"I'll mention your desires," Retief said. "You know, Snop, it seems strange to me that you Crawlies haven't been able to settle your differences with the Creepies peaceably. This skirmishing back and forth has been going on for quite a while now, it seems, with no decisive results."

"Since the dawn of history several months ago, I guess," Snop nodded. "But how can you settle your differences with a bunch of treacherous, lawless, immoral, conscienceless, crooked, planet-stealing rogues like those Creepies?" Dil Snop looked confounded, an effect he achieved by rapidly intertwining the tendrils around his eyes.

"They seem like ordinary enough fellows to me," Retief commented. "Just what did they do that earns them that description?"

"What haven't they done?" Dil Snop waved a jointed member "Look at this office—a diplomatic mission! Bullet holes all over the walls—"

"Some of the shrapnel scars were made by your boys in orange the last time they took over," Retief reminded him.

"Oh, well, these little accidents will happen in the course of foiling the enemy's efforts to ravish our homeland—and this, mind you, sir, after they've invaded the hallowed surface of Furtheron, swarmed over the entire planet, and kept the interior, too! While we're stuck in this crummy valley!"

"Seems like a pretty fair valley to me," Retief said. "Except for the constant bombardment."

"*This* place? Pah! That"—Dil Snop pointed through the floor—is *my* beloved ancestral stamping ground."

"Ever been there?"

"I've been along on a few invasions, during summer vacations. Just between us," he lowered his voice, "it's a little too dark and cold and spooky down there for my personal taste."

"How did the Creepies manage to steal it?"

"Carelessness on our part," Snop conceded. "Our forces were all up here, administering a drubbing to them, and they treacherously slipped over behind our backs and entrenched themselves."

"What about the wives and little ones?"

"Oh, an exchange was worked out. After all, they'd left their obnoxious brats and shrewish mates."

"What started the feud in the first place?"

"Beats me. I guess that's lost in the mists of antiquity or something. Unless the idea that old Doc Ditts over at the Institute knows something is true. I wouldn't bet on it." The Crawlie put down his glass and rose. "I'd better be off now, Mr. Retief. My reserve unit's been called up, and I'm due at the armory in half an hour."

"Well, take care of yourself, Dil Snop. I'll be seeing you soon, I expect."

"I wouldn't guarantee it. Old Lib Glip's taken personal command, and he burns troops like joss sticks." Snop tipped his beret and went out. A moment later the narrow face of Deputy Counselor Magnan appeared at the door.

"Come along, Retief. The Ambassador wants to say a few final words to the staff; everyone's to assemble in the commissary storeroom in five minutes."

"I take it he feels that darkness and solitude will be conducive to creative thinking."

"Don't disparage the efficacy of the deep-think technique. Why, I've already evolved half a dozen proposals for dealing with the situation."

"Will any of them work?"

Magnan looked grave. "No—but they'll look quite impressive in my personnel file during the hearings."

"A telling point, Mr. Magnan. Well, save a seat for me in a secluded corner. I'll be along as soon as I've run down a couple of obscure facts."

Retief employed the next quarter-hour in reading the

Post Report, which was uninformative, and in leafing through back files of classified despatch binders. As he finished, a Creepy attired in shapeless blues and a flak helmet thrust his organ cluster through the door.

"Hello, you must be the new GSO, Mr. Retief," he said listlessly. "Name's Kark. I'm back."

"So you are, Kark," Retief greeted the lad. "You're early. I didn't expect you until after breakfast."

"I got shoved onto the first convoy; as soon as we landed I sneaked off to warn you. Things are going to be hot tonight."

"So I hear, Kark—" A deafening explosion just outside bathed the room in green light. "Is that a new medal you're wearing?" Retief inquired.

"Yep." The youth fingered the turquoise ribbon anchored to his third rib. "I got it for service above and beyond the call of nature." He went to the table at the side of the room and opened the drawer.

"Just what I expected," he said. "That Crawlie slob Snop didn't leave any cream for the coffee. I always leave a good supply, but does he have the same consideration? Not him. Just like a Crawlie."

"Kark, what do you know about the beginning of the war?"

"Eh?" The new clerk looked up from his coffee preparations. "Oh, it has something to do with the founding fathers. Care for a cup? Black, of course."

"No thanks. How does it feel to be back up in the good old daylight again?"

"Good old . . . ?" Oh, I see what you mean. OK, I guess. Kind of hot and dry, though." The building trembled to a heavy shock. The snarl of heavy armor passing in the street shook the pictures on the walls.

"Oh, Retief," Magnan caroled, darting past. "You really must hurry along."

"Well, I'd better be getting to work too, sir," Kark

said. "I think I'll start with the Breakage Reports. We're three invasions behind."

"Better skip the paperwork for now, Kark. See if you can round up a few members of the sweeping staff and get some of this glass cleaned up. We're expecting several varieties of VIP, and we wouldn't want them to get the impression we throw wild parties."

"You're not going out, sir?" Kark looked alarmed. "Better not try it; there's a lot of loose objects flying around out there, and it's going to get worse!"

"I thought I'd take a stroll over toward the Temple of Erudition."

"But . . . that's forbidden territory . . ." Kark was worried, as evidenced by the rhythmic waving of his eyes.

Retief nodded. "I suppose it's pretty well guarded?"

"Not during the battle. Crawlie High Command has called up everybody but the inmates of the amputee ward. They're planning another of their half-baked counterinvasions. But, Mr. Retief . . . if you're thinking what I think you're thinking, I don't think—"

"I wouldn't think of it, Kark." Retief gave the Creepy a cheery wave and went out into the deserted hall.

CHAPTER THREE

FOUR OF THE SEVEN MOONS of Furtheron glowed varied
shades of pink in the sky as the twelve-passenger limousine, with the green-and-white ensign of the *Corps
Diplomatique Terrestrienne* bearing the single star of a
Career Minister drooping from its prow, nosed its way
cautiously through the motley crowd thronging the village marketplace, heedless of the muted flicker and
rumble as of a distant artillery duel. The heavy bombardment had lessened; only an occasional wild shot
caused a momentary flurry as the locals in its path deftly
leapt aside. Colored lights strung on stalls and in the
low branches of the spreading imported heo trees shed
a polychrome light on huts elaborately woven of native
grasses, on quaint native garb, and on the even quainter
natives. The latter appeared in two distinct sizes: squat,
knobby caterpillarlike yeomen, shopkeepers, and trades-
men, their undecorated bodies wrapped in dun-colored
togas adorned with grotesque appliqués indicative of
guild affiliation; and even more knobby seven-foot no-

bles, their upreared thoraxes elegantly swathed in brocaded robes secured by ropes of rough-cut gems, their wormlike hindquarters crisscrossed by harnesses supporting an alarming variety of curved scimitars, businesslike dirks, needle-pointed stilettos, and crude, long-barreled pistols with hand-tooled grips.

"Ugh," First Secretary of Embassy Magnan commented tersely from his place on a thinly padded bench near the rear of the long vehicle. "We must be out of our wits, faring forth to attend a social event while the streets are not only under bombardment but asurge with refugees, spies, undercover beings, DPs, and out-and-out brigands, all lusting for alien blood."

"You mean Chairbeing Pouncetrifle must be out of our wits: it was *his* order," a furtive voice amended.

"I think he feels that a show of normalcy may help to soothe the preinvasion jitters," a sour-faced Econ Officer reminded his colleague. "In some obscure way it's supposed to help put the combatants in a mood to talk armistice."

Magnan wagged his narrow head, peering out through the armored glass at three-eyed alien visages of the color and texture of well-aged salami, which gazed back at the intruders with unreadable alien expressions.

"Pity one can't tell the virtuous Hither Furtheronians from the iniquitous Nether ones," he commented glumly.

"Yes, to the lay observer one salami is much like another, I imagine," said Colonel Otherday.

"Just because you're Military Attaché, that doesn't mean you can tell these Creepies and Crawlies apart!" Magnan retorted sharply.

"Well, Colonel," another civilian commented, "it seems to me we civilians are being shelled just as much as you military types!"

"Don't get the wind up," the officer replied cooly.

"Just a routine artillery preparation, after all. Hardly a bit of a sticky wicket, to say nothing of a spot of bother."

"There are times when I question the wisdom of all this indiscriminate peacemaking," Magnan said gloomily. "I have a feeling their preoccupation with annihilating each other is the only thing restraining these chaps from massacring all foreigners out of hand."

"You underestimate them, Mr. Magnan," Third Secretary Lackluster put in cheerfully. "I've been reading the Post Report, and, given a few more truce proposals like the last one, I'm sure they'll find time to include us on the schedule."

"You know very well that we didn't *really* mean to propose that fifty percent of the planet be designated a demilitarized zone and turned over to the CDT for use as an experimental worm ranch, Marvin," Magnan responded defensively. "It was a mere clerical error, you might say."

"Oh, the Crawlies didn't object to the idea of giving away fifty percent of the planet," the Political Officer pointed out. "It was the fact that it was *their* fifty percent that riled them."

"Well, heavens, how was I to know the globe that presumptuous Nether statesman calling himself Primary Annihilator of Nuisances Swink gave me so blandly was reversible? Who ever heard of a globe printed on both sides—just because these ninnies imagine their world is hollow and inhabited on both surfaces of the lithosphere? What nonsense! Why, we've been here only a few weeks, and already it's clear to us that the Creepies come from just over the mountains!"

"Certainly," Colonel Otherday confirmed. "Spot they call the Scary Place. Job lot of nonsense. 'Scary Place' indeed!"

"But perhaps they have good reason . . ." Magnan's demurral died away as the crowd closed in, pressing against the sides of the limousine, blocking the way completely. After an ineffectual blast of the custom-issue horn, which sounded the first three bars of the William Tell Overture, Fred idled back, allowing the angry growl of the mob to rise above the whines of the turbos, nearly drowning the big-gun sounds in the background.

The huge car rocked, tooting it horns placatingly now as the crown milled around it shaking variously shaped fists.

"Cautiously, Fred, cautiously," Chairman Ambassador Pouncetrifle admonished from his fawn-colored yumphide contour chair amidships, flanked by an inlaid escritoire, a ten-bottle bar, two closed-circuit TV screens, and an attentive cluster of underlings. "We don't want to provoke an unfortunate incident by accidentally nudging one of these chaps. You know their reputation for hotheadedness."

"I don't know nothing about the temperature o' their domes, boss," the chauffeur said over his shoulder to the Chief of Mission, "All I know is, you just run over the odd foot—and believe me, these babies got odd feet, six of 'em on each side—and it's off wit' the doors and onto the chopping block wit' the unfortunate driver which he made the boner—and likewise wit' the passengers. Anyways, when I ram one o' these crumbums it won't be no accident."

"Mere rumor, Fred," Pouncetrifle addressed his inferior with forced democratic heartiness. "After all, not only are we neutral diplomats, we're neutral on their side."

"Frankly, Yer Excellency, sometimes I wonder if these Creepies know which side o' their bagels has got the cream cheese on," the driver demurred. "Like them unruly hoodlums which they put black paint in my window-squirts last week, and the wiseys that glued the pages o' my comic book together. I had a two-hour wait outside the Ministry o' Espionage yesterday, which I had to spend it reading the Owner's Manual, fer crying into yer Alka-Seltzer!"

"I've spoken to you about the use of ethnic epithets," Pouncetrifle snapped. "The locals are Furtheronians-Hither Furtheronians, in the case of the faction among whom we now find ourselves—and anyway, the Crawlies are *our* side."

"What about the Groacis' pals over the mountains? OK if I call *them* 'Crawlies'?"

"You mean 'Creepies,' " Pouncetrifle corrected sharply. "Though 'Nether Furtheronians' is of course the official designation. I suggest you avoid forming habits of informal verbalization which may prove embarrassing if the battle lines should happen to be realigned to the south."

"I was wondering, boss," Fred said plaintively, "how's come we don't supply the Crawlies with a few tactical fractional megatonners, so's they can clean up on the Creepies once and for all? Maybe we'd get some peace around here then, instead of all these here cannonballs which one of 'em throwed gravel on yer limousine yesterday. Coulda nicked the finish."

"I am hardly prepared to discuss the matter of genocide with nondiplomatic members of the staff," the Chairman said shortly. "Kindly devote your attention to getting me to the dedication on time—after all, His Groacian Excellency Ambassador Nith, with his entourage, will be waiting—and you may leave policy matters to those entrusted therewith," he concluded sternly.

"Right, boss," Fred agreed. "Anyways, I got my plate full tryna ease through this here like press without messing up the grill." He gained another foot, occasioning an excited readjustment of rioters.

2

Pouncetrifle helped himself to a stimulating dram from his bar and sighed heavily.

"Sunrise in another ten hours or so, standard," he predicted, eyeing the pale glow in the east, against which the baroque towers of the town loomed in curliqued silhouette. "As we know from bitter experience, the Creepies—that is to say, the Nether Furtheronians—will be launching their confounded *putsch* at first light. I suppose that after the ceremony I'd best begin preparations for a hasty evacuation."

"Drat," Magnan said behind his hand. "Just when I'd almost gotten my voucher files in order."

"Possibly we should consider sliding a two-acre flatbed under the whole operation," Retief suggested. "Then we could gallop off, rock garden, parking lot, and all, every time we heard another rumor the front was shifting our way."

"Why—that might be a notion," Magnan agreed. "That way we'd have tactical mobility without having to bother Sector with all these lease cancellations."

"On the other hand, HQ might start wondering why our homing beacon seemed to be creeping across the map," Retief pointed out, a comment unheard by the Cultural Attaché, who was busy passing the word forward.

"Golly, Mr. Ambassador," a junior political officer, occupying a forward jump seat only a yard from the great man's elbow, eagerly relayed the proposal. "I wonder if Your Excellency's considered mounting the Embassy on wheels? For easier relocation, you know, during retreats—or rather, during the periodic tactical territorial readjustments," he corrected his terminology hastily.

"Wheels, Lackluster?" The Chief of Mission turned a watery eye on the subordinate bureaucrat. "Aside from your unfortunate use of defeatish jargon, the image you conjure of my chancery jolting along the causeway behind a steam donkey like a condemned tenement being transported beyond reach of zoning regulations is not one I would care to offer the undersecretary as exemplifying my progress in pacifying this unhappy planet!"

"A slip of the head, Mr. Minister," Lackluster hastened to reassure his leader. "Actually, it was Mr. Retief's idea. I was just passing it along—sort of as a joke, you know."

"Joke, Marvin?" Pouncetrifle smiled a small, bitter smile. "I suggest you move back a row, my boy—or possibly two rows. That should enable you to exchange japes with your cronies with greater convenience, at the same time making room here for a more serious-minded member of my staff."

"Too bad," Magnan said in a stage whisper, as the displaced junior pushed back through the volunteers jostling for the vacated seat. "Some days one just can't seem to make a point." He smiled sourly at the glare the remark netted from the demotee.

"Go ahead and gloat, Mr. Magnan," the latter hissed over the hubbub accompanying the realignment. "The fact is, it's a profound relief to get out from under the old basilisk's icy stare!" The last three words rang out clearly in a momentary lull in the chatter. Lackluster paled as all eyes turned his way. Forcing a ghastly rictus to his face, he babbled on:

"Yes, there I was on the icy stair of the basilica, and I said to myself, 'Marvin Lackluster,' I said, 'You deserve to fall and sprain your ankle. Ankle? Marvin, you deserve to break a leg! To rupture your spleen! Why, a concussion wouldn't be too severe—or even a compound fracture of the inferior maxillary—'"

"A most diverting anecdote, I'm sure," Chairman Pouncetrifle smiled pityingly at his unfortunate underling. "However, allow me to point out that your voice,

Marvin, while admirably suited for unamplified public address, is somewhat distracting to those of us attempting to cope with the urgent substantive problems confronting the mission. According, perhaps you would be so kind as to select a seat at the extreme rear of the car, where you may continue your monolog, in relative privacy."

"The . . . the *last* row, sir? B-but—"

"The *last* row, Marvin," Pouncetrifle confirmed glacially. "Perhaps Mr. Retief would be so good as to yield his place." A hush fell as the exchange of seats was carried out.

"Well, Chester—any interesting rumors circulating among the lower ranks?" The great man broke the awkward silence to inquire jovially of the nearest toady.

"I heard one," an Econ man spoke up quickly. "They say the Groaci have been ferrying in war matériel to the Creepies—I mean the Feather Nurtheronians."

"Further Netheronians," someone corrected. "Nurther Featheronians? Or—"

"In any event," the Military Attaché spoke up bluntly, "there's an attendant report that the Groaci are supplying the dissident Crawlie element with armaments as well, thus evening things up rumorwise."

"Nonsense," Pouncetrifle stated flatly. "I distinctly hinted to Ambassador Nith some time ago that I would view with concern any undue meddling by third parties in violation of solemn interplanetary commitments."

"Goodness, sir, wasn't that a trifle blunt?" the Chief of the Political Section blurted.

"Oh, I tempered the severity of the warning with a classic 34-b image: a subtle expression reflecting bittersweet recollection of past misunderstanding, leavened by humble consciousness of Terran might, as you doubtless know. Worked like a charm. You should have seen the little devil's expression as he slunk away, all five eyes adroop with consternation."

"Say, it seems like I heard somewhere that when all five of a Groaci's eyes droop, he's planning mischief of the most virulent stripe," an incautious Information Officer mused aloud.

"Indeed, Irving?" The senior diplomat impaled the fellow with a glance. "I suggest you spend more time with your revised edition of Field Manual 76291-D: *Alien Organ-Clusters And How to Read Them*, Irving."

"Let's face it," an Assistant Political Officer said glumly. "The Groacis' objective is to destroy Terran prestige in this end of the Arm by keeping the war going in spite of all our efforts to end it. They only let slip the news about the hostilities in the first place to tempt the CDT into interfering."

"Nonsense, Oscar," Magnan objected. "You call it 'interfering' to end a fratricidal war? Anyway, ITCH is a multiplanetary tribunal, on which the Groaci themselves occupy a seat."

"Oh, sure, Ben, I know all that jazz," Oscar conceded. "But I still don't like it."

"Isolationism rearing its ugly head in *my* mission, Oscar?" Pouncetrifle boomed. "Never mind, I'll keep it confidential, but if the Promo Board should intercept a rumor of such reactionary sentiments . . . I leave it to you to imagine the consequences."

"Sure, *his* next boost—to Career Ambassador rank— might get slowed up too," some bold spirit said in a penetrating stage whisper.

"What's a Chief of Mission to do?" His Excellency mourned. "How am I to stamp out fratricide among the heathen, when in my own official family the rats are gnawing . . .

"Groaci machinations and internal treachery aside," Pouncetrifle went on more firmly, "I came here to end a war, and end it I shall, gentlemen." He ducked as an overripe two-pound dung-fruit opaqued the windshield with an explosive *splorch!* Fred jabbed a button and twin jets of crimson played over the glass, completing the job of blotting out forward vision.

"They done it again!" Fred cried, braking from a creep to an abrupt halt, eliciting sharp cries of alarm from the bureaucrats in the rear. "Only red paint this time," the distressed driver concluded.

"Good lord!" Magnan gasped. "We're under attack! Do something, Retief!"

"Fred—clear that windshield!" Pouncetrifle yelped. "You know the effect stationary prey has on these Crawlies!"

"I'm trying, ain't I!" Fred yelled back as the wipers batted vainly at the tenacious film of scarlet enamel, spreading it evenly over the glass. The car rocked as the crowd surged against it, threshing their laryngeal plates in expression of hilarity. A placard lettered TERRY FALL DEAD pounded against the window. Through the soundproofing, shrill native voices keened urgent exhortations to the Terrans.

Retief, who had been studying the crowd beyond the still-transparent portion of the canopy, tapped the driver on the shoulder. "Fred—put her in neutral and race the engine wide open—now!" he said, and threw open the door nearest him. An ear-splitting scream came from the turbines as Fred complied, the sound rising into a shriek that passed into the supersonic—the Terran supersonic. The Futheronians, sensitive to frequencies in excess of 50,000 cps., fell back as if driven by massed fire hoses, clapping protecting grasping members to tortured auditory membranes. Retief stepped out, with one stride confronted a tall, heavy-set, and flashily-dressed Terran in the forefront of the mob, and accepted a small cylindrical object which the fellow had plucked from his jacket pocket and proffered as if by instinct, murmuring, ". . . little token from Acme Sales Corporation. Oh, hello, Retief."

"I'm surprised to see you here in civvies, Major, in

the middle of a riot in the midst of a war," Retief said casually.

"Damn poor war, if you ask me," the major replied. "I can't seem to find the scene of action, except for this infernal bombardment—and the program of harassing you diplomats, of course, buzzing you with with infernal obsolete aircraft some opportunist has been shipping in here via the loophole in Paragraph 91-2. Confounded nuisance. Good show they spend most of their time dog-fighting with cameras. The troops bet heavily on the scores, I understand. The lawless element has to have *something* to do; and worse yet, of course the basic amenities are unavailable on account of the war effort—but where's the war effort?"

"Keep cool, Howie," Retief said. "Chairman Ambassador Pouncetrifle is a tenacious fellow. He was sent here to stop a war, and eventually he'll find it. He said so himself. Just follow his lead. I assume you're traveling in your usual line of agricultural equipment?"

"Precisely," the Acme red replied smoothly. "After all, one can hardly expect significant production from even the most fertile real estate until ownership thereof has been decided."

Retief went to the front of the car, made a quick adjustment to the cylinder in his hand, and directed it at the windshield. In seconds a stream of superheated ions had scoured a ten-inch disc directly before Fred's staring face. The car moved forward hesitantly, then, gaining confidence as the mob opened before it, sped out of sight, leaving Retief alone, on foot, in the midst of the hostile crowd.

A quarter of a mile distant across the park, the high, peach-colored dome of the university library pushed up into the luminous pre-dawn sky. The darting forms of the ubiquitous fighter planes were silhouetted beyond it, circling each other with the agility of combative gnats. At the far end of the street, clear of the mob, a column of gaily caparisoned Creepy armored cars of French origin, vintage 1918, clattered past, in hot pursuit of a troop of light tanks of equally primitive design flying the Crawlie pennant. The sky to the north and west winked and flickered to the incessant dueling of Blue and Orange artillery. There was a sharp, descending whistle as a medium-sized boulder dropped half a block away, sending a gout of pavement chips hurtling skyward, thinning the audience noticeably. Retief waited until the air was momentarily clear of flying fragments to cross the street and head across the park.

3

The high walls of the Temple of Enlightenment, inset with convoluted patterns in richly colored mosaic tile, reared up behind a dense barrier of wickedly thorned shark trees. Retief used the pocket beamer to slice a narrow path through into the grounds, where a flat expanse of deep-blue grass extended a hundred yards to the windowless structure. He crossed the lawn, skirting a neatly trimmed bed of goggly flowers where a stuffed dust owl lay staring up into the night with red glass eyes. Above, a ragged scar showed in the tilework of the sacrosanct edifice. There were dense scarlet-stemmed strangler vines on the wall.

Aside from the need to fend off the thick pink tendrils which gave the vine its name, it was an easy two-minute climb to the opening, beyond which shattered glass cases and a stretch of murky hall were visible. Retief gave a last glance at the searchlight-swept sky and stepped inside. Dim light glowed in the distance. He moved silently along the corridor, pushed through a door into a vast room filled with racks containing the fan-shaped books favored by both the Creepies and Crawlies. As he did, a beam of light stabbed out, flicked across his chest, fixed on the center button of his dark green early-evening blazer.

"Professor Dits?" Retief inquired.

"Right—and don't come any nearer," a reedy voice quavered. "I've got this light right in your eye, and a bloop gun aimed at where I estimate you keep the rest of your vitals."

"The effect is blinding," Retief conceded. "I guess you've got me." Beyond the feeble glow he made out the fragile figure of an aged Crawlie draped in zebra-striped academic robes.

"I suppose you sneaked in here to make off with a load of historical treasures," the oldster charged.

"Actually I was just looking for a shady spot to load my Brownie," Retief said soothingly.

"Ah-hah, photographing Cultural Secrets, eh? That's two death penalties you've earned so far. Make a false move and it's three and out."

"You're just too sharp for me, Professor," Retief conceded.

"Well, I do my job." The ancient snapped off the light. "I think we can do without this. It gives me a splitting flurgache. Now you better come along with me to the bomb shelter. Those rascally Creepies have been dropping shells into the Temple grounds, and I wouldn't want you to get hurt before the execution."

"Certainly. By the way, since I'm to be nipped in the bud for stealing information, I wonder if it would be asking too much to give me a few answers before I go?"

"Hmmm. Seems only fair. What would you like to know?"

"A number of things," Retief said. "To start with, how did this war begin in the first place?"

The curator lowered his voice. "You won't tell anybody?"

"It doesn't look as though I'll have the chance."

"That's true. Well, it seems it was something like this. . ."

4

". . . and they've been at it every since," the ancient Crawlie savant concluded his recital. "Under the circumstances, I guess you can see that the idea of a cessation of hostilities is unthinkable."

"This has been very illuminating," Retief agreed. "By the way, during the course of your remarks I happened to think of a couple of little errands that need attending to. I wonder if we couldn't postpone the execution until tomorrow?"

"Well . . . it's a little unusual. But with all this shooting going on outside, I don't imagine we could stage a suitable ceremony in any case. I suppose I could accept your parole; you seem like an honest chap, for a foreigner. But be back by lunchtime, remember. I hate these hasty last-minute adjustments." His hand came up suddenly; there was a sharp *zopp!* and a glowing light bulb far across the vast room *poof!*ed and died.

"All the same, it's a good thing you asked," the old curator blew across the end of his pistol barrel and tucked the weapon away.

"I'll be here," Retief assured the scholar. "Now if you'd just show me the closest exit, I'd best be getting started. By the way, is the planet really hollow?"

"Nonsense, of course not. Silly idea."

The Hither Furtheronian elder tottered along a narrow passage and opened a plank door letting onto the side garden. "Nice night," he said, looking at the sky where the glowing vapor trails of fighter planes looped across the constellations. "You couldn't ask for a better one for—say, what *are* these errands you've got to run?"

"Cultural Secrets." Retief laid a finger across his lips and stepped out into the night.

5

Retief quickly overtook the limousine, closed in now by a particularly bellicose-appearing squad of low-caste Crawlies who were boldly swarming over the heavy vehicle, probing its various openings. He plucked two of the most aggressive from their perches and low-beamed the sensitive yatz patches of another who had plastered himself across the entry panel, causing the fellow to retreat with a yelp of astonishment. Retief stepped back inside the car and it surged forward amid a relieved babble from its passengers.

"Quick thinking, Retief." The Military Attaché lowered his voice: "But how did you happen to be carrying a flame thrower?"

"Just a souvenir cigarette lighter all these Bogan gun-runners carry as samples." Retief showed the lettering on the device:

Light up *your* offensive with genuine BAM© weapons systems!*

"You're aware, I suppose, that such thinly disguised weapons are grossly illegal?"

"Certainly, Colonel. That's why I confiscated it."

A moment later the limousine pulled up before the arc-lit site of the newly completed and only slightly bomb-pitted Yankee Stadium-type Sports Arena, the latest Gift of the Terran People to Free Furtheron. The Terran Ambassador and his senior staff peered out nervously at the crowds before the entry, lackadaisically restrained by a squad of bored-looking local police in flimsy but brightly chromed and enameled plastic armor topped with luminescent head-plumes. Pouncetrifle straightened the triple chrome-plated lapels of his

*©Bogan Arms Mfg. Cartel, 2581

midnight-blue late early-evening top-formal cutaway and squared his narrow shoulders.

"Now, gentlemen," he called in a strained whisper to his staff. "Chins up! Look confident! Never give the locals a hint of defeatism in our miens! It might be the straw that breaks their indominable will to peace. Now, as you fellows know, if you've been keeping abreast of my SON's," Pouncetrifle went on, waiting with a show of restrained impatience for Fred to open the door, "I have given the Undersecretary a firm commitment that a major breakthrough in the negotiations will be achieved prior to the arrival here of the Special Inspection Team from Sector." As Fred belatedly came around to swing wide the door, Pouncetrifle emerged cautiously onto the littered sidewalk, clear for the moment of rioters.

"Geeze," the Political Officer grunted. "That's really laying it on the line, sir. If it would've been me, I'd've put a few maybes in that; them SIT teams don't mess around."

Pouncetrifle leaned back in, allowing his 74-y (Compassionate Awareness of Lesser Beings' Shortcomings) to curve his thin lips the regulation .04 mm. "That's why you're an assistant P.O. and I'm Chief of Mission, Oscar," he commented tonelessly. "Nonetheless, inasmuch as the careers of all you gentlemen are at stake, I suggest that a few semi-intelligent proposals are in order."

"—shoulda thought of that before he went and stuck his neck out," the reedy voice of the Press Attaché came clearly through the background matter.

"Let's not forget that little rectangle on our ER forms designated 'Ability to Improvise Viable Strategies on Short Notice,' " Chairman Ambassador Pouncetrifle commented as if not noticing Lester's gaffe. "I shall be happy to hear your proposals immediately after the concert, in time to include any winners in my own dedicatory remarks on the occasion of this gala first night at the Terran People's gift to Furtheron." He shied as a near-miss spattered gravel nearby.

As Pouncetrifle resumed his ceremonial progress, a junior officer from the Political Section tugged at Retief's sleeve.

"Oh, Mr. Retief," he said in a tone of feigned nonchalance, "I was just wondering . . . probably just routine to you old-timers, sir, but . . . why is it that if there's this big war on that we're here to put a stop to, how come we never see any signs of it except the shelling and those crazy old cars and airplanes? Like enemy troops and all, this burg being the Crawlie capital and all—oops, Hither Furtheronian, I meant, sir. Anyways, hows come?"

"A natural enough question, Henry," Retief reassured the lad. "But those officially wiser than us assure us that on the other side of the mountains the action is all that any peacemaker could ask for."

"It's kind of disillusioning, sir. When I volunteered for the ITCH team, I pictured myself holding up a hand and having the tanks halt and the shock troops drop their bayonets and all. But heck—what good is stopping an invisible war?"

"Actually," Magnan put in, "those are by far the best kind, Henry. You see, the Crawlie military plans are so secret it wouldn't do to spill the beans by launching a counterattack right out in the open."

"We're always hearing about the Creepies starting a big offensive that's going to engulf even our sacrosanct CDT area—but all they do is take turns invading the same patch of ground. Pretty dull."

"Such are the vagaries of the Big Picture," Magnan dismissed the neophyte's complaint.

"Oh, we get plenty of refugees to feed," Henry went on, "and of course we're confined to the Mission area and all, so it's *kind* of like a real war, but I was expecting to see the action up close—you know, Mr. Retief, where you get medals and all—"

"I'm afraid the medals will have to wait, Henry," Retief said, "until we've blown the Mission entirely and Terra openly pitches in as a combatant."

While they talked, the Chief of Mission had hurried toward the bright-lit red-carpeted ramp leading up to the gold-leaf grand foyer of the building, accompanied by his aides like a deep-space liner attended by a fleet of tugs. At the top he paused, this time to address the gaily clad throng.

"Come along, Retief," Magnan called as the ambassadorial entourage formed up about its leader. "If we hurry, we can grab the better seats before the Groaci delegation hogs them all; their limousine is bogged down across the square in a herd of slime swine."

"I was designated to lock up the car," Retief reminded his colleague. "Save me a spot behind a post."

As Retief turned back toward the big machine, he heard soft scuffling sounds; Fred, the driver, toppled sideways in his seat. At the same moment two lumpy five-foot figures wrapped in shabby pale-blue togas detached themselves from the surging throng flowing past, and moved to positions flanking the six-foot-three Terran. One flipped back his heavy cloak, revealing the blunt snout of a power gun. "Just keep quiet, Terry," his guttural voice ordered in the local patois. "And get in the car: we're going for a little rideo. Now reach."

"Anything to be agreeable," Retief said in the same tongue, and clamped a hand on the speaker's wrist, causing that unfortunate to drop his weapon and emit a hoarse croaking sound.

"No, no, you don't get the idea," the other alien whispered urgently. "Don't reach for Captain Sprugg! Reach for the sky! Hoist 'em! Grab some air!" The speaker displayed a heavy-caliber needler—a Groaci copy of a Japanese version of a Belgian-made Browning pa-tent 2mm. model, Retief noted. "Now snap it up, before somebody notices!"

"I'll bet I can get you before you can get me," Retief remarked, poking the alien's third toga button, below the owner's line of sight, with his forefinger. "Want to try me?"

"No fair," the dacoit replied, handing over his gun, butt first. "They told me this would be like taking zitz fruit from a meebly bird."

"What's keeping you, Retief?" Magnan's querulous voice punctuated the proceedings; he hurried up, frowning, "Oh, dear, His Excellency's remarks would have been *so* much more effective if the fellow with the dung-fruit didn't have such an excellent aim," he complained. Giving the aliens a disdainful glance, he continued: "This is no time to fraternize with low-caste locals. Why—why, Retief—they're not even *our* locals! These aren't Crawlies, they're Creepies! Didn't you notice? They're wearing blue, the Creepy color!" He grabbed Retief's arm. "Don't you see! They're spies!" He hissed in his ear in Terran: "You engage them in conversation while I go for help. Heavens, what a coup—"

"Hold it right there, jitterbritches!" the nearer alien hissed. "We wun't want the word to get out—"

"Let him go, Leroy," the other growled. "We can always lay for him after."

"Skip it, bub," Retief ordered. "When I want to hear from you, I'll be sure to let you know."

"Retief," Magnan said sternly, "why are you standing so close to that low fellow? You know the Minister's feeling about hobnobbing with the cruder element." He peered closely. "Heavens Retief! Why you are poking him in the short ribs with— "

"With my experimental model Mark II disaster gun?" Retief cut in smoothly. "Oh, just because I didn't feel it would be appropriate to fire it—unless I have to—and have to call in a garbage-disposal squad to scrape up Leroy's component parts right here in the midst of the Grand Opening."

"Oh . . ." Magnan's reply was blanketed by Leroy's excited protestation: "Just take it easy, chief, me and the cap'n here are cooperative fellows is what we are!"

"What about the other one?" Magnan inquired nervously. "He looks mean."

"You're carrying the same armament I am, Mr. Magnan," Retief pointed out. "You handle him."

"To be sure," Magnan replied coolly; he turned to Sprugg and, under cover of fussing with his dope-stick box, sidled behind him and rammed a finger against the Creepy's sausagelike midriff. The officer stiffened. "Rats!" he exclaimed. "That's what I get for forgetting to frisk the subject, like it says right on page two of the Manual. My boner."

"Never mind that," Magnan snapped, jabbing harder. Sprugg fell silent.

"Just refrain from making any sudden moves," Magnan went on in a conspiratorial tone," and I'll endeavor to restrain the impulse to test my Mark II. Just what is it you wanted, anyway? If you intended robbery, you were wasting your time in any case, my man." He sniffed. "I'm wearing only junk jewelry, I assure you—"

"Some guys is too quick to get aholt of wrong idears," the alien snarled, and jerked the car door open.

"Here, none of that." Magnan spoke up sharply, prodding again. The alien froze.

"The Ambassador is very particular about finger marks on the finish—" Magnan warned.

"He'll be lucky if we leave any finish for finger marks to be on," the Nether Furtheronian grated.

"You wouldn't want to mess up this nice upholstery with that Mark II," he added, and slithered inside the car, occupying three seats.

Magnan quickly pocketed his finger. "Retief, I'd best

remain close to the fellow," he commented, and got into the car just as Fred returned to consciousness.

"Cripes!" the chauffeur muttered, gazing into his rear-view mirror. "What'll His Nibs say when he finds out a Creepy's been curled up on his personal tump-leather throne?" He started the engine.

"Oh, Retief," Magnan called. "Perhaps you'd best come along. We'll escort these fellows back to their territory, so as to minimize the incident."

"Good idea," Sprugg exclaimed with alacrity, and ducked inside. Retief followed, hand in pocket.

"Well, here we are," Leroy said comfortably. "OK, let's go, tubehead," he told the chauffeur. "Next stop, Deadman's Pass, and snap it up; we're behind schedule."

"Mind your pedal extremities, sir," Magnan admonished the alien, as the latter rasped six of its sneaker-clad feet on the deep-pile carpet. He glanced nervously across toward the flood-lit ceremony. "If His Excellency should suspect that his official limousine had been invaded by—ruffians—I dread to think of what he'd say."

"Think about it anyways, Terry," Leroy suggested. "Anyways, by the time he notices it's missing it'll be a couple hundred miles on the wrong side of the mountains."

"Congratulations, Mr. Magnan," Retief interjected easily. "You hit upon a sure-fire way to foil their attempt to kidnap us: we're kidnaping them."

"Gracious, I'd no intention—" Magnan protested in a shocked tone.

"That's no chitin off *my* ventral plates," Sprugg commented. "As long as we all arrive on time, my boss won't gripe none. I done my job."

"By the way," he went on, "where'd you guys get the Mark IIs? A usually reliable source told the boss they wouldn't be available for another six months."

"Yeah," Leroy chimed in, "I couldn't hardly believe

my auditory membranes when you said 'Mark II.' In fact if I wouldn't of felt it sticking in my side . . ." He trailed off thoughtfully. "Say, Cap, has a Mark II got hangnails on it?" He turned to look at Magnan in mournful accusation. "You wouldn't of pulled a swifty on me, would you of, Terry?"

"Well, actually, as to that," Magnan responded uncomfortably, "I assure you I was as well armed as Retief was." He threw a glance and the ball to his junior.

"Let's not fall out over a trifle," Sprugg proposed comfortably, "as long as we're all here together and on the way to report to the chief, let's forget the details."

"Am I to understand," Magnan choked incredulously, "that you actually propose to purloin Minister Pounce-trifle's most-prized perquisite?"

"It's a heartbreaker, ain't it, kid?" Sprugg responded off-handedly. Then, to Fred, "OK, let's get going; you're the chauffeur, start chauffing."

"You wouldn't!" Magnan gasped. "That's grand larceny—and in front of witnesses!"

"You wouldn't tell, would you, pal?" the alien said in a menacing tone.

"Whom, I?" Magnan choked. "Why, of course . . . that is, of course, if I were to cross-my-heart-and-hope-to-die . . ."

"It can be arranged, bub," Sprugg stated coldly. "Now just don't do nothing hasty and we can work this thing out so nobody gets hurt."

"An accredited diplomat does not bargain with bandits," Magnan replied coldly.

"You calling us crooks?" the alien snarled.

"Heavens, no," Magnan said faintly. "But why in the world are you bothering with Retief? He's a mere nobody, I assure you—" Noticing what he was saying, Magnan shifted his tack: "Well, I suppose under the circumstances . . ."

"Yeah? The chief'll be glad to hear it," Leroy grunted.

"Now, now, don't be hasty, my man—" Magnan began.

"Hasty is what I aim to be, Rube," Capt. Sprugg concluded. "And I ain't yours and I ain't no man. Now we move out by the count of three, or *blap!?* One . . . two . . ."

"I suppose we must, Fred," Magnan ordered. With a howl of gyros, the big car leaped from the curb, scattering pedestrians as it gathered speed down the avenue. Magnan squeezed his eyes shut.

"His Excellency will never believe this," he groaned. "And if we run over anyone, guess who'll be charged with atrocities!" He opened one eye to glance at Retief, lounging casually now in the ambassadorial chair, from which he had evicted Leroy. "You're taking this with surprising equanimity, I must say," he whispered. "While I was nervily distracting that fellow's attention, why didn't you overpower him?"

"What—and have to sit through an evening of Groaci nose flutes and ritual grimacing after all?" Retief puffed a dope stick alight and indicated the view out the window. "We might as well make the best of it, Mr. Magnan. It's a fine night for a drive."

"But will we live to see the sunrise?" Magnan muttered as the car switched to lift gear, jumped into the air, and headed north for the enemy lines.

CHAPTER FOUR

IT WAS A SWIFT HALF-HOUR flight over the mountains, aglow with ruddy flashes as of heavy artillery. The lights of a small settlement appeared ahead; at a curt command from Leroy, Fred banked the car, circling for a landing. The silver thread of a small river meandered past the town and through a pass to the edge of the city.

Retief turned to address Sprugg, spread comfortably over a pair of jump seats two rows back.

"What's next on the program, Major?"

"Captain," the Furtheronian corrected blandly. "The headquarters boys are hogging all the promotions. As for the program, I suppose I'll turn you over to Colonel Yan. He's the chief of our commando unit, staked out here east of town. He'll run you through Phase One Interrogation: you know—a few socks on the chops, a few dumb questions like 'where is your regiment?' Then he'll shift to Phase Two: cigars, drinks, sympathy, a couple of kindly inquiries about troop deployments—

just to save casualties, you understand. Then on to Phase Three. That's where we'll get down to business. By the time they get through you'll be remembering stuff you never knew."

"T-torture?" Magnan quavered. "But that's in violation of Interplanetary Accord Number 958473625465-7483920-B, as amended—"

"Sure. Remind me to file an official apology."

"Your boss is only a colonel, eh?" Retief said. "That's pretty small tubers. Still, I admire a patriot who places his commanding officer's press notices above mere personal glory."

There was a lengthening silence.

"How's that again?" the captain said uncertainly.

"Well, here you are in a position to earn a planetary reputation as the intrepid agent who delivered a pair of genuine Terry diplomats to Supreme Creepy Headquarters, intact, ready to be ransomed for incredible sums—to go to the Nether Furtheronian War Chest, of course—and instead you're going to hand us over to an obscure regimental commander in the hopes of squeezing out a few hints on local tactical dispositions. Noble, I call it."

"Ah . . . what would you call an incredible sum?" the captain inquired in a cautious tone.

"Ten million Galactic Universal Credits?" Retief offered blandly.

"I don't believe it!" the alien gasped.

"That's the ultimate test of incredibility," Retief agreed.

"Retief!" Magnan blurted. "Are you suggesting . . . I mean, do you intend to convey the impression—"

"I hope so, Mr. Magnan."

"Ten *million* GUC?" the captain whispered. "Great galloping globs of gorp goo, that's enough to launch an offensive that will knock the Crawlies back into the rear echelon, plus leave me a tidy retirement fund."

"Retief, have you taken leave of your senses?" Magnan wailed. "Can you picture Ambassador Pouncetrifle's reaction to the idea of a ten-million GUC payment, for just a couple of subordinates? Why didn't you make it—"

"Ten billion?" Retief cut in. "You're right, Mr. Magnan. No point in trying to save a few hundred million where our necks are involved."

"Ten *billion?*" the captain squeaked. "F-fantastic! What in the world would make a couple of civilians worth a sum like that?"

"Shall we tell him, Mr. Magnan?" Retief inquired judiciously.

"Yes . . . why don't we?" Magnan faltered.

"Oh the other hand," Retief mused, "maybe we'd better save a few surprises for Supreme Headquarters."

"Don't be like that, fellows!" the Netheronian cried, leaning forward eagerly. "Haven't I always played square with you?"

"You call trying to kidnap us at gun-point playing square?" Magnan said tartly. "I think it was sneaky in the extreme, even though you failed."

"How about it, Cap'n?" Leroy inquired plaintively from the front seat. "Do we land, or keep going?"

"Keep going, you idiot!" Sprugg snarled. "You think I'm going to hand a plum like this over to Yan?"

"Up to you, Cap'n. *He's* the one that makes out your Annual Disposal Reprieve. If you want a transfer to the fertilizer pens, it's no epidermis off my crouch pads."

"Umm. You've got a point, Leroy. Maybe the smart play would be to turn 'em in to the colonel with a recommendation—in front of witnesses—to pass what's left along to the general after he gets through squeezing 'em."

"Right, chief," Leroy said. "You heard him, Rube," he added, addressing Fred. "Just aim this heap for the landing strip."

"What about it, Mr. Retief?" Fred inquired in a voice with a slight quaver. "He's got a gun on me."

"On the other hand, Cap'n," Leroy put in in a less enthusiastic tone. "There's them cannibals down there, too."

The car rocked wildly as an antiaircraft shell detonated a few feet off the port bow. "Take her down, Fred," Retief said, as the machine regained an even keel.

"Now, gents," Captain Sprugg remonstrated,, elongating his neck to peer downward into the blackness below, "we don't wanna do nothing hasty and like that. Colonel Yan ain't a fellow to take this here affair light, you know. If we louse up the detail, he'll have all four of us pounded out flat for rugs to swap to the natives for some o' their neat electronic gadgets they handmake in their grass huts." Then without further conversation, and as the car banked for final approach, Sprugg lunged. Retief pocketed his Mark II finger and thrust the alien aside easily. "Naughty," he said, and aimed his cigar lighter on narrow focus at the Crawlie's thoracic plates.

"Can't we just be reasonable about all this?" the captain pleaded. "Suppose we just sort of declare a truce, and pretend like Leroy and me are bringing you boys in, instead of the other way around—just in front of Colonel Yan, I mean; with the cannibals it won't matter."

"Best attend to your steering, Fred," Magnan advised tartly. "A hundred-and-eighty-degree turn should put us on course back to friendly territory."

"Friendly—hah!" Sprugg muttered. "If you Terries really knew— "

"Let's not be hasty, Mr. Magnan," Retief advised. "After all, the captain has gone to considerable effort to get us here. Think how it would look in his 201 file if he wound up in a CDT jail charged with grand larceny, mayhem, and gross inefficiency."

"That's his problem," Magnan sniffed. "I, for one—"

"—wouldn't want to see a promising career blighted by a premature hanging," Retief finished for him. "Your sentiments do you credit, Mr. Magnan. So I suggest a compromise."

"You mean dump them out right here and let them take their chances? Oh, very well. After all, it wouldn't exactly be murder; they might just happen to land in a haystack."

"I was thinking of a more dramatic gesture of good will. We'll return the captain's gun to him—minus the power cell, to avoid accidents—and continue on our way—to Supreme Headquarters."

"Yes, but I'd just decided to take you direct to Colonel Yan, remember?" The captain brightened, straightening his tunic. "I'm glad you decided to be reasonable; I'll put in a good word with the colonel to go easy on the nox box and stick to more conventional interrogation methods like red-hot pincers."

"Too bad," Retief said. "In that case, I suppose we'd better go ahead with that one-eighty."

"But on the other hand," Sprugg hurried on, "if the prisoners want to go to Supreme HQ—why, Supreme HQ it is! Even if that means violating the Scary Place."

"Retief!" Magnan tugged at his junior's sleeve as the craft bored through the night. "What's going to happen when we get to this Scary Place? What's your plan?"

"Frankly, Mr. Magnan, I thought we'd improvise as we go along."

Magnan sank back with a groan. "We'll be improvising our own ceremonial dismemberment!"

"Not if the captain is half as sharp as I think he is," Retief said in a stage whisper. "If anybody starts to squeeze us, the first thing that will come to light is that someone's been tampering with his gun, which may lead some hothead to accuse him of introducing spies into Supreme HQ. I'm sure he wouldn't want a misconception of that sort noised abroad."

The unhappy alien uttered a mournful croak. "Look, Mr. Retief, you better give me your personal word you got no plans to blow up headquarters; otherwise I'll just have to order Leroy to grab the wheel and drive this heap into the ground and get it over with."

"That's the farthest thing from our intentions," Magnan hastened to reassure the officer. "I'm convinced it's vital to the future of Terry-Futheronian relations that HQ remain intact, at least for the present."

"Well, if you change your minds let me know," Sprugg said glumly. "So's I can commit ceremonial sprog throttling—or at least make good my escape before she goes."

"I'll regard that as a solemn commitment," Retief reassured the alien officer.

Suddenly Leroy gave a sharp cry, a sound which in his species resembled the impact of an omelette against a freshly tarred road, as Fred threw the limousine into a vertical bank. There was an actinic flash, a dull report, a concussion which slammed the big car into a wild aerial skid.

"It's a Crawlie patrol boat!" Leroy yelled. "Hey, you Terries—got any armament aboard this tub?"

"Nothing but a few blank ER forms," Retief said, "but I'm afraid those constitute a threat only to career bureaucrats."

"Hold on for a crash landing!" Fred cried grimly, and nosed into a steep dive.

"We're still over cannibal territory, you cretin!" Captain Sprugg yelled. "Make a run for it!"

"Nix, Cap'n. Our chances with the Crawlies on the ground ain't good, maybe, but they're better'n they're gonna be when the next torpedo zeroes in on us." Fred held the dive. The captain scrambled forward as if to overpower the driver, but Retief pitched him into a rear seat.

"Better not try to change horses in the middle of a catastrophe," he suggested. There was a sudden crushing weight of inertia as the car pulled out at treetop level—or slightly below. A leafy crown loomed darkly; Fred tried to pull up.

With a rending crash, the heavy car ploughed through branches, vines, massed foliage, careened off a major trunk, upended, and came to a halt, nose down, while the battered turbos whined down into a dismal silence.

2

"Good lord," Magnan groaned, extricating himself from the ruins of the inflight autovalet, "How can I ever explain this to Ambassador Pouncetrifle?" He plucked at the jagged rent in the ambassadorial mauve-and-cirrhosis demi-informal kilt draping his narrow shoulders. "His Excellency's entire traveling wardrobe ruined at a stroke?"

"Don't even try, Mr. Magnan," Retief advised as he assisted the senior diplomat to safer footing on what had been the door of the ambassadorial comfort cubicle.

"Are we alive?" The muffled tones of Captain Sprugg emanated from the aft end of the car. Amid a stirring of debris, the alien's oculars emerged from a heap of official CDT forms, followed by a number of groping tentacular members, some his, some those of Private Leroy, fumbling blindly over his commander's twitching gestures as the latter struggled to extricate himself both from the treacherous paper drift and the familiarities of his subordinate.

"Heavens, he's running amok!" Magnan cried, recoiling from the unfortunate alien.

"He's only temporarily unhinged," Sprugg sputtered

as the private's manipulative members felt over his verbal orifice, "I hope."

Leroy, suddenly boosted free of the entanglement as his superior rose up beneath him, paused abruptly in his aimless groping, and swiftly scanned his surroundings with suddenly alert oculars.

"What—where—how—?"

"We crashed," Magnan said breathlessly. "Thanks to your interference," he added tartly.

Leroy groaned. "Yeah—it's coming back to me—"

"Are you, ah, yourself now, Private Leroy?" Sprugg called from astern.

"Oh, yeah, chief," the alien said uneasily. "Did I, uh, do anything to, uh—?"

"Nothing that would hold up at a court-martial," the captain snapped. "Now let's get out of this before those treacherous Creepies arrive with their skinning knives and basting forks."

"Creepies?" Magnan echoed. "But aside from the epithetical aspect, I thought this was Crawlie territory."

"Same difference," the officer replied indifferently. "All the villagers eat each other."

Retief had forced the forward hatch open. It was a clear forty-foot drop to the jungle floor. Magnan peered down cautiously.

"I suppose we'll just have to wait here for rescue," he said unhappily. "Luckily, there's a modest stock of gourmet items in the ambassadorial larder, so we shan't starve—"

"*We'll* be the gourmet items if a bunch of wild Creepies gets to us first," Sprugg predicted. "They'll feed us to the snart-worms, which will be eaten by the gid-grubs that they use to fatten the fomp-fowl, and on to the garg-worms—the lousy cannibals-by-proxy!"

A distant rumble became audible, quickly swelled to the full-throated roar of a bright red biplane bearing Crawlie insignia on its flank; gunfire twinkled from its twin Spandaus. Bullets rattled among leathery leaves, smacked into plastic and metal; ricochets whined as the attacker hurtled past, pulled up sharply, and headed for town.

"Here, you madman!" Magnan called after the departing attacker, shaking a fist. "As a representative of civilization, you should be rendering aid, not shooting at us!"

"No use, Ben," Captain Sprugg pointed out. "Us Creepies—and Crawlies too—*enjoy* shooting people up."

"But we're friendly!" Magnan expostulated. "If civilized Furtheronians—and *our* Furtheronians at that—propose to riddle us, just for fun, what can we expect of wild Creepies?"

"I know how to find out," Sprugg offered. "Let's get outa here before the Red Baron comes back."

"But . . ." Magnan looked down into the blackness yawning below. "If we jump . . . We may as well stay here and be shot to bits in comfort," he added.

"Here he comes again, boss," Fred and Leroy said together.

"We need a rope!" Sprugg bleated. "And I'll bet my pension to a plate of ripe garg that's one item your Big Cheese didn't bring along in this traveling joss house!"

Retief, rummaging in the remains of the desk, produced a large reel of scarlet polyon ribbon, a full inch in width, embossed at intervals with the great seal of CDT.

"This ought to do the job," he suggested. "Captain Sprugg, since you seem eager to meet whatever welcoming committee might be awaiting us down below, perhaps you'd like to go first."

"Not me," the officer declined. "Leroy, you go—you're expendable, remember."

"Are you kidding, sir? Anyway, that stuff looks pretty flimsy to me."

"It's served to hold many a planetary government

together," Magnan said loftily. "I daresay it will support your modest weight."

Ignoring the debate, Retief tied one end of the scarlet tape to a seat stanchion; he tossed the reel out the open doorway, grasped the slender red strand, climbed over the balustrade, flipped a turn of the line around his leg as a brake, waved to the worried faces staring down at him, and pushed off.

It was a fast descent through the filtered moonlight; he slammed into a thick layer of mouldering leaves, rolled twice, and came to his feet. Somewhere a wild creature called shrilly in the treetops. Near at hand, a twig crackled sharply.

A squat shape separated itself from the deep shadows before Retief—a curiously truncated Furtheronian whose neck sprouted directly from his paunch without the intervention of a chest. His exoskeleton, dull mauve in color, was decorated with elaborately painted patterns, including concentric rings around the bases of the prominent eye-stalks. His maroon head-cilia writhed slowly. The grasping members—thick, sturdy tentacles likewise adorned with colorful designs—held an assortment of edged weapons, one of which, a broad, stone-headed spear, was aimed at Retief's ribs.

"You-fella speakum Pidgin?" The native inquired. Retief conceded the point.

"Good. You nice for eat? You not poison?"

"Actually, I just might sour on your stomach," Retief said pleasantly.

"No good be pessimist," the aborigine said encouragingly. "Look on bright side. Maybe make-um cheese sauce, you be plenty OK. Me sport, willing make attempt." The creature poised the spear. "Hold still now, me try for perfect sprong shot—"

"Oh, Retief!" Magnan's reedy voice floated down from above. "Are you still . . . did you . . . that is, can you hear me?"

"Come on down," Retief called cheerfully. "It seems we're invited to a native feast."

"Perhaps I'd best remain here; one never knows just how one's tummy will react to these native dishes. Remember the garg."

"A stirring thought, Mr. Magnan," Retief replied respectfully. "One to rank with the *Maine*, Pearl Harbor, and Leadpipe."

"On the whole," Magnum's voice came back dispiritedly. "I think perhaps we'd all best remain here for the present, until you've made arrangements for our transportation back to the city." After a pause he added, "The others agree."

Before Retief could reply, a crudely made spear shot from the blackness toward him. He caught it, snapped it in two, and faded back into the deep shadows of the surrounding jungle as his would-be captor, with a yell, pounced on the underbrush whence the spear had come. "Hey, you keepum digital members off, this one *my* lunch!"

An answering native voice protested its benign intentions: "Me only try helpum stick foreigner! Him pretty big, maybe too much for you to handle, Seymour!"

Muttering, Seymour reemerged from the underbrush, to utter another yell of outrage as he saw that Retief had departed the scene. "Terry! You no wantum trouble with my union, you get back in position for sprog shot fast!"

"No use, Seymour," his erstwhile opponent commented. "Terry gone, and my spear ruin, too!"

Finding a faint trail, Retief soon moved out of earrange of the wrangling locals. Orienting himself by the Third Moon, a pale green orb gleaming through the treetops, he set his course for the city, moving quietly. Then, from ahead, he heard large native feet padding toward him down the trail with a sound resembling a radio depiction of Tom Mix's horse crossing a wooden bridge. Retief eased behind a tree until the two cannibals had passed. Then he took two steps and, with a grab from behind, twitched the matches from their owners' grips and tossed them aside. As the astonished natives whirled, he seized one limber eighteen-inch eye stalk of each, and deftly knotted them together.

"Now, boys," he said soothingly, "as long as you're here, you may as well earn a little pocket money by showing me the fastest way back to town."

"No gottum pockets, Terry," one sullen captive said. "But maybe got basis for deal anyway. You Terry heap nosy fellas, so maybe you arrange nice CDT pension for information leading to capture and conviction of notorious warmonger on foot somewhere here in jungle same like you."

"The dialect needs work," Retief said, "but the general idea is clear. I'm interested. Just who and where is this warmonger, and how does he go about his warmongering?"

"Foreigner, only got more eyes," the other local volunteered. "Beauregard, no pullum eye! Take it easy."

"*Me* pullum eye?" Beauregard protested. "Me no pullum, *you* one pullum. Hold still, whilst I dicker with this Terry! And you keepum yap shut before you spill legumes with no pension plan!"

"Hurry up—no time for sharp dealing. Give him whatever ask for—except . . ."

"Yeah, *except!* Even in dire emergency, loyal cannibal no mention taboo stuff to stranger."

"Yeah, but—no fun have eyeball tied in square-knot. Got to get free, even at expense of violate old tribal taboo!"

"I'll tell!" Beauregard threatened. "Then *you* be sorry you no tell first!"

Retief edged past the pair, who were shifting gingerly from foot to foot, emitting shrill cries and fingering their entangled oculars in an exploratory manner.

"Not pullum that way, you blood-wit!" one cried. "Pullum *this* way!"

"I guess I knowum which way pull own eyeball!"

"Not your eyeball, goog-brain, *my* eyeball!"

"Well, I hope you gentlemen can agree to see eye to eye on the matter," Retief said soothingly. "But never mind the taboo areas for now. Just tell me where Colonel Yan is encamped."

"Oh, you mean city slickers make caves out of sheet metal good for magic talisman, to keep local Crawlies out of own territory. Sure thing, Terry, no taboo on that." Beauregard responded enthusiastically. "Just kind of untie Morris and me and we'll put you right on to him. But look out. He's got two battalion of sharp Green Bloomers, armed to the gills with the new Mark X rubber-band guns—and believe me, those babies *sting!*"

Retief urged the now cooperative pair to the nearest tree and, using the cannibals' barbarically ornamented artificial alligator-hide belts, strapped them securely, embracing the stout bole from opposite sides. Then, with a deft twitch, he untied their eye stems.

"Wow, some relief, get eyeball back," Beauregard sighed, exercising the newly freed organ by rotating it dizzyingly. "Still, it's a bummer to be strapped to this here zum-zum tree, where a fella can't hardly relax. You pretty smart, Terry. We figgered you to turn us loose and then we'd both jump you, tie *you* little sunk-in eyeballs together. You loused that up by tying us up first. Got to tip hat, if I knew what 'hat' was, to such acumen. OK, Terry, now, to get to Yan's camp, just—uh, say, Morris, how *would* a feller get there from here anyways?"

As the two discussed the matter Retief reconnoitered the trail for a few yards ahead, pausing at a bend beyond which he heard the careless sounds of water gurgling over rocks. He advanced far enough to see a fallen log laid across a narrow ravine, at the bottom of which was a rapidly flowing stream. Beyond were the tents and shacks of what appeared to be a semipermanent settlement of quasimilitary nature, with armed Further-onians in baggy magenta pants and brown tunics bus-tling about camp duties. Retief returned to the tree where his two captives waited, silent now, slumped disconsolately against their bonds. They brightened as they saw their captor returning.

"See, Morris, I *tole* you Terry no leavum here to be eat up by googly-bugs! Him OK, turn us loose now, we get on with secret mission."

"Like fun, Beauregard," Morris replied. "Terry just come back gloat a little, maybe poke eyes out with sharp stick, like we do him if sneaker on other pedal extremity."

"I just thought we could take time for a little chat, boys, before the googly-bugs scout you out," Retief said easily, selecting a sharp stick from among the forest litter at his feet.

"Sure, Terry, we *love* to talk to foreigners, even if they do talk funny. Go ahead, what we discuss? Anoma-lous weather pattern got lately? Strange way bombard-ment let up all of sudden?"

"What's the war all about, anyway?" Retief asked.

"Maybe Terry notice big rocks fall from sky a lot," Beauregard suggested. "Even down in town, alla time big chunk stone come down maybe knockum brains out while out for stroll down avenue or like that."

"Are you sure its the enemy who's throwing the rocks?" Retief asked.

"Anybody throw big stones at *me*," Morris contrib-uted, "is enemy."

"Sure," Retief conceded, "but who's throwing them? And at whom?"

"Don't know about this feller Hoome," Beauregard pointed out, "come close *me*, same like *intend* for me.

Don't matter who throw em, *any*body throwum big rock me, him enemy."

"We ain't picky," Morris confirmed righteously.

"Down in town," Retief said, "they've got the idea it's the Hither Furtheronians against the Nether Furtheronians. Which are you?"

"Right now one's political orientation is a matter of complete indifference, I should say," Beauregard stated. "Both in the same kettle fish, whatever that mean."

"They saw the Nether Furtheronians—" Retief started.

"You mean Crawlies—or is it Creepies?" Morris broke in.

"Nether is Creepy," Retief explained. "And they're called Nether because they're supposed to live underground. Only they keep trying to emerge and take over the surface, which belongs to the Crawlies."

"We don't know nothing about these here like subtleties," Beauregard snorted. "We're just the slob in the trail, you know. Who tells *us* anything?"

"Coloney Yan, maybe," Retief suggested.

"Terry make humorous remark remind me Terry wantum know where find old friend Creepy big shot," Morris remarked. "Makum deal, Terry. You cut us loose, we tell where findum."

"Never mind," Retief said. "He's camped just up the trail. You boys just came from there. You wouldn't be playing it cagy, I suppose?"

"Unsophisticated native not know how play it cagy," Beauregard put in. "Us only simple jungle-dwellers."

"In that case, I'll have to be going now, fellows. Try to see the true beauty lurking deep in each other's being."

"Hold on, Terry," both simple jungle-dwellers cried as one. "Expectum report from city-type spy any time now. Him givum all dope on next big offensive!"

"If you mean Sprugg, I'm afraid he won't be coming for some time," Retief informed the pair.

"Oh-oh, somebody talked," Beauregard said mournfully.

"Still," Morris pointed out, "him bringum special HQ-type troubleshooter along: him sharp, deal with any emergency. Anyway," he added, "lone Terry on foot in jungle not get far."

"I won't be on foot, thanks," Retief said, and went quickly back to the bend in the trail. Concealed by thick brush, he made his way to the rude bridge and, lifting one end of the big log, eased it down-slope. He waded across the foot-deep stream and lowered the other end of the log to a temporary lodging on a projecting rock ledge. A yell rang out as Retief scaled the ravine on the far side, pushing through a skimpy screen of brush to emerge openly at the end of the company street defined by parallel rows of patched tents. The alert sentry, a medium-sized Crawlie—or possibly Creepy, Retief was unsure—advanced stone spear-head first, still howling the alarm, stirring the somnolent camp to reluctant activity. When the sentry was within reach, Retief grasped the spear below the head and gave it a powerful jerk, causing its owner to stumble precisely into the arc of a right uppercut which dropped him in his tracks. Reversing the weapon, Retief advanced casually, as if unaware of the excitement occasioned by his arrival. Amid the babble of excited talk, he caught a few words:

". . . big-shot HQ type foreigner."

". . . all these foreigners look alike to me."

". . . no, him only gottum two flat eyes. Big Shot gottum five, or maybe nine, on nice stem, same like us."

Retief approached a fellow in an ornate robe in blue-and-orange stripes, bearing elaborate rank badges.

"You may conduct me to Colonel Yan at once," he ordered the officer, who made bobbing motions and at the same time fingered a nine-inch dirk in his belt.

"Colonel no seeum now, Colonel havum lunch." The

major bobbed. "Tough E-pores Mr., ah, I didn't catch the name—"

"Just tell him the time has come," Retief said firmly.

"Sure thing, Mr. The-Time, sir," the adjutant agreed. "What'd Yer Excellency come for?"

"A reckoning," Retief replied, yawning. "Get moving. I'm not here to gossip with underlings."

"We're fresh outa reckonings, but I got over a hunnert crack troops and strit orders to slice up any unidentified stranger comes around. But you're identified, Mr. The-time, so that's OK."

"Even Colonel Yan sometimes gives imprecise orders," Retief replied patiently. "After all, he's only human, or the local equivalent thereof."

"Sure, Mr. The-time, my boner. I'll tell him." The officer fled and Retief followed him, peeling off at an ornate tent with two slack sentries half-dozing at its fly. He walked into the dim interior, where an obese Furtheronian lay snoring in a rude pallet, his fancy toga and jeweled trimmings of rank draped over a camp stool at one side. Retief seated himself at the small table and began to peruse the papers piled there. Colonel Yan snorted and rolled over, then resumed his rhythmic snore. Retief softly whistled a few bars of *Reveille;* the sleeping colonel sat up abruptly, looking wildly about.

"Good afternoon, Colonel," Retief said easily. "I think it's time now for an explanation of certain matters."

"Not expect HQ Big Shot so sudden," Yan said. "Me just restum eyes, and—blooie! Big Shot practically in my lap. Explain what?"

"Just come to attention there, Yan," Retief ordered the flustered colonel. As the latter rose and clumsily complied, Retief casually squared up a stack of loose papers from the desk and laid it aside.

"I think we can skip over the routine matters," he said, and opened a leather-backed notebook also gleaned from the disarray on the colonel's desk. Frowning intently, Retief leafed through to a blank page, which he studied with a grim expression, finally miming jotting a note.

"Now, all this about the taboo," he said sternly. "We at Headquarters are not all sure this is the correct way to play it. Your idea, Colonel, or did one of our fellows suggest it, perhaps?"

"Intrepid adviser name of Leroy say good idea use old Scary Place legend, help keep ignorant villager in line."

"Umm," Retief said sadly. "For your personal information, Yan, Leroy is now dangling head-down over a cannibal's pot about one mile from here. Clumsy fellow, Leroy. I do hope he didn't unduly influence you in matters of policy."

"Heck, no," Yan replied firmly. "I told lousy HQ stoolie me plenty old veteran, not need foreigner tell me job."

"Oh," Retief said coldly. "Ignored the advice of a duly appointed specialist dispatched from HQ precisely to keep you from the type of blunder in which you're now so deeply involved." He made another note.

"Yeah, but you said—" Colonel Yan began, then changed his tack. "Lucky thing, too. Run into plenty opposition here in so-called 'pacified' area. Just send two good boys off to town to bring in reinforcements."

"If you mean Beauregard and Morris," Retief put in coldly, "they're fighting off googly-bugs two hundred yards down the trail from here. So don't expect any aid from *that* quarter."

"Hey," Yan said, "I just count and you only got three eyeballs—and little flat ones at that! Why HQ Big Shot wear disguise?"

"To refrain from questioning your betters," Retief said shortly in breathy Groacian.

"Me no savvy foreign-talk," Yan stated. "Anyway,

who say five-eyes better'n high-class Creep field grade officer?"

"All right," Retief said crisply. "I want the whole story now, all about this sacrosanct Scary Place you've dreamed up, and where it is,"

"Gettum order direct bossy little foreigner. Him say part of Big Picture."

"Too bad, Colonel," Retief said, gently extracting the officer's ceremonial sidearm—a late-model 2mm needler—from its holster. "Now give," he said, aiming the gun casually toward its owner.

"Well, you know, ignorant savage already got all old legend about spook come up out of ground; all demon and devil live down below, fight alla time, make big rumble and sometimes shake ground, so we just dress story up and spread word big portal to underworld just over hill, next to poorhouse; anybody go there, spook gettum; not even need post guard, all ignorant cannibal plenty scare, and givvum plenty boost to prestige foreigner, only foreigner go over hill, never come back. Plan workum good, expect maybe boost to general officer rank, not reprimand in middle nap."

"Now you'd best give me the precise coordinates," Retief said, moving over to the chart of the local area pinned to a board against the tent wall, noting as he did the disposition of Yan's troops, indicated by blue rectangles clumped in a short arc, open to the east.

"Over east, off map," Yan offered. "Not far, but plenty rugged terrain. Me pickum spot, self," he finished with a note of pride. Retief jotted quickly and flipped up the chart to reveal another beneath it, a continuation of the first. He pointed to what appeared to be an indication of one of the volcanic craters with which the area was thickly studded.

"This one, Colonel?" he inquired in a tone of mild interest.

"Nope, HQ type got that one wrong," Yan said with

satisfaction. "Not biggest fire-hole. Second biggest, foolum spy. Tricky, not use obvious one, take little bit smaller one over just to west of Old Treacherous. Foreigner say OK, Leroy report, so why Big Shot here now, chew out chicken colonel do great job? I almost scare go over there self!"

"Still, I'm afraid you'll have to," Retief stated firmly. "I'll be making an inspection, of course, and I have no intention of setting off without a guide, to clamber over the crags in search of it."

"No searchum," Yan declared fervently. "Nice path, plain marked whole way; only last few feet look out for puddles melted stone." He came to Retief's side and pointed out a thin red line leading to a medium-sized caldera. "You findum, no sweat. Needum couple my boys honor guard?" he added slyly.

Retief declined the offer. "By the way," he asked casually, "What do you hear from Ambassador Nith?"

"Shhh!" Yan clapped a hand over his mouth, miming silence. "Orders from top, never mention name Big-Shot foreigner," he hissed, then, uncovering his mouth, he added in his normal tone, "Got to keepum big secret Groaci got digital member in huckleberry cobbler."

"You mean you were ordered not to discuss the fact that the Groaci are meddling in Furtheron's internal affairs?"

Yan nodded vigorously, a gesture which sent ripples along his entire seven-foot length. "Penalty for mention, chop up and dump in garg-pits."

"Very well, we won't discuss it again," Retief agreed. "Now I really must be getting along; wouldn't do to be late for the attack in the city, you know, so get busy, Colonel. I have new orders for you: instead of an assault directly on the city, you're to take all your fellows on an extended forced march in the opposite direction."

"No gettum," Yan stated firmly. "Crazy order. Troops all ready attack, this move dampen martial ardor."

"Sure," Retief agreed, "but just think how confusing it will be to the enemy."

"Got point there, sir," Yan conceded. Retief returned the Colonel's weapon, nodded curtly, and left the tent, pushing through a curious throng. A growing mutter grew behind him:

". . . not *our* foreigners!"

". . . all lookum same to me."

". . . look like Terry in my comic book."

"Here, Sergeant, takum detail and block—"

"Stop that foreigner!"

As an ominous crowd began to close in before him, Retief broke into a run, bowled over an eager Creepy who attempted to block his way, and sprinted along the path, the mob baying at his heels now. At the log bridge, he veered aside and scrambled down into the ravine, splashing across the stream, just as the first of his pursuers pounded out onto the log, whose insecurely propped end promptly dropped and dumped the front runners into the icy water. They were joined a moment later by new arrivals, as the posse, carried forward by its momentum, piled over the edge. Retief waited until the fallen log had been pushed clear of obstruction by the swift-flowing water, then made his way to it, and as the buoyant bole moved off downstream, Retief stepped aboard and rode it past a swirl of rapids and out into a larger stream, flowing swiftly toward a water-cut gap in the surrounding hills. Outraged cries and a few halfhearted spears followed him.

Two hours later, the log grounded on a sand bar at the edge of the warehouse section along the city's waterfront. Retief waded ashore and made his way up through noisome, crooked alleys to the upper street, empty and silent in the bleak light of a lone moon.

3

It was a brisk ten-minute walk through eerie, deserted streets to the Embassy; the offices were dark, but Retief went at once to the garages where the small official fleet of high-powered CDT vehicles were stored, and selected a fast-moving one-man courier boat; a moment later the lift deposited the tiny craft on the roof. He checked over the instruments, took a moment to pit twin Spandaus into the swivel mountings, and took to the dark sky. Steering by the glow of village lights lining the river along which he had passed only half an hour before, Retief swung to the east to check on Yan's troop dispositions and saw the armed columns moving along at double time, bound for the hinterlands, well out of the way of the coming battle. Turning the car's finder to the code of the CDT limousine, he soon saw the running lights of the once ostentatious vehicle, still wedged nose-down in the crotch of a majestic zum-zum tree. Carefully, Retief dropped his car in to a landing in the concealment of a dense clump of brush. After scanning the area beneath the battered limousine via I-R screen and finding it deserted, he directed the powerful beam of the carrier boat's searchlight upward to bathe the official car in its blue-white glare. All was dark and silent there. The car was deserted. Retief switched off the light and, locking the boat securely, advanced on foot to look over the ground. The broken stone-headed spear lay where he had dropped it. He picked up the business half of the crude weapon, at the same time noticing that the scarlet line of the ribbon on which he had descended from the limousine had been hacked off at spear's length from the ground. Just as Retief was about to move on down the trail leading west from the clearing, he heard a lugubrious groan from the underbrush. Investigating, he found Seymour, identifiable by his purple head cilia and mauve hide decorations, securely strapped up in lengths of tough, thorny vine. Retief poked the Creepy gently with the spear, at which Seymour's oculars erected with an audible *snap!* One bloodshot organ gazed mournfully at Retief as the other two lapsed back into somnolence.

"Oh-oh," the trussed Furtheronian said sadly. "You again, just my luck. How you escape throw-net King Yox drag out when hear fancy car down in jungle? Just cuttum loose, pal, and me puttum in word with His Majesty—which him and me are practically drinking buddy—and get wiggle on, googly-bugs find me soon."

Leaving the unfortunate local's six pairs of sneaker-clad feet trussed, Retief cut the bonds holding his grasping members cruelly cinched up behind him, as well as those binding his sinuous upper torso to a log of tough thornwood. Seymour instantly attempted to throw a loop of his extended, snakelike lower body around his rescuer's legs, a move which Retief countered by administering a sharp jab to the ungrateful creature's sensitive zotz patch, at which Seymour yelped sharply and declared his intention to "no tryum no more snappy trick, be pals Terry, tellum plenty high-class inside dope!"

"Where did they go, Seymour?" Retief asked. "Why did they come down?"

"You come down too, Terry, some wise guy throw hive full zing worms through busted window!"

"Who threw it?"

"King Yox's boys, picked troop of loyal Household Guards Detachment, plenty sharp discipline, those boys: take plenty order, shine sneaker, keep spear polish, do Queen Prudelia drill—not even drop spear. Sometimes salute, even; get wear special fancy imported imitation ostrich-hide harness, real genuine simulated zivian jellybeans, know how march in step, do 'bout face, fall out, smoke if you gottum. All time police area, asses and elbows!"

"Impressive," Retief agreed. "Was everyone taken, even Leroy and the captain?"

"Sure, big haul. Gettum one five-eyes, too, sneak ride in trunk of fancy car."

"A Groaci hitchhiker was aboard the limousine?" Retief pursued the point.

"If Groaci foreigner same like Terry, only nice eyes, on handy stem same like local boy, five of 'em, maybe two too many. Him plenty mad, gettum truss up same like Terry, doomed suffer dire fate of all those who violate Sacred Scary Place of Beginning."

"And precisely what fate is that?" Retief pursued the interrogation relentlessly. "Death by torture?"

"Nobody know. Tribe leavum incorrigible bad hat in Old Treacherous, come back later for gloat a little, nobody there. Maybe he carry off by spook, gottum plenty spook Scary Place."

"Let's go for a walk, Seymour," Retief proposed jovially. "Over in the direction of this Scary Place."

"How come walk, foreigner got nice boat hid in bush?" Seymour protested.

"We'll just scout the way first." Retief reassured his captive.

"Sure, boss, you bettum," Seymour agreed enthusiastically. "Only cuttum loose, Seymour showum way."

Retief released the fellow, who spent half a minute groaning and rubbing his twelve ankles. Since he had only two hands with which to perform the chore, considerable agility was required. At last he assembled his feet under his long, lumpy body and reported himself ready to travel.

"This way," he stated confidently, and set off into the deep underbrush on a heading of 95°. "Go on foot, no takum boat Terry hide in brush, sneak up, foolum all spook," Seymour decreed.

"Let's take the short cut," Retief said, and started off in the opposite direction. Seymour hastily reversed and came undulating up alongside the Terran, offering protests.

"Where Terry gettum idea short cut?" he demanded. "Seymour number-one guide, take foreigner right to destination, avoid cameo factory, miss all ravine, desert, impassable mountains, river, all same ocean."

"Doubtless," Retief conceded, "your route would get us there eventually, but I don't have time to circumnavigate the planet. The taboo area is about two and a half Burundian squiffs northeast by north." He pointed ahead.

"Strange," Seymour commented in a shocked tone, "how Terry get all top-classified inside dope even loyal Crawlie only find out by dread initiation ceremony, make head-tendril jump like foop not on hot plate."

"Ever heard of a fellow called Colonel Yan!" Retief inquired.

"Oh, Old Yan three-time recipient Security Risk of Year, always treat every spy like favorite shrink, tell all. But duty simple native guide warn Sahib taboo area plenty bad medicine. Spook take away, never come back." Seymour glanced about at the humid, insect-infested jungle and added: "Maybe good deed at that, plenty tired life in drafty hut in woods. Maybe go nice snug place underground where spook live, be nice maybe spook lettum stay, run errand for tip, get rich, be big shot."

"Good thinking, Seymour," Retief said, noting as he spoke a sudden odor of woodsmoke. Ahead a crackling sound was rising steadily in volume.

"Tough E-pores, Bwana," Seymour exclaimed, halting abruptly. "Big fire ahead, consume all in path, even foreign meddler and faithful guide. Sign spooks in bad mood. Better head for river, maybe get off with only

singe hide. No good makum spook madder than already
is."

But rather than heeding this advice, Retief led his
trusty native guide off on a wide circle to the right,
following the rising ground, until they gained the vantage of a bare, rocky ridge from which was visible a
panorama of open volcanic pits, smoking fissures, and
blackened vegetation growing from weathered drifts of
volcanic ash, the whole laced with the scarlet tracery
of rivulets of molten lava. Beyond the gaping fissure
bisecting the raggedly aligned row of active cones, a
well maintained path was visible, leading from the heat-
withered jungle edge down around the bubbling lava
lake filling the hollow below the ridge. Seymour briskly
pointed out the access road.

"All same regular interstate highway leadum right
into middle spook," he stated, as if in satisfaction. "Seymour wait here, Terry got honor violate sacred taboo
own self. Too narrow squeeze boat between big rock,
all same loyal guide say in first place, but plenty room
for lone Terry walk in, shake spook hand or other
member as appropriate, get all glory, name in papers,
nice memorial tablet in cemetery, too bad no find body,
give proper burial."

"Your road seems to lead right into a big puddle of
lava," Retief pointed out. "Somehow I doubt that even
the elite guard would step into that."

"Sure, gottum high-class fireproof sneaker, provide
by foreigner want help, hire plenty simple native do all
hard work while foreigner stand around give order. Not
bad deal, though, unsophisticated local boy get plenty
green stamp, spend all free time lookum catalog, find
plenty fancy consumer goods want have pretty bad, you
bet. But plenty hot work; fireproof sneaker not keepum
cool."

"What sort of work is going on down there?" Retief
inquired.

"Oh, all same movum big rock, smooth up wall, puttum special fancy genuine imported magic tube where foreigner say."

"How long has this been going on?" Retief asked his voluble cicerone.

"Ever since union get on foreigners, do own work, not join union; make deal pay back dues join up special honorary member, hire deserving local labor, bail union boss out hoosegow, givum all worker few nice present. Now all OK, work go top chop, no more sudden rockfall make lava spill down hole where foreigner; get job done, labor force get nice pay packet, union boss stay in new mansion and count take."

"Why did you quit?" Retief asked.

"No quittum, get fire, say too nosy, go looksee what foreigner do in special off-limits area, sanctum sanctorum or something, you know."

"What *were* they doing?"

"Too bad, not find out, gettum bum's rush soon as open door, lousy burglar alarm go off like devils in bad place. Wreckum eardrum." Seymour fingered his elaborate external auditory membrane. "That's how come elite guard manage sneakum up, catch trusty native guide with longhi up."

"How do the Groaci come and go?" Retief inquired next. "Their sneakers are no more fireproof than anyone else's."

"Oh, sure, foreigner got plenty smarts. Not wade through hot rock, flyum over top wall, land inside, all clear, closum big gate behind. All fix so big fly-car fit hole in rock like key in keyhole. Nobody else get through. Pretty nifty arrangement, keep out all snoopy villager come poke around, maybe pick up nice garbage, old sneaker got hole in, but plenty mileage left. All local soon learn stay clear, big taboo highly effective. So we better clear the area, Terry, before one of their roaming squads of security boys gloms onta us."

Retief's eye was caught by a small patch of dead white lodged in the prickly branches of a low thorn tree just off the well-worn path along the rocky ridge. He retrieved it, unfolded a Trip Ticket, CDT Form 2768 (1) as amended 6/4/92. On the back in block letters inscribed in soft pencil well lubricated with spit was the terse appeal: HELP. THESE DEVILS MEAN TO ROAST US ALIVE. TURN THIS NOTE OVER TO ANY TERRY EMBASSY PERSONNEL YOU CAN FIND—QUICK. YRS TRUELY, FRED POCKENHEIMER, DRIVER FRI-1. PS LOOK OUT FOR MORE NOTES. FP

"So far so good," said Retief. "The note is in the hands of the CDT. Now what?"

"Oh, rush in intrepid troops rescue all Terry in hand or equivalent of native bad hat," Seymour proposed. "Put bad hat in jail, feed good, get sleep dry, on bed even, not scratchum too many bug, have nice rest; all ignorant native rogue want get bum-rapped, give up easy."

"Sounds like a faultlessly thoughtout plan," Retief conceded, "except for one detail. You and I are the only intrepid troops available for the chase."

"Oh, did I forget to tell boss?" Seymour replied eagerly. "Union rule very strict, faithful native guide not allow get kill on job. Louse up insurance rates or something. So—good luck, chief. Be interest see how come out."

"Just drop by the Embassy next week," Retief suggested. "And I'm sure Ambassador Pouncetrifle will be glad to settle up at union scale."

"No gettum vacation in nice hoosegow?" Seymour inquired mournfully.

"That depends on just how glad His Excellency is to see Mr. Magnan and me back on the job."

"Bad news:" Seymour declared. "Hear plenty rumor Terry Bwana M'kuba Trouncepiffle or whatever pick up right after you, Sahib; him and whole crowd at dedication, lodge in durance vile down there someplace. So—

let's just let it ride, maybe someday you repay favor."
Then he was gone among the crannied rocks.

4

As Retief turned back to scan the view below once
more, a faint cry sounded from above. He looked up,
saw nothing at first except for the striated face of a rock
spine jutting upward into the sky, now lightening with
approaching dawn. The sound came again, this time
clearly a human voice in distress: "Yoo-hoo—up here!
Quick, Retief!"

It was Magnan's reedy tones, joined almost at once
by a glutinous Furtheronian voice, that of Captain
Sprugg, perhaps, yelling for haste: "If no ladder, say
goodbye old pal, officer of Creepy National Army of
Liberation, sad fate die here next Scary Place."

At last Retief was able to make out a row of oddly
assorted heads in silhouette at the edge of the tiny
plateau formed, apparently, by the breaking off of the
last few yards of the tip of the spire. A tiny fleck of
white floated gently outward from the position of the
maroonees, drifted in a lazy turn, came sailing gently in
to land at Retief's feet. He picked it up: another trip
ticket, folded into the shape of a paper glider such as
schoolboys launch stealthily across classrooms. It bore
the message: BEEN PERCHED UP HERE 21 HOURS NOW. NO
EATS. NO WATER, SWELL VIEW. NO COMPANY. AND NO WAY
DOWN. NEED ROPES OR BETTER YET, A SPINNER CAB. YRS
TRUELY, FRED POCKENHEIMER, CDT DRIVER FSR-1. P.S.
HURRY UP.

Retief waved, made his way across loose rubble to
the base of the spire, then followed it around to the
north side, where in a broad hollow a pocket of dust
and snow lay drifted. He tested it, found it as soft as

down. Looking up, he saw that the cluster of heads had followed his progress.

"Soft spot," he called. "Can you see it?"

"Barely," Magnan's voice came back with a quaver. "Whatever do you have in mind?"

"Better jump, Mr. Magnan. It seems to be that or a worse fate in the fire pits."

"Well, get busy, Retief," Magnan replied urgently. "Talk me into it." A moment later, with a wild yell, a spearbearing local savage charged down from a nearby ledge: Retief stepped aside, allowing the Creepy to impact against the rock spire and rebound, dazed. Retief took the spear and gently prodded its owner.

"You tender, juicy?" The cannibal inquired dazedly.

"That, again?" Retief inquired. "We're already decided I'd give you a severe case of heartburn."

"Not me, some other bum," the Creepy declared, producing a late-model crater gun which he aimed at Retief quite steadily. "I'm Irving, gladda meecha." He thrust out a hand and Retief hoisted him to his feet. "You must be Retief," he went on, "the one that got away. But looks like I got you now. Got problem, though—turn you in for bonus, or proceed to dinner at once." Irving's final words were drowned by a terrific impact accompanied by an explosive burst of icy grit, as a heavy body struck the snow-and-dust-patch dead center. A moment later, Magnan, hardly recognizable in a coat of floury white muck, tottered to his feet.

"Heavens!" he exclaimed. "So that's what being brave feels like. Can't say I like it, Retief. And, ah, was that yet another dinner invitation I overheard just as I arrived?" He leaned to a confidence-imparting closeness and added, "Such hospitality indicates unmistakably the high regard in which we Terries are held by these simple unspoiled primitives."

"I think that's an accurate assessment," Retief agreed.

"Still, if we linger in the area he's likely to renew the invitation."

"Retief, I think you're showing signs of developing a true diplomat's subtlety in these matters," Magnan said approvingly. "Now, we don't want to hurt their feelings by openly rejecting their overtures, so why don't we just slip quietly away, and—"

Magnan's proposal was interrupted by the abrupt arrival of Sprugg, who, on the first bounce, bowled over the cannibal, and impacted with considerable force against the bole of a stout green-barked tree. Leroy arrived in time to assist his chief to his feet.

"Tsk. The Captain seems to be one of those accident-prone types," Magnan observed as the Furtheronian officer stood, tottering, fingering an abrasion on his jaw and slapping halfheartedly at his coating of dust. "Come along, fellows," Magnan encouraged his erstwhile captors, "We're ducking a tiresome invitation—"

With a soft, whistling sound, still another new arrival shot into view from above, barely missing Sprugg and rebounding into a tangle of springy underbrush.

"It's Fliss!" Magnan cried as if delighted. "But I thought you'd decided to sit tight."

"To have taken further thought," the Groaci explained. "Our captors were less than scrupulous in their respect for my person. And would you have me linger there above to concoct explanations for your escape to Ambassador Nith?" the Groaci bureaucrat whispered as he extricated himself from the entangling vine. "Though to be capable enough in his chosen sphere, His Excellency is not one to hearken kindly to alibis."

"You, Fliss?" Magnan gasped. "Alibis? You suborned the kidnaping of fellow diplomats?"

Fliss recoiled as several of his eyes fell on the squat Furtheronian, rooting for his spear under the bushes, where Retief had tossed it, minus the stone head.

"A cannibal!" Fliss whispered. "Quick! Blast the thing before it utters an alarm!"

"I suspect the blast would give the alarm even more effectively than an utterance," Magnan demurred. "Anyway, it's only Irving. We were just about to steal quietly off into the night," he went on, "to avoid the necessity for protocol, you understand."

"Is that anything like a barbecue?" Leroy inquired dazedly, feeling over the ground as if in search of missing parts.

"In this case, quite possibly!" Captain Sprugg contributed. "With ourselves serving as *pièce de resistance!*"

"Nonsense," Magnan said shortly. "As it happens, Retief and I have already established most cordial relations with Irving."

"You delude yourself, sir. These dacoits are on nobody's side but their own!"

"Oh, fellow neutrals," Magnan said smoothly. "Better and better. Possibly I'd better wait until he reemerges from the brush and just spend a moment cementing relations."

"You still fail to grasp my meaning," Fliss muttered furiously. "The wretches will devour anybody, regardless of consanguinity or political affiliation. I therefore propose a truce, whilst we remove ourselves from the imminent prospect of participation in the local cuisine."

"I'm afraid we waited a bit too long," Retief said, noticing a stirring in the underbrush. "Unless you're good at fending off invitations, I think we're stuck with a dinner party." As he spoke, a deep rumble vibrated the rock underfoot, and a new gush of lava overflowed a ridge and came trickling down, nearly drowning the trail and the ridge it lay on.

A dozen low-slung natives, generally similar to Irving, stepped silently into view on the level above the new lava flow, with spears, harpoons, bows-and-arrows, and machetes held at businesslike angles.

Magnan, Sprugg, Fliss, and Leroy continued to stamp and to slap at the floury dust with which they were liberally coated.

"See spook come up out of ground," one of the new arrivals announced. "You payum bet, Arbuthnot: silly idea spook fly."

"*Seeum* fly!" Arbuthnot rejoined indignantly. "*You* payum!" He edged closer to the capering foreigners. "Hey, spook," he called. "You fly, right? Only not too˙ graceful: see come down clobber in pretty hard. Only spook already dead, survive hit rock like bale of yup weed falling off tailgate."

"Spook no tell truth," his comrade-in-arms pointed out. "Anyway, we seeum come out of ground. Pay up, chiseler!"

"Killum spook," another suggested.

"No can killum," Arbuthnot protested. "Everybody know spook spirit of dead Creepy. Can't killum dead fellow."

"Stickum anyway," the bloodthirsty one persisted. "Even spook no likum spear in zotz patch." He advanced, spear first. The others followed down the broken slope to surround the pasty-white group.

"Oh-oh, that does it," Sprugg announced. "Compared with these babies, Colonel Yan and his interrogation team would be like old pals!"

"Well, ah, speak up, Retief," Magnan muttered. "Explain to these simple fellows that we're on official business, before they do something hasty."

"No stickum," Sprugg exclaimed in the local patois, as the nearest savage gave him a tentative prod with his spear. "You no wantum stick me-fella, same like you, indigenous life form!" He pointed at Magnan. "Stickum Terry interloper, no gottum business here in the first place!"

"Well, I like that!" Magnan gasped. "And after we

were gracious enough to offer to put in a good word for you with His Excellency."

"Sorry, Terry—in this spot it's every life form for itself—" the captain yipped, and executed a nimble leap as the spear jabbed again, more vigorously.

"Him-fella spook hop high," the jabber stated judiciously. The spear carrier to his left edged forward and gave Magnan a none-too-gentle dig in the haunch. Magnan leaped, uttering a shrill cry and barely avoiding a puddle of red-hot magma.

"Retief! Do something!"

"Mine jump better," the second native declared firmly.

"Gottum two skins say *mine* best jumper," the first sportsman affirmed. He assayed a further jab in support of his assertion, but Sprugg eluded the point.

"Hey—no fair. How I winnum wager, you no jump?" his sponsor inquired in an aggrieved tone.

"I'll jump! Just don't jab!" Sprugg cried, and executed a creditable bound.

"Now my turn," Magnan's sponsor announced, and drew back his weapon for a determined prod.

"You're likely to spoil him," Retief pointed out, stepping forward. "His kind of spook jumps but poorly if at all with a stone spear head in the kidneys."

There was a stir among the rank and file as an imposing native of wider than average diameter, wearing a broad synthetic alligator belt cinched about his neck and a matching wrist watch, came thrusting through the circle to confront the prisoners.

"They-fella gottum cash in kick?" the newcomer demanded peremptorily.

"No checkum yet, boss," a machete-bearing local confessed. "Still scare of spook."

"No spook, only Terry and five-eyes, got plenty moola. Checkum fast, then chop up, make sweet and sour." The chief reached out to prod Fliss in the ribs. "Keep this one, fatten up. No likum lean meat."

"Help!" the Groaci shrilled. "Somebody stop him!"

"He's bluffing," Retief said; "He wouldn't pass up the ransom a diplomat in functional condition would bring."

"Ransom?" Magnan blurted. "But where would this uncouth savage get a sophisticated idea like that?"

"Easy," Retief said. "We'll suggest it."

The cannibal leader waved Fliss away.

"Ah—he's not as skinny as he looks, Your Chieftainship," Magnan put in hastily. "There's actually a lot of nourishment on him—"

"Cretin!" Fliss cried. "Explain to him that I'm an alien dignitary, worth quite a lot if delivered to my Embassy alive!"

"Shh! Don't give him ideas!" Sprugg hissed in a stage whisper, stepping between Magnan and the chief. "Ah . . . you keepum us-fella all one piece, we givum plenty gratitude, slap on back," he assured the local.

"Those are hardly overwhelming inducements you offer," Magnan snapped, stepping to a slightly higher ridge as lava lapped at his perch. "Quick! Tell him about the billion GUC reward!"

"You take me for ignorant savage?" the chief inquired with dignity. "No need spellum; I know it's 'guck.'" He turned to an aide. "What's guck?"

"Uh—sour fruit with tough rind, plenty seed," the adviser hazarded. "Grow on plenty tall tree, you bet."

"No likum peel fruit, spit out seeds," the chief stated flatly. "Also, no likum climb tree. Sour fruit pucker up buccal membranes."

"He was just being jocose Your, er, Majesty," Magnan volunteered. "Actually, we're worth a good deal more than mere fruit—"

"Vast sums will attend my intact return," Fliss whispered.

"Skinny meat, no talk," the chief cut him off. "Got too much on plate now, digest conflicting claim. Anyway, I heard no good eat Terry—"

"Why, bless you chief," Magnan gushed, stepping up beside Retief. "We're the Terries!" He nodded contemptuously toward Fliss. "He's a mere Groaci. Now, if you'll just arrange for our transportation back to town, preferably before the lava reaches us." He coughed gently, demonstrating the suffering occasioned by the fumes swirling about them.

"—might give bad case heartburn, or equivalent, eat alien meat," the chief conceded thoughtfully, "so—throw Terries away instead. Skinny meat, too. Make do with city hotshot." He turned away abruptly, "Private, too!" he added, indicating Leroy, who had crept behind Fliss.

"Wha-what does that imply?" Magnan plucked at Fliss's sleeve.

"It implies the imbecile means simply to discard us! Poof! Like that!" Fliss said, as the cannibals jostled him reaching for Leroy.

"Well—I suppose it could be worse, eh, Retief?" Magnan said hopefully. "We can make our way back to the city on foot—"

"Not that easy, Terry," a native armed with a hatchet said. "Chief plenty neat fella. Give orders always bury garbage."

He snapped an order and three squat jungle dwellers armed with machetes fell out to flank the diplomats, as others let Sprugg and Leroy away, expostulating vigorously.

"Come 'long," the hatcheteer said. "Nice hike to municipal sanitary fill."

"Retief! What are we going to do?" Magnan quavered as they set off down the ridge, followed by their escort, while Sprugg was hurried off in the opposite direction, Leroy trailing disconsolately behind.

"For the present," Retief said, "it seems we're going for a stroll in the crater of an active volcano."

"Retief, what's the matter?" Magnan demanded. "You seem so . . . so passive. It's not like you."

"As long as matters are going so well, why interfere?"

"Going well? Retief, have you taken leave of your senses? We're being marched off to be buried among the broken bottles and old bham-bham-fruit rinds—if we're not incinerated first!"

"No, burnam garbage," a guard put in. "New antipollution measures in effect, you know."

"I suggest we just be patient until the right moment comes, Mr. Magnan."

"The right moment? When will that be?"

Retief glanced casually behind them as they approached a turn in the path; the native foursome was trailing by a dozen feet, whacking idly with their machetes at the shark vines that draped the rock, and chattering among themselves; no other locals were in sight.

"Now," Retief said, and, rounding the abrupt corner, ducked behind a rock spire. Magnan and Fliss dithered for a moment, then dived for concealment in a crevice as the guard appeared around the bend.

". . . so I say, 'No, why *does* goom fowl crossum road?' And he say—Hey! Where Terry go?"

"Not gettum point. What Terry got do with goom fowl?"

"Story over, dum dum! Garbage consignment gone!"

"Quick! Beatum brush!" Brisk flailing sounds ensued, culminating in a sharp yelp from Magnan's direction, followed by a faint cry from the spot chosen by Fliss.

"Unhand me, ruffians!" the Groaci said. "One day you'll rue this outrage!"

"Your orders were to deliver us to the municipal dump in good condition!" Magnan expostulated.

"Condition immaterial, Terry. Where other Terry go?"

"Why, he's right over—I mean, ah, he, er fled. *That* way."

"Right here, chum," Retief supplied, emerging long

enough to lay a length of ironwood smartly alongside the hatchetman's skull just above the ear patch, at which the unfortunate fellow's three helpers fled, gibbering.

"No fetchum garbage to dump, boss consign faithful garbage detail fill quota!" one predicted.

"Terry disappear like puff of smoke from juju pipe," another pointed out, and whirled to look behind himself, cantering like a dog chasing its tail until he spun out and collapsed. The last hurried back uptrail, to report: "All Terries turn into goom fowl and fly away, give plenty loud horse laugh, chief."

"Shall we go, gentlemen?" Retief said to Magnan and Fliss.

"C—certainly," the senior bureaucrat agreed, edging nervously into the trail. "How in the world are we going to find our way back, Retief?"

"I rather thought we'd visit Colonel Yan's headquarters before we leave the area. I know the way from there."

"Heavens, this no time for courtesy calls, particularly while fleeing a barbarian who's already consigned us to the local equivalent of a Dempster Dumpster!"

"The woods are swarming with appetites," Retief reminded his senior. "A Creepy field HQ is the last place they'll look for us. Besides which, it seems like an excellent opportunity to gather a little behind-the-scenes intelligence."

"Hmm. There *is* that. Quite a feather in my cap, actually, if I were able to toss some dramatic findings into staff meetings Tuesday morning. Gracious, can you picture the expression on Colonel Otherday's face when I announce I've conducted a reconnaissance behind enemy lines?"

"A moving scene, Mr. Magnan."

"But hardly likely to occur if we're dismembered by these headhunters, Retief. Come along. With my unerring sense of direction, I'm sure we can reach the foothills by dawn . . ." Magnan paused uncertainly. "Which raises the question of how we're going to negotiate the mountains between us and safety . . ."

"I think Sprugg can help solve that problem."

"But he's in no better case than we—or possibly worse."

"Unless we're able to improve his status."

"Why should we exert ourselves on behalf of an unprincipled kidnapper who planned to hold us for ransom?" Magnan grumbled.

"We can hardly carry out that plan if he's playing a central role in a case of indigestion," Retief reminded them.

"To demand instant repatriation under the rules of diplomatic usage!" Fliss keened. "To forbid any peripheral adventures designed to curry favor with inferiors!"

"Come now, Fliss," Magnan sniffed, "it won't hurt to just take a peek before we go."

It was a brisk ten-minute walk back along the winding jungle trail, past the spot at which they had been captured, to a clearing crowded with imported plastic huts, based on a beehive design once popular among the less advanced tribes of the lower Limpopo region, but featuring packaged air conditioning, indoor plumbing, and rickety tridee antennae which clustered in a picturesque pattern against the moonlit sky. A few dozen spear-carrying savages were visible, busy at arcane tasks, while Sprugg, in shackles, harangued them unheeded, until suddenly he was bustled away.

"Ghastly," Magnan whispered as they surveyed the scene from concealment behind a screen of vines. "Once they're pacified, I daresay the alert diplomat who pro-. poses a jungle slum-clearance program will make valuable points at Sector—will earn the natives' undying gratitude, that is to say."

"A proposal already embodied in certain recommendations Ambassador Nith plans to dispatch to our government at the first opportunity," Fliss whispered sharply.

"We'll let the thought sustain us while we sneak up for a closer view," Retief said.

"Of what? The skinning knives?" Fliss inquired acidly. "I suggest we withdraw now, and—"

"And leave a former associate in distress?" Magnan inquired with raised eyebrows.

"Exactly. Glad to see you're going to be reasonable—" Fliss broke off as an agonized yell went up from a point near the center of the village.

"Poor Captain Sprugg," Magnan whispered. "We're too late. I suppose that was his death cry."

"I doubt it," Retief said. "It sounded much too cheerful." He started forward. "I suggest we get out of sight as soon as possible. There's likely to be a stampede along this way very soon."

"Retief, wait . . ." Magnan hissed, but he skittered along in his junior's wake as the latter went quickly to a darkened hut and slipped inside.

"Retief, this is madness!" Magnan peered through the gloom at the rude decorations adorning the walls: plastic antelope heads, New Jersey-made serapes, grotesque local deities of Groaci manufacture.

"There's not even anything worth stealing," Fliss whispered. "Appropriating for official use, that is."

"Let's get out before the owner returns—" Magnan's proposal was cut short by a sudden burst of cheering, followed at once by sounds of a crowd dispersing hurriedly.

"Alas! Trapped by the aboriginals!" Fliss shrilled.

"Maybe not," Retief said softly. "Stand fast; I don't think anyone's going to stop off here for a change of socks at this point."

"What point? What's going on?"

"I suspect that Sprugg violated security and convinced the chief we were too valuable to discard out of hand. That will be the posse passing now."

"It s-sounds like the whole village!" Magnan whispered in despair. "Now we'll never get away."

"But we don't really want to get away, do we, Mr. Magnan? Not before we've had our talk with the chief."

"T-talk with the chief?"

"Certainly." The sounds of running feet had faded into the distance. Total stillness had settled over the village. "Shall we go?" Retief proposed. "I think if we can locate the chief, we'll find him available for an interview now with a minimum of formalities."

CHAPTER FIVE

CAPTAIN SPRUGG LEANED IN ONE CORNER of the royal hut, picking his teeth. Leroy squatted as far from him as possible, eyeing the savage chieftain obliquely and muttering to himself. Retief and Magnan were seated beside the royal banquet board—a three-legged card table of Groaci manufacture—across from their host, who was securely trussed in a length of purple fringe borrowed from the royal wardrobe. Though not gagged, he maintained a sullen silence.

"I really feel that, er, those lacking diplomatic credentials should be excluded from the proceedings," Magnan said, eyeing Sprugg and Leroy severely.

"You're not holding a grudge, are you?" the Furtheronian protested. "Sicking them onto you was the only way I could stop them from popping me into the cooking pot," he went on reasonably. "No hard feelings, I hope, Retief. After all, I *did* side with you once you had the drop on 'em."

"Unless *we* end up in the cooking pot," Magnan reminded his part-time ally.

"But you goofed, assaulting Chief Yom in his own banquet hall," Sprugg continued. "Actually he's not a bad sort of guy, for a mere savage. We were about to agree on a deal for my release—"

"While we were fricassed as a consolation prize, I presume?" Fliss put in.

"You give a little, you get a little," Sprugg said. "You didn't expect the chief to go hungry after getting his salivary pumps all ready for a feed, did you?"

"No internal bickering, please," Magnan said severely. "We still have to devise a route of escape from the area before the villagers come back."

"I think the chief will help us with that detail," Retief said. "Right, chief?"

The chief made rippling motions with those portions of his anatomy not immobilized by his bonds, and muttered aloud.

"How would you interpret that, Captain!" Retief asked.

"Obscure dialect, but offhand I'd say it indicates that as soon as he gettum grasping member on any one of us, he usum to gouge out chunk," the Furtheronian guessed.

"Even after we explain to him how he's going to become the biggest independent warlord on the planet?"

"Sure. You don't think he's going to be robbed of his revenge by a trifle like . . ." He paused. "Did you say the biggest warlord on the planet?"

"That's right."

"Well, after we explain *that* to him, maybe he'll feel more like talking deal. Ah, by the way, how *is* he going to become the biggest warlord on the planet?"

"Very simple. He'll use the stockpile of munitions he gets from the Groaci."

"Eh?" Fliss spoke up. "What's this? You suggest that the Groacian state would aid and abet the depredations of this miscreant?"

"Nonsense, it's just the sort of *coup* Ambassador Nith dreams of," Magnan snapped. "But I hardly see—"

"Once the chief fully understands the situation," Retief went on, "I'm sure he'll be eager to get on with arrangements for the ransom."

"Retief—a word with you in private." Magnan looked coldly at Fliss and Sprigg until both withdrew to neutral corners.

"Now," he whispered, "am I to understand you're proposing to assist this savage in extorting funds from the CDT?"

"That sums it up rather neatly, Mr. Magnan—except that I'm not talking about CDT funds."

"Then what funds *are* you talking about?"

"Groaci funds."

"But how do the Groaci get into this?"

"Very simply. Sprugg sells me to them."

"Sells *you*?" Magnan gasped. "Whatever for?"

"A few beads and a safe trip to the coast."

"But—I mean—I *need* you. That is to say, shouldn't we stick together, shoulder to the wheel and bolder and bolder and so on?"

"I'll be all right—and I'll keep them occupied while Chief Yom's boys lead you and Fliss through the mountains."

"But, Retief, can we depend on these locals? As we've seen, Terries are no more popular here on Furtheron than we usually are . . . " He cleared his throat. "That is, while in time they will no doubt come to recognize the selfless role the Corps is playing in Furtheronian affairs, I can't quite see them risking anything important, on our behalf, at this point in our developing relationship."

"They will," Retief reassured his superior, "once it's suggested to them that we're in a position to let them in on the Groaci battle strategy."

"But what do *we* know about a Groaci war plan, Retief?" Magnan demanded.

"Nothing," Retief said. "There isn't one."

"No wonder our military intelligence people keep coming up blank," Magnan muttered. "But see here, Retief, how will the threat of disclosure of this nonexistent intelligence serve to coerce anyone?"

"Ah, that's the fine point, Mr. Magnan. Three will get you five the Groaci on the scene don't know they don't have a war plan."

"Possibly—but it's risky, Retief. From all evidences, they've taken leave of their senses. Why, Fliss even threatened *me* with a choice of dire fates!"

"Oh, they'll behave once it's suggested to them that we're in a position to let them in on rebel battle strategy."

"We are?"

"No—but they don't know that."

"Why, I daresay you're right. Capital notion, Retief. And once I'm safely back among civilized bureaucrats, your release can be simply arranged, no doubt." He rubbed his hands together briskly and favored the captive native leader with an affable smirk. "All clear, Generalissimo?"

"Me no generalissimo, my Chief Yom, plenty Big Shot, you bet!" The Chief broke his silence at last, and threshed his laryngeal plates impatiently.

"Who, me?" Sprugg protested when his part in the plan was explained to him. "I'm supposed to play the treacher for a hatful of beads?"

"Close enough," Magnan confirmed. "And you get to keep the beads."

"It's nuts," Leroy said gloomily. "Especially the part about me sticking my head back in that nest of foreigners." He shook his head. "If it wasn't for the ransom, I'd say the whole idea is a bunch of yatz foam."

"You'll be privileged to participate in a negotiation

carried out by professionals," Magnan said sharply. "A neat finesse, if I do say so myself."

"You call that a negotiation, with the chief trussed to the eye stalks?"

"Tsk. I see you're unfamiliar with the history of diplomacy." Magnan dismissed the objection.

"Yeah—but what's going to keep Yom from running outside and yelling his head off the minute we cut him loose?" Sprugg persisted.

"Don't give it a thought, my dear Captain," Magnan said smugly. "My experience of chiefs of state assures me that the Generalissimo will be most eager to join in a modest conspiracy of silence regarding the events of the past hour."

His guess was confirmed when Retief cut the chief free. The latter stretched his limbs gingerly, massaging various spots where his bonds had chafed.

"Well, what about it, Generalissimo?" Retief inquired. "Do we join forces, or shall we call the Grand Vizier in and explain to him how we tied you up in your second-best sarong?"

"Xunk not gottum sense of humor," Yom replied lugubriously. "On other hand, I like idea sell you-fella foreigner, get plenty wampum, buy plane, tank, rubber-band gun. Then royal chestnut bringum big laugh, you bet."

"In that case, shall we go?" Magnan suggested briskly. "I suppose Your Excellency can supply some sort of rude transport?"

"Rude good choice of word, Skinny-meat," Yom said. "Only chance, catchum giant froodle grub, get free ride." The native leader went to the exit and extruded an eye through the opening in a cautious manner.

"OK, coast clear—for moment," he called softly, "come 'long, showum secret route known only to royalty." He stepped from view; Magnan followed, then Sprugg and Fliss, with Retief bringing up the rear. The major moon was high in the sky now, shedding a pellucid magenta light on the well-trodden village street, on the towering trunks of the ancient trees looming all around, on the polished lacework of leaves casting complicated patterns on the scene. Yom ducked back, waving his guests to immobility as a pair of villagers hove into view.

"Old Yom lose grip," one commented as they paused to flap their respiratory membranes, catching their breath. "Sendum off on wild choob chase in middle of thousandth anniversary rerun *I Love Lucy*."

The other ran a dozen or so digital members along the edge of his machete.

"Probably trick so he get hog entire stranger," he said morosely. "Probably sopping up gravy right now, having good chuckle over nifty way he make dumbbell out of rank and file."

"Maybe few slice left for enterprising citizen," his companion said in an ominous tone. "Time for change administration anyway."

"Not bad idea, Depew. When I new chief, make you number one back scratcher."

"You little mixed up, Zop. Me takum over top slot, you gettum crack at position of royal hut-keeping staff—"

"You try steal my job?" Depew demanded, hefting his weapon.

"Ha! You got big idea, you expect outrank betters!" Zop retorted, and whipped his own blade up.

"Heavens," Magnan said disapprovingly. "Someone *do* something, quick. These two are about to murder each other in hot blood."

"So?" Fliss rejoined coolly. "Would you have them dispatch each other more dispassionately, Ben?"

"That's not the point, Fliss," Magnan came back tartly. "You, as a diplomat, should evince more concern with saving the lives of sentient beings!"

"I am, Ben, I am," Fliss reassured him. "Mine being the life I hope to prolong."

"Heavens, Chief Yom," Magnan whispered in what he hoped was the native ruler's auditory orifice, "it appears your retainers will hack each other to bits unless you act quickly."

"Just as well let treacherous bums dispose of each other," Yom replied grimly. "Save expense of official execution."

"But that will leave us without the troops you promised," Magnan expostulated. "Your whole army will revolt when they observe how unfeelingly you watch their comrades perish!"

"Not unfeeling," Yom protested, as the two soldiers' machetes clashed and clashed again. "Feel plenty satisfaction, watch little bout; Zop and Depew pretty evenly matched. Still, I'll put five on Zop this time. Him madder cause him wronger."

Retief stepped out of concealment and approached the combatants, who, intent on their contest, failed to notice him until he had grabbed both by the sword arm, at which they dropped the weapons and embraced each other for mutual comfort in the face of this shocking intrusion.

"Sorry, boys," Retief said. "I can't afford to have you dead right now, because I've got a use for you."

"Hey, Depew," Zop whispered hoarsely, "ain't this one o' them Terries which they wanna louse up our war and all?"

"Looks like one, according to what old Five-eyes said," Depew agreed. "Let's take him; you go for his legs and I'll go for help."

"No deal, Depew," Zop dissented. "You still wise guy on make, think you can sucker me. Why you not offer honest deal, like *you* go for his sword member and *I* go for help? Oh, hi, Yer Majesty," he interrupted himself as Yom emerged from concealment, accompanied by Sprugg, Leroy, and Fliss, while Magnan hung back. "Me and old Depew here was just warming up a little before we come see what keeping you. The boys missed you at the barbecue—and there's the menu, big as life, right behind you!"

"Never mind the smokescreen," Yom addressed his subjects. "I know you two slobs were plotting treason. Go ahead and hack each other to bits. You have the royal assent."

"Yer Majesty prolly noticed me and Depew here are in hot pursuit of one o' them fierce Terries we heard about—" Zop went on, unheeding the reproving note in his sovereign's tone.

"—and just stopped long enough to kill each other, so as to travel faster, I suppose." Yom interrupted.

"I caught that there like sarcastic crack, my liege," Zop returned. "Me and old Depew was just kind of kidding around, right, Deep old kid?"

"Wrong!" Depew replied. "Have at you, varlet!" At once the two trusty retainers clinched, organ cluster to organ cluster, said organ clusters set in fierce frowns of concentration while their eye stalks writhed in complex patterns which added to the inscrutability of their faces, rendered even more complex by the impulse to observe progress, which caused the dizzily writing ocular organs to pause in their struggles from time to time to stare fixedly at their own exertions.

"Stop!" King Yom commanded. "You're making me sick to my stummick! First guy mentions ripe garg gets a plain funeral at state expense," he added ominously.

"You boys better knock it off before you arouse the royal ire any further," Retief said.

"Just another coupla seconds," Zop demurred. "If this bum would just hold still for a minute, I got a neat *redoublement* I want to try."

Retief reached out and separated the combatants with a hearty shove. The two at once hurried off into the brush, and a moment later Furtheronion voices could be heard raised in contention, then the tramp of multiple feet returning.

"Oh-oh, we've—that is, you've—muddied the waters, Retief," Magnan complained. "Having made mortal enemies of Depew and Zop, to say nothing of Seymour and his partner, you've released the scoundrels to summon a necktie party which is even now descending upon us."

"No such luck," Yom corrected glumly. "Them ain't *my* boys my boys run inta; sounds more like a bunch o' them lawless savages from the next valley, which they deny my sovereignty and all."

"Good," Retief said. "Lots easier than having to beat the brush looking for them."

"*Looking* for them?" Magnan protested. "Whatever for?"

"To arrange our deal," Retief reminded his senior.

"Oh," Magnan recalled, "you mean about selling you to them as a sop to their ferocity, in return for a trip home for the rest of us. A most noble gesture, I'm sure, Retief, but somehow it seems a trifle selfish to accept—"

"Never mind the conscience searching, Ben," Fliss broke in. "Never give a sucker an even break, in the words of the great Foosh."

"Nonsense," Magnan returned. "Great Foosh indeed. Why, Foosh was merely one of your early Groaci warlords, and everybody knows that feelingless motto was coined by a Terry charlatan named Peetee Barnum!"

"Regardless of chauvinistic theory as to the origin of the saying," Fliss replied crisply, "its wisdom is not to be doubted." He eyed Retief assessingly. "What do you think he'll bring, Ben?"

"Why, we'll merely demand safe transport to the coast," Magnan decreed. "In a situation of this sort, one mustn't be greedy."

"Indeed? Why not?" Fliss demurred. "Ah, heart-warming greed, the noblest of emotions, one of our chief Groacian virtues."

"You not only openly acknowledge the well-known greed of your species," Magnan countered, breathless at the Groaci's audacity, "but indeed claim it as a virtue?"

"Greed," Fliss replied complacently, "is the noblest of emotions, my dear Ben, because it is invariably honest." He broke off as the first of the savages emerged, spearfirst, from the surrounding underbrush.

"Hey, fellows," the newcomer called over his shoulder, "Looks like we caught em with their longhis up!" He advanced another step, poking his razor-tipped weapon ahead. Retief stepped forward, grabbed the shaft below the head, with a sharp jerk pulled the aborigine within reach, and took a firm grip on the latter's first thoracic laryngeal plate, giving that sensitive organ a sharp tweak, at which its owner yelped and halted in his tracks, dropping the spear, which Sprugg at once picked up.

"Think I oughta stick the slob out of hand, Retief?" he inquired casually, fingering the sharp edge.

"Not yet, Captain," Retief replied, urging his captive closer to the little group watching in shocked silence.

"Why did you do that?" Magnan moaned. "Now we'll find it doubly difficult to convince them of the benignity of Terry intentions."

"Hah!" the captive cannibal interjected. "We know all about you Terries and your benign intentions! Why there's even a hot rumor going you plan to put a end to our war, which it's about the only fun we got!"

"A base canard," Magnan countered deftly. "That is," he added, belatedly realizing what he had denied, "of course we hope soon to bring about a termination of the fratricidal hostilities which now make life on the unfortunate world so hazardous for Creepy and Crawlie alike."

"See, Corporal," the prisoner cried over his meager shoulder to the noncom just emerging from the shadows, a full squad at his back, bristling with spears. "He admits it! I tole ya I got it from a hot source. By the way," he went on, "if you could see yer way clear to make this sucker leave go my chat flaps, I'd be much obliged."

"After a while, Irving," the NCO replied indifferently. "Teach ya to keep a sharper eye on the opposition, maybe, if ya suffer a little first. Now—" he faced Retief truculently— "why're you picking on Irving here, which he's one of my most inoffensive boys?"

"Tell the rest of your boys to drop the spears, lie down and roll over," Retief ordered. Irving made a lunge for freedom, tripped over the foot Retief extended, and went sprawling, his stubby legs pawing the air helplessly.

"Thanks, Irving," Retief said, then to the corporal, "just follow Irving's example, and I'll give you another chance."

"Don't do me no favors, Terry," the noncom replied, backing into his front rank. "A chance at what?" he asked, with an inquisitive tilt of his oculars.

"To beat King Yom's bid," the diplomat explained.

"Yeah? What on?"

"Me," Retief replied.

"You? What good are you? You're only one o' them Terries."

"It is precisely in my Terryhood that my cash value resides," Retief pointed out. "The CDT wouldn't pay ten billion guck for just any old species, you know."

"It figures," the corporal conceded, coiling on a rock in traditional haggling pose, while he plied his fangs with an ivory toothpick. "What's a guck?"

"A most rare and valuable fruit," King Yom supplied, "normally reserved for the delectation of those of royal rank."

"Never heard of it," the noncom said, dismissing the subject.

"In that case," Yom spoke as one taking over, "it's clear that the prize is mine."

"Whattaya talking 'prize'?" the corporal came back hotly. "Me and my boys has got the drop on you this time, Yom, and any prizes in the picture go to me. In immortal words of the great Spud, 'To the victor belong the spoils,' and all that, right?"

"In that case, you better get a wiggle on, Corp," the fallen King advised gloomily. "These here Terries spoil fast if they don't get enough food, water, air, nookie, and berb berries, you know. And the Big Cheddar down in town ain't likely to fork over the guck for spoiled goods, saying or no saying. Anyways, it was *our* former Beloved Leader, Werner, originate spoils system."

"Like fun!" the corporal riposted deftly. "Old King Werner never originate anything more ingenious than the chip transponder; I'll give him that one, but it was prolly a accident at that. But trivialities aside, *I* got the valuable goods here!"

Yom gave Retief a gloomy look, characterized by the unevenly canted ocular stems diagnostic of deep depression due to outmaneuvering by a wilier antagonist. "Too bad, Terry," he commented. "Looks like our palship will never have a chance to develop."

"Pity and all that," Fliss put in briskly. "But now that the matter is settled, let's get on with the payoff."

"Oh, I *knew* I fergot sumpthin," the corporal said. "Just what did I agree to pay for this here Terry, which he's spose to be worth all them guck?"

"It's quite simple, actually," Fliss explained in his heavily accented Furtheronian, "and cheap. You merely escort me and possibly an associate, in safely, to the Groacian Embassy at Furtheron City."

"Cripes!" The corporal exclaimed in dismay. "Are you real sure I signed on to do *that*?"

"Beyond preadventure of a doubt, my good fellow," Fliss reassured him.

"Except it's really *me*—and the hitchhiker Fliss, here—you're to escort," Magnan put in. "After all, it was I who proposed the deal."

"Now, Ben, easy," Fliss cautioned. "Are you sure you're ready to go before a Board of Inquiry and swear that it was you who proposed to go off and abandon your colleague Retief to his fate?"

"Perhaps I was a bit hasty," Magnan concurred. "Actually, I protested the deal, didn't I, Retief? Not that it isn't equitable enough: we salvage a senior diplomat, *plus* a Groaci functionary, all in return for a *junior* diplomat. Clearly an example of enlightened negotiation."

"Never mind all that," the corporal broke in. "The problem is, me and my boys are surrounded by about six sets of rogues, which I dunno why old Tom here ever wanted the responsibility in the first place, which he can have it back any time."

"Keep it, wise guy," Yom replied loftily. "I'm retired. I'll be interested to see just how you extricate yourself from this here like dilemma and all. Rots o' ruck, in the words of Admiral Higeshima just before the mob got him."

"Look, so OK, I was impulsive," the corporal offered. "I was just a young fellow which I was led astray by bad companions and running a strong-arm squad for Yer Majesty, insteada doing postgrad work in fifth grade and all, so I din know what I was getting inta."

"Very well," Yom said promptly, "we extend the royal clemency to you."

"Is that anything like a assagai?" the corporal queried nervously.

"On condition," Yom went on, "that you employ your squad of fellow traitors to disperse the rabble now encumbering the path of the royal progress."

"With only these six or eight coat-turning goldbricks, I gotta put to rout six invincible armies o' cutthroats?"

"That's one goldbrick per army," Yom pointed out.

"A ration sure to challenge the mettle of any true warrior."

"Actually, I'm more the administrative type," the corporal complained. "I didn't get these here two stripes going around looking fer trouble, after all."

"The time has come," Yom intoned impressively, "to look for trouble."

"Oh, I just remembered," the corporal said. "My boys didn't exactly capture this Terry; *he* captured *them*. I didn't like to mention it before, you see, but under the circumhooches— "

"You gettum big word wrong," King Yom cut in. "You no talkum good, like me, you no fit be king anyways."

"I'll make a deal, Corporal," Retief said. "You assign me to attend Mr. Magnan and Fliss when you escort them back home, and I'll release your boys."

"Deal!" the corporal said at once. "That'll keep the old T.O. filled up, and get me out of the war zone, and with all them gucks I can stay in town and set up a fruit stand." He swiveled a baleful eye toward Depew and Zop, standing by trying to look invisible. "You two are promoted to Temporary Acting Assistant Cadet PFC," he stated. "Now shape up these bums into a honor guard and let's get moving! I got a big career waiting down in town!"

"Better duck first," Retief said, an instant before a sonic boom struck with shocking intensity, trailing out into the shriek of a slightly out-of-tune atmosphere engine of the type associated with low-level attack craft. An instant later, the craft itself appeared as a glimpse of glittering red-and-black enamel and bright metalwork flashing overhead at treetop level—or a trifle lower, it became apparent, as the shriek faltered amidst a prolonged crashing of breaking wood.

"Ha!" Yom and his heir presumptive said as one, rising from their prone positions to dust leaf mold from thier ventral surfaces. "I tole you boys one o' them wise guys was going to outsmart hisself one o' these days," Tom exulted.

"Let's go look for the rewards!" Without awaiting assent, the corporal plunged into the underbrush. Magnan made an abortive lunge, as if to block his way, and was thrust back against Fliss and Yom, who stood dumbly by.

"Retief!" Magnan yelped. "Do something! They're getting away!"

"I don't think we'll miss them, Mr. Magnan," Retief replied coolly. "After a while it would have occurred even to the corporal that they outnumbered us three to one, and *they* had all the weapons in sight."

"He's right!" Ex-King Yom spoke up. "Good riddance to scurvy knaves!"

"And just when the virtuosity of my negotiation had them at the point of agreeing to give us safe escort," Magnan mourned.

"*Your* virtuosity?" Yom objected. "It was me, with a little help from Retief here, that had the bum on the ropes. You didn't say hardly nothing!"

"That's the subtlest form of negotiation," Retief explained to the primitive. "Now I suggest, with Your Ex-Majesty's permission, that we get the party headed toward town at once."

"Good idea," Yom agreed. "Whattaya mean 'Ex-Majesty'? With that usurper outta the way, my sovereignty is restored, unchallenged."

"Except maybe by Zop and Depew."

"Aw, we was just kind of kidding around, like we said," Zop explained. "Right, Depew?" the latter nodded.

"OK, so I've just put down a mutiny plus I repelled a invasion, or maybe insurrection," Yom recapped. "Not bad for one morning, eh? And I also worked a deal where I stand to collect a few billion guck; and like the corporal said, a fellow could make it big in the fruit game with a stock like that. I guess that demonstrates who's got the qualities o' leadership around here! So what do we do, boys, check out that clown in the go-boat, or head for town?"

"Never mind," a harshly accented voice came from the underbrush. "Just spread out in a line there, and get your manipulatory members back o' your heads; you know the routine."

"That sounds like 'cop' to me." Sprugg spoke up, having remained unobtrusively in the background during the negotiation. Now he bustled forth, Leroy trailing, and raised his forward set of hands.

"Now," the strange voice continued, as the little group complied with his orders, except for Retief, who casually lit up a cigar, "you people are lucky: happens I need some slave labor, so you get a chance to stay alive for another hour or two, if you follow orders precisely." He pushed his way past leafy boughs into the clear, a squat, heavy-set near-human alien dressed in a well-cut Eisenhower jacket over plain gray-green 'alls, with bits of bright metal on his massive shoulders, and a heavy power gun in a fist like a bluish ham.

"As I live and breathe," Magnan said in a choked voice, "a Bogan gunrunner, and as such under automatic sentence of brain scrape. Such cheek! Openly showing yourself here!"

"You can call me General Snart," the newcomer said, "and it matters little how many corpses know of my presence here—" He broke off as his eye fell on Fliss, at the far end of the row. "Well, excuse *me*, sir," he said in a suddenly deferential tone, "I failed at first to recognize you among these low-lifes. Please accept my apologies, and do me the honor to fall out and take a position on my right." He executed a medium-snappy salute, his features set in an expression indicative of shocked surprise (341-a).

"To presume too far, fellow," Fliss muttered in

Groacian, "when you imply some collusion between an outlaw and a Groacian bureaucrat!"

"Oh, I get it, sir," Snart responded brightly. "Ooyay ont-day ant-way ese-they obs-slay to ip-tay ise-way."

"Eecisely-pray, eneral-Jay," Fliss replied loftily. "Now you may offer me a chair and a cooling draught."

"I'd be glad to, yer honor, only wouldn't that tend to blow yer cover? as we say in the eye-spay game."

"Drat the eye-spay game," Fliss replied irritably. "I wish to be seated and imbibe an iced isky-whay and oda-say."

"Say," Sprugg spoke up as, at an inconspicuous gesture from Snart, a servitor appeared to offer Fliss a camp stool and a tall amber glass on a silver tray. "That there's a Scotch and soda, or I'll trade in my olfactory membranes, only he called it a 'isky-whay and oda-say.' See, it's a kinda code. Gimme a minute and I'll have it doped."

"Oh-oh, boss," the servitor commented to his chief. "It looks like security's blown again. How could this savage of got aholt of our top-classified crypto so quick, which the Big Boss only thought it up yesterday?"

"The rot runs deep, Private Burb," Snart replied gravely. "But I'll soon have their secrets out of them."

"A moment, please!" Magnan spoke up in an icy quaver, confronting Fliss. "In spite of your protestation, Fliss, I still infer that you are in some fashion in collusion with this Bogan criminal! Shocking indeed to imagine that an official representative of a civilized state could lend aid and comfort to such a degenerate, a gunrunner, an enemy of life itself—"

"Look again, Ben," Fliss countered cooly. "I'd say it was General Snart here who supplied aid and comfort to *me*." The Groaci leaned back cheekily on his stool and took a long pull from his frosty glass. "If you'd played your cards right, my dear Magnan, you too might now be lolling at ease, pouring soothing balm into your interior arrangements, rather than standing out in the hot sun as a condemned prisoner humbled before your executioner. A lesson in finesse for you."

"B-but anyway," Magnan quavered, "it appears your duplicity will afford you scant advantage, your colleague having crashed here in the deep jungle in the midst of the formidable peaks of the Lousy Mountains, known to all to be impenetrable territory."

"Still, *we* appear to have penetrated it," Fliss murmured.

"Certainly, getting *in* is easy enough," Magnan conceded. "But getting out is another matter. Pity this chap seems to have wrecked his boat; we could have made good use of it."

"Not so fast, Terry," the Bogan spoke up. "Dja ever stop to think maybe I always land like that? Makes a big impression on the locals when I step out, not a scratch on me. Spikking which, I estimate there's about a zillion of 'em closing in on this spot right now. So you'll have to excuse me, fellows, if I hurry the process of justice along a little, and just zap you where you stand, except for the little fellow, of course, which he's sitting down."

"I must insist, my dear General," Fliss came back hotly. "That you refrain from implying that I am in some way in league with you! Like these other poor clods, I am simply another victim of your lawless depredations. I'll relinquish this chair at once, lest my colleagues imagine I'm the recipient of special favors." He finished his drink in a gulp and resumed his place at the end of the line, next to Leroy.

"Very well, your worship, if you insist," Snart said in a rebuked tone. "A little to the right, please," he suggested as he made a fine adjustment to the aperture control on his Groaci-made blaster. "So's I can get the lot of you in one clean shot, you know. If there's any part of the job I hate, it's going around finishing off the wounded."

"Do you mean," Fliss inquired coldly, sidling closer to Leroy, "that you actually propose to immolate a diplomatic member of the staff of the Embassy of Groac?"

"Since you insist, boss," Snart concurred reluctantly.

"I think you must have misinterpreted my remarks," Fliss retorted tightly, abruptly resuming his chair and signaling for a refill. "So just get on with whatever it is duty requires you to do with regard to these riffraff." He indicated the lineup of Terrans and Furtheronians with a negligent wave. "There-after," he went on, "you may address yourself to the problem of providing me with suitable transport back to what passes as civilization on this benighted planet."

"Fliss!" Magnan gasped. "Does this mean you admit to Groaci complicity in the heinous crime of gunrunning?"

"Figure the angles, Ben," Fliss said offhandedly. "In my spot, what would you do? Hi, you there fellow!" He interrupted himself to address the servitor hovering nearby. "Move my chair over into the shade, eh? And I'll have a chocolate-banana dope stick."

"Say something," Retief urged his supervisor. "Keep 'em occupied."

"Well," Magnan whimpered to Fliss, "In your spot I think I'd at least have the decency to plead with this criminal for the lives of my former colleagues—the diplomatic ones, anyway."

While Magnan spoke, Retief made an inconspicuous adjustment to his cigar lighter while holding it carelessly aimed in the general direction of the contact cap on the exposed end of the spare power cell clipped to Snart's belt.

"Any chance of repairing your boat?" Retief asked the Bogan, casually.

"As to that, my dear fellow," Snart replied smugly, "what can be disassembled can be reassembled, eh?"

The detonation threw the general backward, his natty tunic torn and blackened, as was a patch of the horny hide beneath. Retief pocketed his lighter and stepped forward to collect the fallen terrorist's side arm, a moment before Captain Sprugg lunged for the same object.

"Lucky break he was carrying cheap after-market reloads," the captain said. "I've been expecting one of them to go off any second."

"Do me the honor to accept his Mark XI as a memento," Retief said, offering the compact crater gun. Sprugg took it eagerly.

"L-look!" Magnan squeaked from a supine position, having fallen backward at the shock of the explosion. He pointed with a trembling finger. All around, scared-looking Furtheronian faces were peeking through the underbrush. One of the newcomers, bearing fancy hide decorations indicative of leadership, slid awkwardly forward into the clear. "OK, boys—" he began.

"Nice work, Mr. Retief," Fliss commented as he swaggered forward to confront the bold native. "As for you, fellow," he addressed the newly arrived Creepy confidently, "good job you and your chaps arrived promptly. This little company of nobles acting as my escort of honor requires a well-armed squad to lead us by the most expeditious route back to the town. Sedan chairs, though desirable, will not be required. Ergo, you will at once select those personnel most deserving of the honor, and we will set out immediately. As you see, I have found it expedient to chastise this alien ruffian"—he indicated General Snart with a casual wave of the hand—"and you may have him, as well as the remains of the vessel in which he arrived but now, to do with you as you please." Fliss glared at the local with all five eyes at full-stalk extension, expression 721-x (Rightful Wrath Restrained Out of Nobility, But About to Burst Forth). The chieftain slunk away to give the appropriate commands.

"Hey, arf a mo," Leroy spoke up. "Just a minute, boss," he addressed Fliss. "Before you go giving away that go-boat, leave me take a look at it. If the general here got out without even disarranging his medals, maybe it ain't broke up so bad after all. Better'n sedan chairs," he added.

"Hey!" Zop blurted abruptly. "Me only dumb private, don't know where Big Shot headed, but me no go this direction—lead direct to Scary Place." He pushed his way through to confront the corporal. "You in charge of this outfit?" he inquired in an almost hopeful tone.

"Who, me?" the corporal objected in astonishment. "Heck, me only humble two-striper, and we got a genuine king in the bunch, and two or three other top three graders, outrank me six ways from the deuce!"

"OK, then who in charge?" the recalcitrant private demanded.

"Don't looka me," Yom protested. "There's been so many changes of administration in the last few minutes that I've lost track."

"Must be skinny foreigner, sittum special VIP chair, smokum dope stick," someone suggested.

"Insupportable!" Fliss keened. "To so twist matters as to make it appear that a Groacian dignitary, merely because he accepted a few of the amenities due his station, is thereby rendered responsible for the doings of an ill-assorted gang of dacoits! Is this *your* doing, Magnan?" the irate diplomat demanded, turning on his Terran colleague.

"Whom, *I?*" Magnan declined the responsibility. "That's perfectly silly, Fliss: I'm a mere captive just like everybody else."

"If everybody captive everybody else, then me free gettum out of here!" Irving declared, and disappeared into the underbrush.

"Quick! After him!" someone yelled and started in pursuit. In a moment such order as had existed in the group disintegrated, various impromptu groupings darting off in as many directions until, besides the foreign diplomats and a few ill-assorted locals, only Snart was left, a bit scorched and tattered but still a commanding presence.

"All right, you people have had your fun," he declared. "Now it's time to shape up and get moving!"

"Where to?" a number of voices chorused.

"To recover my command, of course,"

"We tie plenty rope," a small chap addressed by his comrades as Ambrose muttered, "draggum heap back to town, get fix at Enco station. Me helpum fix; me number one grease monkey, too, fix plenty skateboard and stuck zipper!"

"Nonsense," Snart barked. "I'm the only one in this neck of the woods knows how to get that tub going."

"Splendid," Magnan contributed. "You may proceed at once to lead us to the vessel, and there set about preparing it for VIP use."

"No goum Scary Place," Zop muttered doggedly, but fell in nonetheless. "No stayum here in spooky woods alone either," he explained to himself.

"Hey, what about our deal, boss?" the newly arrived local chief, still hovering nearby, demanded of Fliss, who flicked imaginary lint from the lapel of his bush jacket and muttered, "It seems you missed your chance. Another time perhaps you'll respond with more alacrity."

"Alacrity?" the dejected native echoed. "We can't get none of that stuff out here in the boondocks; the headquarters types in town hog it all."

"Quite," Fliss agreed. "A not unfamiliar phenomenon among the military. But let us carry on and perhaps another opportunity will present itself."

"Cheeze," the chief replied. "That's grayish-green of you, pal. Just keep the oculars at the alert; maybe I'll spot a way to trip up this here hot pilot yet."

"But not until he has effected repairs to his former command," Fliss cautioned.

"Sure not, boss," the chief agreed readily. "Fer the nonce, I'll ack like he's got us by the sneakers, right?" He gave a slovenly salute and headed his flock along in the wake of the Terrans, Snart at the head of the ragged little band.

"Oh, Retief," Magnan said, tugging at his junior's sleeve. "I'm a little mixed up. Just who has captured whom? Is our side in charge now, or what?"

"Offhand, I'd say we've all captured each other," Retief offered. "But since at the moment we seem to be going in the right direction, I suggest we accept the status quo."

2

Moments later, they struck the trail of shattered trunks and fallen boughs which marked the final approach of the go-boat.

After another few minutes of slow progress through the dense undergrowth, Snart paused and waved a manipulatory member toward a smoldering hulk of fire-blackened scarlet-and-black enamel upended amid leafy debris.

"There she is, gents," he announced superfluously. "And I'll wager a carload of guck against a half-used chocolate-banana dope stick you'll never lift her without a dock-crane."

"Just leave me take a look," Leroy said aggressively, and started forward. Retief fell in beside him. "Do you mind if I watch?" he inquired mildly. Leroy glanced at him dubiously. "Just don't get in my way," he admonished, forging briefly ahead.

"In your way is where I intend to be, Leroy," Retief replied, pausing beside the soot-smeared curve of cracked red enamel that was the fallen boat's port quarter. "Like this." He reached over the low-slung Furtheronian to grasp an inconspicuous panel of curled stainless-steel trim, and gave it a hearty pull. It came away, exposing a pristine metallic surface beneath, in which was set an emergency port. Retief operated the countersunk release lever, and the panel cycled open.

"Neat job," he commented. "Built by a little firm in the Belt owned by a chap named Leatherwell. It would have fooled me if I hadn't once had them run up a fake wreck a lot like this one for my own use." He stepped past Leroy into the spick-and-span interior of a small cargo lock. As Leroy attempted to follow, Retief put a foot between the Creepy's wide-set oculars and pushed. Leroy fell back in a heap, his horny carapace splitting at the impact. A curl of acrid smoke and an angry electronic buzzing emanated from the dark cavity thus revealed, within which vague movements were visible.

"Come on out, Nith," Retief suggested calmly. "The masquerade's over."

"But how . . . ?" a faint voice whimpered from the depths of the shattered carapace.

"You were careless," Retief said coldly. "I poked your supposedly sensitive yatz patch three times and got no reaction. A real Creepy would have gone into shock, at least."

"One can't cover everything," the breathy voice said defensively as a skinny leg emerged, groping for purchase. "Is it safe?"

"Come on," Retief urged. "It's not safe, but come on anyway."

"To see your dismembered remains thrown to the tiger ants at Yone." The breathy Groaci voice replied. Then a slight, spindle-legged figure with all five eye stalks laid flat (All Right, This Is It) clambered out through the rent in the false Creepy carapace.

"You're wasting that 79-w on me, Mr. Ambassador,"

Retief said casually. "The time for idle threats is past. For the moment, if you're *very* careful to mind your manners, I'll let it ride. Just keep quiet and keep those notoriously sticky fingers of yours to yourself. We're going to look this tub over and make certain everything's shipshape."

"You think to impose conditions on a Groacian Chief of Mission?" Nith/Leroy hissed. "To take care, vile Terry! Should you precipitate an incident which unleashes the wrath of all Groac on this unspeakable world, your chances of advancement in your presumptuous CDT will dwindle away to naught."

"Oh, they did that the first time I proved to an ambassador that he'd made a fool of himself. Come on, get moving—but carefully. If you try anything I haven't ordered you to do, it will be a long time before your remains are discovered."

"To have the audacity to propose that I, the ranking Groacian representative to this stink hole, would supinely accede to your demeaning proposal?"

"Oh, it wasn't a proposal, Nith; it was an order."

"Sir," the Groaci said loftily, "I must refuse to dignify your presumption—"

"Sure," Retief said, taking the undercover being by the neck and tumbling him inside. "We can fix up the paperwork later. Right now, there's work to be done, and you can graciously assist by telling me how the sucker trap is set up."

"Sucker trap? By this coarse term I assume you refer to the measures taken for circumventing interference by unauthorized personnel with certain arrangements?"

"Neatly put—for a Groaci bureaucrat," Retief said. "Tell me."

"We'd best along to the auxiliary stores hold at once," Nith said coldly. "That Snart fellow is something of a hothead, as we've seen. I suspect that an elapsed-time device on a minimal setting is even now humming away its final moments of existence. He seemed in something of a hurry to return here."

"Good thinking, Nith," Retief acknowledged. "You first, Your Excellency," he ordered, prodding the Groaci ahead. Nith braced his spindly legs to resist. "On more mature consideration," he whispered hoarsely, "to reflect that it were well to vacate the premises entirely. To recall, vile Terry," he added threateningly, "that you too will perish in the holocaust if the device is not disarmed in time."

"So we'd better hurry," Retief replied, and boosted Nith ten feet along the narrow passage with a shove of his foot applied to the Groaci's midsection. Nith, retaining his footing with difficulty, proceeded without further conversation. At an inconspicuous hatch set in the bulkhead, he halted, and began feeling over its surface as if searching for the latch.

Retief eased him aside and pressed the lower left-hand corner of the panel; it swung inward at once on a dim-lit compartment stacked nearly full with heavily banded cartons marked FIELD RATION ZZ-100 S. CLASS A EMERGENCY USE ONLY. GFM-100-3. Nith fingered the tight-stretched steel band securing the nearest box. "Headquarters types," he said disgustedly. "Considering that a Class A emergency can be declared only when all surviving personnel have sustained wounds of the second degree or worse, and only a champion athlete in his prime, equipped with the Type-ZZ cutter, could hope to remove these infernal straps, after which the carton, weighing seven hundred pounds, would have to be man—er—Groaci-handled through that narrow hatch, and the five layers of virtually impenetrable wrappings removed, what possible use could an invalid make of his emergency rations?"

"Still," Nith mused on, "it doubtless discourages frivolous use by the healthy-but-bored. After all, these Type ZZs are luxury items all the way. If any Tom,

Dick, and Irving could dip in at will, there'd soon be naught but empty husks remaining for a *real* emergency."

"Or, on the other hand," Retief pointed out, "it's just possible some crafty Supply type has substituted a little contraband for the disaster goodies. To me, those look a lot like Type G-7 limited-access crates."

"Are you mad, Terry interloper?" Nith objected sharply. "The use of G-7s is limited by solemn interspecies accord to category ultimate cargo accorded duty-free entry as destined for the personal use of Chiefs of Diplomatic Mission."

"What are they, Nith?" Retief asked in a man-to-man tone. "What kind of contraband is important enough to coax a full Career Ambassador out to make the meet?" He put his hand in the side pocket of his horizon-blue hemi-semi-demi-informal, early-late-mid-afternoon blazer, and took out a small brassy cylinder which he casually tossed up, caught and tossed again, interposing an elbow as Nith, three eye stalks canted at a sharp angle, lunged to intercept it.

"Naughty," Retief said. "This thing looks to me like the prime charge for a late-model Bogan hand blaster. I don't suppose the weapons it's meant for could be boxed up in those G-7s."

"Impossible!" Nith keened. "Surely this Snart person is aware that the penalty for such blatant defiance of interplanetary accord, as well as local criminal law, is brain scrape without anesthetic, followed by ritual dismemberment!"

"Certainly," Retief agreed, "and the same rather harsh measures apply to rogue ambassadors who get themselves caught red-handed mixing in the action."

"To imply?" Nith began indignantly, then more matter-of-factly continued in his fluent Terran: "Look here, Retief, I know we haven't always been the best of chums, but surely as a fellow bureaucrat you could see your way clear to quash this routine matter, just quietly. After all, no harm has been done, and no one but ourselves is privy to the circumstances. Let this one pass, and I'll see to it you'll find the Groacian Autonomy not ungrateful."

"It's tempting, Mr. Ambassador," Retief acknowledged, "but I'm afraid this time you'll have to take the rap."

"But why me personally?" Nith protested. "After all, it was that scamp Fliss who actually—"

"Am I to understand, Mr. Ambassador," Retief inquired coldly, "that a Groacian Chief of Mission is not responsible for the activities of his subordinates? That Fliss arranged to smuggle the stuff in in defiance of your authority?"

"Why, of course not!" Nith objected indignantly. "He wouldn't dare! He's a mere lackey, or Vice-Consul and Third Secretary, you know; he helps out in the Admin. Section. In any case, surely there's no need for heroic—or shall I say desperate—measures . . ."

"Now that the matter of who's boss at the Groaci Embassy has been clarified," Retief cut in, "it's time to get on to the desperate measures without further delay."

"And what form, vile Soft One, will these desperate measures take?"

"A modest mushroom cloud, I'd predict, unless we find out in a hurry where the demolition charge is set," Retief replied.

"Let's assume we have thirty seconds remaining in which to find it," Nith said in a practical tone. "Or, alternatively," he went on, sidling toward the exit, "we could employ that self-same half-minute in placing a discreet distance between ourselves and the detonation."

"No dice, Mr. Ambassador," Retief said. "You forget that this is no wreck—it's just disguised to look like one—which means General Snart had every intention of using it to get back to his base—which means it's not a time bomb but a booby trap. It won't go up until we meddle with it. Let's meddle."

"Are you mad?" Nith inquired coldly. "Must you include the person of the Groacian Ambassador Extraordinary and Minister Plenipotentiary in your madness? Why not avoid an interplanetary incident by permitting me simply to slip quietly away whilst you pursue your immolation?"

"I'd like to," Retief said. "But there's only one way I can keep an eye on you, and this is it."

"But suppose I just step into the passageway? I shall still be at hand if you should have need of me—"

"Sorry. I can't watch you through two inches of bulk-·head." Retief studied the Groaci thoughtfully. "But it occurs to me you're excessively eager to get out of this compartment. Could it be that it's stashed in here?"

"Nonsense," Nith came back crisply. "Why, clearly there's nothing here other than these few crates—be they G-7s or otherwise—plus, of course, the usual standard equipment, like that fire extinguisher and the intercom. Where could this imaginary infernal device be hidden?"

"Thanks for the tip, Nith," Retief said easily. "So it's not in the phone or the foamer. But you rather pointedly left out the security screen, for example. But why bother with all this conversation?" Retief stepped to the door. "I'll just leave you here to meditate while I give the rest of the boat a quick check. If you think of anything, just give me a call. Ta." He went out, closing and latching the hatch firmly behind him.

"Retief!" Nith's breathy voice rasped from the nearest intercom outlet. "To reconsider! To have a proposal! To let me out at once and . . ." His voice faded. "What's to be gained by imprisoning me here?" he resumed. "If indeed there *is* a charge planted here, awaiting a slip on my part, how can you be sure you yourself will escape the blast—and anyway, as you said, Snart expected to make further use of this, his only lifeline to safety."

"Yoo-hoo, anybody home?" Magnan's thin voice came

playfully from the stern. Retief opened the compartment door, reached in, and plucked the distraught Groaci from the intercom. Herding Nith ahead, Retief went aft to meet his immediate supervisor.

"Why, hi there, Mr. Ambassador," Magnan cried at sight of the Groaci. "Whatever brings Your Excellency out to this remote spot?"

"Your colleague, one Retief," Nith replied sourly. "And you may be sure the matter will arise in my next conversation with His Excellency Ambassador Pouncetrifle."

"I noticed that poor Leroy had given his last full measure of devotion," Magnan said solemnly, glancing back out the open port at the empty plastic carapace discarded by Nith. "Disemboweled, poor chap." Magnan mused. "What happened, Retief? How is it you escaped injury? Surely you didn't leave poor Leroy to his fate when the hostiles attacked?"

"Hostiles?" Retief queried. "I hadn't heard about them."

"Oh, yes, that's what General Snart and I were hurrying ahead to tell you. Just when I'd reached such a charming accord with Field Marshalissimo Wump—he's the chap who took to Fliss so readily—an absolute *gang* of unspoiled primitives came boiling out of the jungle and forced everyone, at spear-point, to form up in a column of ducks. Even the poor corporal and his little band of thieves were included. Wump must have made a sweep of this entire area, and just sort of swept *us* up by misadventure. I tried to point out that he'd be wise to reconsider and let diplomatic personnel go, but he seemed to have some dire scheme of his own. Anyway, General Snart eased over and quietly proposed that I make a disturbance under cover of which he'd slip away, and then he'd do the same for me. Sound chap in spite of all, Retief, though perhaps he *did* overdo a bit. Climbed up in a humzum tree and shot himself—and in

the excitement I got clear. But whatever are you lingering here for? Those savages are doubtless beating the
brush for me—or *us*, I should say, I suppose."

"Are you dead certain Snart pulled the chain?" Retief
asked. "It seems out of character."

"Well, first he yelled he was going to do it—as a
protest, you understand—then there was the shot, followed at once by the most dreadful cry and the sound
of a heavy body crashing down through the foliage. And
as everyone dashed away to investigate, I took my
departure. A most impressive distraction, I must say—
and all in aid of a Terry diplomat! I must make a note to
mention the matter to the Ambassador. It will make a
nice Interbeing Chumship item in the Quarterly Sum-
mation to Sector next month."

"Meanwhile, where is General Snart?" Nith put in.
"Weren't you to rendezvous after your escape?"

"To be sure," Magnan confirmed. "Over here, by the
ship. But the general's weakness in jungle navigation
detracts not a whit from the nobility of his action."

"If his action was as noble as you say, Snart won't be
making that rendezvous," Retief pointed out. "After all,
Mr. Magnan, suicide is a permanent sort of thing—
shouldn't be resorted to lightly."

"I suppose there *is* that," Magnan conceded. "But
the general was adamant: 'By the port tubes,' he insisted."

"Kindly keep an eye—and your Mark X—on Ambassador Nith while I take a look, Mr. Magnan," Retief
said, and moved off into the tall grass to round the stern
of the vessel. He paused at a faint sound ahead, then
advanced silently until he could see, through the thinning undergrowth, the burly figure of General Snart,
busy at an inconspicuous access cover adjacent to the
heat-eroded and blackened orifice of the port main
steering tube.

A moment later the Bogan closed the panel, looked
carefully around, noticed nothing amiss, and set off

toward the bow of the fallen vessel. Retief advanced to the spot where the Bogan had been busy, checked the jet-access cover, which opened easily, its latch sprung.

Inside, neatly wired to the ignition circuit relay, was the characteristic pink-and-yellow-foil wrapping of a woopee bomb of the type manufactured on Groac for use by practical jokesters bent on inducing coronaries in acquaintances owning late-model ground cars. GUARAN-TEED HARMLESS read block letters on the side of the compact siren, smoke, and blast device. Retief detached the toy and made his way back to where Magnan and Nith stood, deep in devious conversation by the open hatch.

". . . so impressed by Your Excellency's bold policy of personal activity in the field! Why, Ambassador Pouncetrifle hardly ever stirs from his chancery."

"What's that, some kind wisecrack, Ben?" Nith responded coldly. "One's duties sometimes require activities at odds with the conventional—just as one's duties sometimes require close attention to the paperwork back at the office. I trust no slur was intended, either to my colleague, Ajax, or to myself."

"Heavens, no, Mr. Ambassador," Magnan hastened to reassure the senior diplomat. "Oh, Retief," he said as the latter reappeared. "We were just wondering what in the world had become of you. Don't you agree we'd best be off at once before our former captors arrive and resnare us? I *do* find durance vile uncomfortable!"

"Not yet, Mr. Magnan. Let's wait to see what, or who, turns up," Retief shooed the two frail bureaucrats back inside the lock, over a flutter of ineffectual protest.

"Whatever were you doing off there in the brush?" Magnan cried plaintively around the edge of the half-open hatch. "Why, we might have been savaged by some wandering headhunter while you were off poking about out there!"

"But you weren't," Retief pointed out.

"Perhaps," Magnan suggested, poking his head from the open entry, "we—you, that is—had best go in search of the general. We wouldn't want him to be recaptured by those horrid natives."

"Too dangerous," Retief demurred. "You might be savaged by headhunters while I was away."

"There *is* that." Magnan conceded. "Hark!" he added, withdrawing quickly. "Here they come!" The hatch slammed shut.

Retief waited as General Snart disengaged himself from clinging vines which had already begun to creep up the prow of the fallen boat; he advanced boldly toward the waiting Terran.

"Ah, good day, sir," the gunrunner cried in a jovial tone. "How fortunate to meet you here, my dear fellow. I was hoping to rendezvous with your colleague, Master Mignan, or something, but he seems to have outdistanced me. He was instrumental in effecting my escape from the cannibals, a deed for which he will find Boge not ungrateful."

"That was careless of him," Retief said. "By the way, where is he?"

"Ah, poor fellow, he was savaged by headhunters. I interposed my own body in an effect to save him, but, alas, to no avail. Doubtless his noble features are even now being shrunk over a slow fire."

"Too bad," Retief commented casually. "You know, he was a great admirer of yours."

Snart preened visibly. "Indeed?" he said. "A capital judge of character."

"And since he's under the impression you kamikazied just to help him escape captivity, it would be a pity to disillusion him by turning up hale and hearty."

"True," Snart conceded, looking grave. "But surely you don't mean that I should, er, make good on my little deception—in cold vascular fluid, so to speak?"

"Regardless of the temperature of one's vascular fluids,"

Retief pointed out, "it would be a pity to forfeit the esteem of a First Secretary of Embassy of Terra just out of squeamishness."

Snart conceded the point with a nod.

"You may borrow my Mark IV if you like," Retief offered, "to insure a quick, if not neat, job."

"Look, pal," Snart said. "This matter is getting out of hand. I came out here on a routine delivery of disaster relief goods, OK? And when I land a little off-target, I get mobbed by a bunch of underprivileged Crawlies, and before they can get a good hot fire going, here comes another bunch—these characters are all at war with each other—even worse out here in the unspoiled wilderness than back in town where they got the bombardment going day and night. So anyway, I play my last ace, and get clear and aloft again, and then I decide to break out the old junk-yard routine and put her down nice—and what happens? I walk smack into three more sets of savages—plus you Terries and that five-eyed sucker, which you wanta stop a guy from making a honest buck supplying a few modern handguns to these bums which they're gonna beat each other to death with a blunt instrument if somebody don't step in to modernize 'em a little. So now *you* gotta come up with a idea I oughta croak myself. Have a vascular pump, fella; seein' we're in the same boat, sorta, let's join forces and get the heck outa here!"

"Not a bad idea," Retief said. At his back, Magnan nudged the hatch open half an inch and peeked out to contribute: "Capital notion, General. Perhaps you'll be kind enough to come aboard and attend to the technical chores involved in lifting off—quickly, before that horde of rogues arrives."

"With pleasure to be of service," Snart replied briskly. "And now sir," he added, addressing Retief, "if you'll just step aside—"

"Nope," Retief said flatly.

"I trust, sir," General Snart said grimly, "you'll not oblige me to employ force."

"Suit yourself." As Retief spoke, the vanguard of the mob of which they had so recently been involuntary members appeared, halted to stare, then turned and set off at a clumsy gallop to report back to their assorted leaders.

"See?" Snart muttered. "They've spotted us. In another three jerks of a snoof organ they'll be all over us like stink sauce on a plate of garg. So I decided to make another big sacrifice. I'll stay here and hold 'em off whilst you and yer pal go ahead and lift her outa here. When you get back to the port, tell Ogru I said hang loose. Par me," he added in a chocked voice. "When I think about how noble I am, I sorta lose control. Bye, pal." He turned away as if in deep dejection.

Behind Retief, the hatch popped again and Magnan's nose appeared.

"We're in luck," he whispered hoarsely. "Ambassador Nith assures me he knows how to operate this thing. So come aboard quickly."

"Give me five minutes," Retief replied. "The general has decided to stay close." He overtook the Bogan in two steps. "I suggest you move back to the shelter of the thick growth, General," he proposed. "You can hold 'em off there." From within the vessel came the low hum of fuel pumps starting up. In another four hundred and eighty seconds, Retief knew, the automatic sequencers would ignite the main drive. At that moment Magnan emerged, smoothing his somewhat rusty lapels, Nith at his heels.

"I—that is, we've—decided to just have a word with that mob," he said, swallowing with difficulty. "After all, one *is* a diplomat; no need for violence when a bit of conversation will serve as well or better. Right, Mr. Ambassador?" he concluded, turning to assist the spindle-legged Groaci down.

"Too right, matey," Nith replied. "You first, Ben. I want to watch your technique. And you better order Snart back before he louses up the negotiation!"

"I say, General," Magnan called thinly. "Do return at once. General Snart!" he added more vigorously. "It's been decided that an escalation of hostilities is contraindicated at this point."

Snart's broad flat face reappeared through the screen of brush at the edge of the swath cut by the landing of the go-boat. "You mean I don't get to scrag these suckers till after the big shots give up?" He hauled two struggling Creepies after him as he emerged into full view.

"Precisely, my dear General," Magnan confirmed. "You may release them, as a gesture of our benign intentions." Snart slackened his grip and the pair drew back out of arm's range and began to jeer, contorting their features in expressions conveying ridicule. "Sucker" was the kindest term they employed before they turned and disappeared. Magnan advanced as if casually, passed Snart, and proceeded in the direction taken by the two parolees.

"Ben's aplomb should be an inspiration to us all," Nith commented solemnly. Magnan disappeared into the deep jungle shadows; shouts and the crashing of heavy bodies among dense growth ensued at once, but faded quickly. Then the head of the column of jungle dwellers thrust into view, carrying Magnan, trussed and slung head-down from what Retief recognized as a ceremonial Torture Pole, an even more elaborately carved one than that on display in the State Museum across the street from the Terran Embassy.

3

As the native escort halted at sight of the three foreigners, Magnan, managing to twist so as to see what it was
that had halted the savages, yelled, "Retief! Farewell!
This time there's no escape. They're taking me to the
top taboo Scary Place, there to subject me to torments
undreamed of even by the Grand Inquisitor of Haterak.
A trial to exceed the Tsugghood rituals of bleak Oberon.
It's no use trying to help—this time I'm done for. Our
partnership is at an end. Save yourself, and tell Mother
I died game."

"Pretty good wind for a sucker hanging downside-up,"
Snart commented. "Let's go."

"Almost, Retief," Nith hissed harshly, "almost I rejoice to see you thus impotent in the face of the certain
destruction of your colleague. Though of course it is a
bit rough on Ben, a harmless bureaucrat whose record
is unblemished by any affirmative action whatever—an
ornament to the high calling we share!" Nith shed a
crocodile tear from the tip of an ocular with a deft flick
of that member.

"Hang loose, Mr. Magnan," Retief called. "I'm going
to put our Category Ultimate plan into effect—the cata-
clysm bomb, remember?"

"Still," Magnan croaked as there was a stir among the
cannibals, "to destroy an entire planet—nay, a whole
solar system, perhaps even an Arm of the Galaxy—isn't
that perhaps too severe?"

"How can man die better?" Retief inquired rhetorically, waving Nith and Snart back as he advanced a few
paces. By now the entire band of marauders had come
forward to stare threateningly from the jungle edge,
spear points foremost. Retief planted the woopee bomb
carefully in a patch of zitz weed, ignited it with his cigar
lighter, and walked away. At once the main body of the
besieging cannibals melted away.

Nith and Snart had retreated to the illusory shelter of one of the artfully scorched atmospheric guidance vanes of the pseudo-wreck, but they emerged as Retief approached.

"Why bother hiding," Snart said, "when the whole planet's going up, eh, Retief?"

"But on the other hand," Nith continued, "if it's maybe a dud—" But an eardrum-piercing screech cut him short as greenish-black smoke boiled abruptly from the infernal device. The last of the villagers fled.

"Farewell, Retief!" Magnan's reedy voice called over the clamor of the astonished savages. Then there was a detonation which rattled windows a mile away in a rude shack on the inner curve of the extinct crater known as the Scary Place. A lone administrator, sitting at a desk, looked up in annoyance.

"Drat!" he exclaimed. "That wasn't on the schedule! What's keeping the beggars?" He rose to look out into the night. "All is ready," he muttered. "Let the sacrifice appear."

4

At the battered hulk which had been Snart's Class A go-boat, Retief urged Nith and the general aboard. He went quickly forward and reset the motor drive sequencer on HOLD, then motioned Nith to a gear locker.

"Retief," Nith protested in a choked voice, "are you so unmoved at the passing of your old comrade, your companion in so many adventures, one with whom you have so often met—and mastered—disaster, as we Groaci have good cause to know? Does it not temper the harshness of your judgment to contemplate the dismal fate of one with whom you have shared hardship and danger? Do you feel no impulse to mildness in your handling of the trifling offense we discussed so perfunctorily earlier?"

"If you mean am I going to let you off the hook in memory of Mr. Magnan, I doubt that Mr. Magnan would appreciate the irony of it," Retief said bluntly. "Right now you're going to help me pull off a raid that will make Mr. Magnan's secret mission to the Quornt look like a visit by the tooth fairy."

"Doomed!" Nith keened. "To have suspected that all was up as soon as I recognized your lineaments among the functionaries aboard the limousine! Why did I not then turn back?"

"No time for vain regrets," Retief said. "General Snart, would you mind defusing your little self-destruct gadget? After all, if we go, *you* go."

"Quite a reasonable assumption," Snart said, and withdrew with commendable alacrity.

"'To lapse into catatonia," Nith said in a calmer tone. His oculars snapped erect, then tilted to stare intently into each other's depths. Nith's breathing became fast and shallow, and his hide, under Retief's hand, turned cool and clammy. Retief gave him a slight shake, then a more insistent one.

"It's no use." A monotone issued from the unconscious Groaci's vocal aperture. "I'm a third-degree master; I can make deep coma in four seconds flat. I'm not coming out again until I'm safe. Good luck, rash Terry!"

"But you hear my voice clearly," Retief stated firmly. "And you will do precisely as I command. Understand?"

"Of course," Nith concurred blurrily. "I await your command."

"You will remain in a deep hypnotic state until I say 'inscrutable.' Meanwhile you will hear, understand, and obey whatever suggestions I give you. You will not be afraid, and you will tell me everything you know about the situation here on Furtheron, especially the role played by Groac. Start now."

"When Admiral Slizz reported that the newly explored world Ynnezadoog was potentially habitable, a full Survey Party was dispatched at once. This was some twenty years ago, Standard. The landing party was greeted by a heavy bombardment to which the admiral responded by hastily erecting the fortified camp which has now come to be called Furtheron City. The early discovery of valuable mineral deposits provided sufficient incentive to remain, in spite of the hostility of the place. I say 'place' advisedly, since the 'bombardment' is a natural phenomenon, due to an eccentric sort of vulcanism, and had been proceeding continuously for at least some millions of years. Investigation by Groacian geologists revealed that gas pressure within the porous crust constantly expelled particles from surface pores, these particles ranging in size from dust grains to multiton boulders. Once expelled and having fallen back to the surface, such an object tended naturally to roll or slide downhill until it encountered an open pore large enough to admit it, in time wearing well-refined grooves which thereafter channeled later objects to the same orifice. These returning particles clogged the gas vents until reexpelled, the repeated expulsions occurring along the most convenient channels, in time smoothing and strengthing them until they attained the appearance of well-polished gun barrels. So much for outré natural phenomena. Now let us consider the local population. Having evolved under constant bombardment from an unknown source, they not unnaturally developed a sense of hostility toward whomever it was who was attacking, as they imagined. Since the enemy could be anyone, mutual hostility became the norm. Thus spurring the growth of intelligence, while the natural conditions kept the population small and prevented developments of any cooperative nature, such as organizing socially. We Groaci found conditions of complete anarchy here, and of course set about creating local government institutions in the hope of ameliorating the universal impulse to attack on sight any fellow Furtheronian—foreigners, of course, being exempt, since clearly they could not be at the bottom of an assault which predated their arrival by eons. In the end, we arrived at two major factions, which we not unnaturally called Hither and Nether, based on the location of the parley sites at which the protocols were hammered out. We appointed Lib Glip as Premier here aboveground, and one Barf, self-styled 'General,' as the Nether leader."

"Swell," Retief said. "Later you can explain the explanation. And all this was just for sheer love of your fellow beings?"

"Precisely," Nith confirmed promptly. "Selfless Groac has brought this plague spot as near to a condition of nonbelligerence as is possible. We have cooperated with the instrusive Terry-sponsored Tribunal as a gesture of amity, knowing the efforts of ITCH to be futile."

"Why didn't you tell Chairman Pouncetrifle the whole story?" Retief demanded.

"We tried, we tried, but Ajax could see no prospects of advancement in rank arising from a totally negative report to Sector—ergo, he goes through the motions."

"What did kidnapping Mr. Magnan and me have to do with all this? But you were trying for the Ambassador, of course."

"Obviously, my dear fellow. But your interference upset the assault on the car. Thereafter, before I could regroup, my associate, Captain Sprugg, was a bit too impetuous, thus landing us all in this sorry contretemps. Of course, later Chairman Ambassador Pouncetrifle was indeed to come along. Tsk, it would all have been so much simpler if he'd come voluntarily, as invited . . . But no need to grieve over unrealized potentialities, eh, Retief? We've our own plates full, merely struggling to survive in this hell spot into which your intransigence has dragged us all." Nith glared sightlessly, his eye stalks at half-mast.

"Why?" Retief pressed on. "Not just for ransom, surely. And it must have some connection with your own august presence so far from your cozy sandbox back at the Embassy of Groac."

"Of course. We were to meet with a foreign dignitary of awesome magnitude, all in the interests of poor bleeding Furtheron, of course. Pity Ajax wouldn't come along voluntarily, thus earning haughty Terra a place at the bargaining table later."

"I believe our friend Snart is coming back," Retief said. "You will act normally, but with loyalty to my cause at all times, got it?" Then, as General Snart entered, he said, "General Snart, will you take the co-pilot's position?"

"Madness," Snart barked. "Co-pilot indeed! To what end, mad Terran? Little do you dream that even as we natter of trivialities, the detonation of an awesome device called a Termination Bomb is rapidly approaching S-second. Farewell to vanity! I tried, in my magnanimity, to lead you from this fatal spot, but you, rash Terry, insisted. Now let us wait our fates with dignity." Snart folded his arms, elevated his massive chin, and assumed what he imagined to be a noble expression. Retief took him by his thick neck and the seat of his whipcords and threw him through the entry to the front office.

"Your kind have an unfortunate habit of interpreting courtesy as weakness," he said. "Now strap in and keep your hands off that board."

Snart quickly jerked back his hands and tried to reassume the noble look.

"If you imagine, poor deluded Terry," he grunted, "that you have any conception of the operating procedures for a new-model Bogan Class One go-boat, you are in for a rude shock."

"Never mind that," Retief said, taking the pilot's position, while Nith tugged in vain at the hand grip to which Retief had secured him with a strip of braid from the unfortunate Chief of Mission's bedraggled informal hip cloak. As Retief studied the auxiliary panel somewhat crudely riveted in place over the elaborate factory-installed communications group, Snart uttered a bark of his less-than-hilarious laughter.

"Peer well, fool! Never will you penetrate the cryptic arrangements devised by Boge's picked Deep Think teams to circumvent unauthorized usage of Bogan state property."

"Don't kid me, Snart," Retief countered offhandedly. "That lockup was installed by one of Leatherwell's shifty operators named Bunny de Mand, at a hot-drop shop in the Belt. It's what he calls his October Thirty-one Special. Not even recoded."

"Madman!" General Snart grated. "But touch that dire device and violence undreamed of in your philosophy will rend your very atoms, my own position being insulated from the effect. Still, out of respect for your recent bereavement I offer you one last chance: Leave me here alone and withdraw and I'll be inclined to forget all this."

"Me too!" Nith wailed. "Make him unlash me first. After all, there's no need to create an interplanetary incident by vaporizing a harmless Groacian diplomat, eh? And once returned to Groac safe and sound, I can put in a good word regarding certain negotiations concerning recognition of the *de facto* Bogan regime at Fournoy and a few other places—plus, of course, a tribute to your own impeccable handling of this unfortunate matter, good for a two-star boost at the minimum."

"See me after," Snart said stonily. "Now, Retief," he went on, "I can see you're a practical fellow. You know how to get things done, and when to keep the old nostrils out of something which you'll just get 'em packed full of lint. So just be reasonable and get on to something else. OK, you got the drop on me, even got inside what's left of my official go-boat, and old prissy-britches here is pretty well run out of dumb ideas—so why don't you just buzz off like a smart guy which he knows next time the sneaker may be on the other pedal extremity, hah?"

"This little installation interests me," Retief said as if Snart had not spoken, indicating a large but inconspicuously mounted lever beneath the main panel, secured open with a loop of wire and a large blob of black sealing compound.

Snart uttered a humorless chuckle. "Just test it out, chum, and maybe, just before the last brain cell vaporizes, it'll dawn on you that a Bogan go-boat's not so easy to hijack."

"A black seal means lethal category in Bogan usage," Retief mused. "That's a security classification. So what's so secret about a lever—especially one that gets vaporized as soon as any unauthorized personnel mess with it? And it's pretty clear they didn't send you in here just to clobber-in less than a mile from the Scary Place." Retief turned to look steadily at Snart's leathery face. "If I hadn't recognized your Chief of Technology down in town, I might not even have realized I was dealing with a Bogan Top Person," he conceded. "The cover was fair, but you boys have gotten careless because you've had it too easy for too long." He grasped the big lever firmly, and the Bogan began a lunge which turned into a back flip when Retief's free fist connected solidly with his wide, bony jaw.

Nith, tugging at his bonds with suddenly renewed vigor, protested. "Retief! Are you mad? First you state that we are in the presence of a member of the Bogan Imperial Family, then you assault His Imperial Highness! Need I remind you that this is a breach of protocol which will have your Sector HQ, and even the

Department back on Terra, writing official apologies for the next decade?"

"Old Snart here is actually His Imperial Highness Lieutenant General the Prince of the Blue, former head of External Operations in the Bogan Ministry of Espionage," Retief said. "I finally recognized him from the mug file back at Sector. He was thought to be working under cover back on Vroom 12; it seems he's widened the scope of his operations."

"To be sure," Nith said severely. "Our security people were equally at sea; we understood he had returned to Boge to participate in a palace revolution intended to place his branch of the imperial family on the throne in the person of Grand Admiral the Archduke Gorg. Curious that he should be here in this backwater, conducting a solo operation on foot in a cannibal-infested jungle."

"You forget, Mr. Ambassador," Retief said, "we're only a mile from the Scary Place."

"Oh, yes, I've heard of it, some sort of volcanic fissure from which issue fumes and oracular pronouncements, eh?"

"Close, but I'd like a better look," Retief said, and threw the big lever.

5

For a moment nothing happened; then a deep rumbling started up, growing to a vibration which shook the heavy vessel as if it were afflicted with *agitans gravis*. The needles on the instrument faces swung wildly; the seats, with their occupants, bounced and swayed until the Bogan's chair fell backward, even as a communicator deck fell from its mounting.

"Ch-cheap construction," Nith commented, as the stanchion he was gripping came away in his hand. "So we see the vaunted Bogan war machines are but flimsy, after all."

"By no means, my dear Mr. Ambassador," Snart rejoined as he got to his feet. "These items are by design affixed but casually. As they fall off, they are carefully gathered, tagged, and placed in stores. Thus we avoid the necessity for carrying redundant spares, as our supply always matches demand precisely. A triumph of Bogan logistics."

"Maybe," Nith conceded. "But what if something important falls off just when you need it?"

"There are trifling flaws in any system," Snart returned. "One can't demand absolute perfection of mortal creatures."

As they spoke, the shaking had increased both in frequency and in amplitude, punctuated now by heavings and lurchings, and loud clattering sounds from without. Retief extruded one of the machine's external viewers and turned it so as to scan the length of the hull. Great sections of the camouflage covering had fallen away, taking with them dummy gun ports and beam apertures. The inner hull thus revealed was that of a sleek atmosphere craft of antique design; that it too was false became apparent as the surface split longitudinally to expose a squat, functionally ugly bulk with immense flexible treads for surface traction. More bits and pieces dropped away until the vehicle's true form was revealed in its entirety: a Yavac battle unit, the famed Bogan copy of the Groaci version of the mighty Bolo Combat Unit.

"Clever," Retief affirmed. "Two layers of disguises— and so far we've stripped off only *one* of your own, Your Imperial Highness. What's *really* under that rugged exterior of yours?"

"To pry no further, rash Terran," Snart said in accent-free Groaci and the whisper characteristic of that tongue. "To let well enough alone. To release me and this unfortunate functionary, Nith, as well, and to go your way. Your fate shall be one with which to discipline the recalcitrant of generations yet unborn."

"Nith"—Retief addressed the Groaci, now hanging listlessly in his bonds—"I'm going to take a look at the inscrutable Scary Place. Now's the time to decide which side of the fence you like best. Would you like to get off here among the cannibals or come along to guard the prisoner?"

"Why, as to *that*," Nith stated indignantly, "would you presume to coerce a Groacian Chief of Mission? You, a mere Second Secretary?"

"Sure," Retief replied cheerfully. "Just take him back and lock him up in that cozy little storeroom we found. Use your Mark X." He cut the diplomat's bonds.

"Very well," the unmasked Groaci agreed, rubbing has cramped limbs. "To do as you suggest, but under duress—not that I do not fully support the investigation of this Scary Place, in due course, by duly constituted officials." He motioned apologetically to the Prince of the Blue, and they started aft.

A moment later, Nith was back. "The miscreant to have overpowered me!" he gasped. "To have leaped clear and fled into the jungle! In *that* direction." He pointed a shaky finger. "Straight toward the Scary Place!"

"We'd better beat him to it," Retief said, and slammed home the big drive-control lever.

CHAPTER SIX

IT WAS A JOLTING HALF-HOUR ride for Retief and his reluctant ally, as the giant fighting machine drove relentlessly forward, dozing its way through any obstacle it could not pass over. Immense trees toppled to be crushed undertread. Rocky ridges crumbled to gravel, and at last they emerged from the dense growth at the base of the foothills culminating in the sawtoothed rim of the great crater, halfway around its periphery from the vantage point from which Retief had surveyed it earlier.

"This formation appears to be a major meteor strike," Nith commented, "rather than a volcanic crater. Curious. But now that we've seen it, let's go home."

"Not quite yet, Mr. Ambassador," Retief demurred. "They still have Mr. Magnan in there, remember? And then there's our ex-prisoner, His Imperial Highness Lieutenant General the Prince of the Blue, and whatever mischief he's up to."

"True enough," Nith agreed. "I shall regret leaving Ben to his fate while permitting Prince Blue to go free to continue his depredations, but there you are. 'One can't win 'em all,' as King Zont remarked on the occasion of his decapitation by a party of wretches recently freed from durance vile by his royal clemency. Pity he couldn't have celebrated his accession by some less spectacularly liberal ploy."

"The difficulty with being an Uplifter," Retief remarked, "is that it involves contact with the upliftees, who invariably regard their benefactor as one of the Oppressors, and a fool to boot. And as soon as he gets within range, well, someone on whom to vent one's righteous indignation is better than just sitting around packing bomb casings and complaining."

"Of course," Nith agreed. "But one mustn't speak of it; if it were generally recognized, Uplift as we know it would suffer."

Retief gunned the Yavac up the slope toward the nearest notch, while Nith clung to his seat and made keening noises as the angle of climb increased to 45 degrees before they topped the rise to squeeze between towering rock faces and look down at close range on the Scariest Place of all.

From this position Retief had an unobstructed view of the precipitous drop-off to the wide expanse of hardened magma below, where a numerous black-uniformed cadre of several species moved like ants among storage huts, stacked crates, rubbish piles, and heaped tailings, around the gaping cavity at dead center. Far across the crater, the peaks of the opposite rim stabbed up in stark silhouette against the pearly white of predawn.

"It's been a long night," Retief remarked. "You'd better lock in your shock frame now, Mr. Ambassador. From now on the going will be rough."

"You *don't* propose to drive over the cliff, Retief?" Nith hissed. "Pity and all that, but our gallant attempt to rescue our colleague clearly ends here." He extended his three long-range oculars to survey the cliff edge extending both ways, while his two close-in visual organs gazed morosely at the instrument readings.

"We've a full charge on the plates, I see," he noted. "That should take us safely back to town and our respective Missions with power to spare."

"Perhaps, Mr. Ambassador," Retief said, manipulating various levers, causing instrument readings to fluctuate wildly. "You've forgotten that this is a copy of a Bolo Mark XV Model Y, and thus has a limited lift capability for maneuvering in rough country." As he spoke, the deep hum of the converters dropped to a bass growl; the heavy vehicle shuddered, creaked, and rose some inches above the rock ledge on which it had rested. As it began to drift sideways toward the drop-off, Retief threw in the autopilot, which checked the slip immediately. Nith, his oculars quivering with the effort of focusing on the shifting perspective of the near-vertical slope, uttered a thin wail and began to finger an elaborately engraved kiki stone, uttering breathy invocations to the discredited pantheon of ancient Groac.

"Don't make any vows that will oblige you to spend the rest of your days in the ice mines to pay off," Retief suggested. "I hear those old idols like Yhang the Insatiable and Fross the Needle-fanged are a vengeful lot. You wouldn't want to start down the cliff hoping you don't make it."

"One should never speak thus lightly of these old demons so naïvely worshipped in times past by primitive Groacians; I was just getting in a little insurance, so to speak."

"We can't have too many demons on our side when we hit the Scary Place," Retief assented. He engaged the drive, and the giant machine floated off along the edge until Retief saw a break ahead, where the fallen rubble made a crude ramp, minutely less steep than the adjoining vertical rock face. Nith shifted his wails to the near-supersonic as Retief guided the Yavac over the rocky edge and down the incline; he checked its slide and, after a precipitous descent of some hundreds of feet, regained the solid rock slope. Continuing the descent at a more moderate rate, now under the inaccurate fire of mortars, the heavy vehicle soon reached the heavily fissured lower slopes, where deep gullies, cut by the slurry of pumice which washed down after every rain, had eaten away the hard stone as if it were sugar. Retief maneuvered into the coverage of a relatively wide, shallow ravine and extended a periscope to check the scene below, but found the panoramic view blocked by a heap of fallen rock, thrown down by a near-miss.

"I'm going out to reconnoiter," Retief told Nith. "If we sit here blind they'll eventually zero in and we'll be buried in rubble."

"You'd leave me here alone to suffer living immurement, whilst you suicide thus dramatically?" Nith objected half-heartedly.

"Come along if you like," Retief replied, as he cycled the overhead hatch open. The Groaci declined as the sound of nearby detonations came loudly through the opening. Retief waited until the clatter of falling rock fragments had dwindled, then climbed out, jumped down from the lofty turret, and went forward to scale the barrier of new-fallen rock. The mortars, he noted, were lobbing their missiles consistently wide, just on the far side of the ravine, so that only small rocks and gravel, wide-scattered by the blasts, were falling into the narrow crevice. From the top of the heap which had blocked his view, he saw a column of spear-bearing Creepies moving up-slope toward an isolated construction hut no different from the others but for a small purple-and-yellow pennant adroop from the TV antenna which appeared to be the chief support of the structure. At the rear of the advancing party, he was barely able to recognize the distinctive somatotype of a Terran-

Magnan, no doubt, still slung, head down, from the torture pole.

As Retief turned back to the Yavac, the entry hatch slammed shut and the huge machine stirred, backed a few feet, and high-centered on a rock slab; for a moment the great tracks threshed impotently; then the growl of the engines faded to an idle and the treads came to rest. Retief went to the stranded monster, crawled under, and manually activated the emergency jacking systems. As the blunt jacking rods extended, to bear against the rock with a fingernails-on-a-blackboard squeal and a puff of rock dust, Retief emerged, surveyed the situation, picked up a slab of volcanic rock six inches thick and two yards long, and wedged it under the left track where it hung clear of the underlying stone. After repeating the procedure with the other track, he crawled under and retracted the jacks, allowing the big machine to settle down, its belly plates almost against his chest. Emerging, he took out his cigar lighter and applied a beam, at fine focus, to a perforated area just aft of the forward gun blister. A moment later, the hatch sprang open, and Nith's distraught features appeared, eye shields awry, all five oculars canted at extreme angles, indicative of incipient mania.

". . . to get it over with," he was keening, over and over. Ignoring Retief, and shying violently as a shell exploded on the canyon rim above, the Groaci set about clambering awkwardly down to the rubble layer. Once down, he looked about wildly and set off at a run back up the ravine, away from the mortar fire. Retief overtook him easily, gathered in the alien's wildly gesticulating arms, and brought him back to the Yavac.

"You don't understand, Retief," Nith was yelling in his accent-free Terran. "To be in deadly peril," he continued, reverting to Groaci. "To be deep in a lethal zone, and at any moment . . ." He fell silent as he made a desperate last attempt to escape the Terran's powerful one-handed grip, and, failing, went limp.

"Nith," Retief said, "I really don't have to put up with all this. Why don't you go back into your catatonia routine?"

Nith immediately went through the routine, and subsided into coma. Retief carried him inside the tank.

Retief engaged the drive and the Yavac moved forward, not without some slippage and vibration from the tracks, and advanced to the point where the ravine debouched onto the gullied down-slope. Below, he saw gun crews maneuvering heavy tracked-artillery pieces into position in a shallow crescent centered on the gaping aperture at the center of the lava plan. Moments later, bursts of flame and smoke signaled the firing of the first barrage.

"They're through playing, Mr. Ambassador," he addressed the catatonic Groaci. "Now we're going to be getting aimed fire. Hold onto your hat." With that he gunned the machine off in a tread-wrenching curve to the right, then left, and as the volley erupted behind him, charged at full speed down on the enemy stronghold.

2

While Nith, slack in his seat harness, blindly fingered his kiki stone, Retief locked shock frames in place as the hurtling combat unit rocked to the blasts of direct hits from fractional megatonners, smashing aside or bounding over obstructing rock formations, leaping gullies, taking a twisting course to evade the brunt of the defensive fire, which ravaged the slope all along the intruder's erratic back trail as the guns' computers lagged by a vital microsecond in tracking and aiming.

At last, knocking aside the last few scattered boulders, the Yavac reached the level floor of the center. Retief slowed, pulled aside to permit the avalanche to pass behind him, and switched the forward spotter screen to full gain. Low sheds built of corrugated metal, heaps of crates lettered KAKA priority UTS, broken stone, and scurrying crewmen leapt into crisp clarity. The artillery battery, looking cross-eyed, with muzzles fully depressed, had fallen silent after firing a final few rounds into the ground before them. Retief saw nothing of Magnan or General Prince Blue. A crowd of excited Furtheronians clustered about a small hut at one side, where a blue-and-orange pennant fluttered in the fitful breeze sucked in by the rising hot-air mass created by the intense gunfire. As Retief watched, the hut's doorway was slammed from the inside.

"Quickly!" Nith hissed. "To recognize the colors of the DBU! To take cover in the great pit yonder!" Then he lapsed back into his defensive coma.

"You may have had a good idea for once, Mr. Ambassador," Retief said, as from all sides blue-and-orange-uniformed commandos converged on the Yavac, moving with a crisp purposefulness at variance with the erratic movements of the milling mob, from which they were now emerging to form a double column which in turn split to flow around the intruding machine and rejoin at its rear, leaving an open space directly ahead.

"They think to use our finer sensibilities to herd us where they will!" Nith hissed. "To assume that rather than run them down, we'll take the path they leave clear!"

"So they do, Mr. Ambassador," Retief agreed, executing a sharp left turn toward the hut, which caused the encircling troops to redispose themselves hastily. Rather than roll over the hut, Retief halted his mighty steed beside it and fired a relatively mild antipersonnel blast from the apertures low on the side of the war hull, a discharge of buckshot which riddled the flimsy sheet steel, nearly knocking the hut from its foundations. A Furtheronian scuttled from the blasted structure, whether Creepy or Crawlie was unclear because of the enveloping robes of blue and orange zigzags in which it was wrapped, and fled into the mob. A moment later a second occupant appeared in the now sagging doorway, this one a slight, spindle-legged being in a dusty hip cloak and unpolished greaves, wearing a partial set of the jeweled eye shields of a Groacian dignitary of the primary degree. At sight of him Nith uttered a cry.

"A Boss of Ten Thousand Bosses!" he yelped. "Doubtless held prisoner here by these vile savages," he added. "Oh, boy! When we, that is, I, return His Superiority safe to his estate at Groac, what rewards will be mine! Excuse me, Retief, I'll just nip out and welcome His Superiority aboard. You'll observe proper protocol, of course: lie flat, face down, until His Superiority graciously condescends to step on or across you, thereby signaling you to rise, facing the nearest wall."

"Before you do anything hasty, Mr. Ambassador," Retief said, "notice that nobody appears to be holding a gun on His Superiority."

"Who can say what subtle measures of duress have been employed, so to trepan an official of such lofty rank to these dismal environs?" Nith returned, and opened the hatch, letting in a puff of rock dust, the battlefield reek of explosives and hot metal, a cacophony of yells, falling masonry, fitful small-arms fire, and a shrill voice shrieking in outrage:

"To supervise the ceremonial dismemberment of the cretinous scoundrel responsible for this contretemps! To express the utmost dissatisfaction! To vow revenge worthy of my majesty!"

On the side screen, Retief saw Nith execute a complicated leg salute as his voice was picked up tinnily by the aft monitor.

"To offer Your Superiority the full resources of my

Mission, together with the *apologia universalis,* with full embellishments! To suggest Your Superiority take shelter at once within my conveyance."

"I suppose you're Nith, our AE and MP. Very well, you may rise and disentangle your limbs, in order more efficiently to be of service to ourself."

"To caution the Boss of Bosses that I have aboard a creature, a Terran diplomat to wit, to whom I have assigned the task of monitoring the control system, in view of which perhaps the High One will, just this once, suspend full protocol, since he would find it difficult, if not impossible, to operate the machine while lying face-down in the passage. Ah, there you are, Retief," he added as the Terran jumped down beside him. Hastily, Nith offered introductions.

"Enough of these trifles, Nith," the Boss said coldly. "You've been guilty of a serious blunder in charging down on us here like an army bent on conquest. Chairman Gith is quite undone, and as for Gloob the Obtuse, he's gotten the impression that in some curious fashion the Other Side has gotten wind of our arrangements, and he's dithering over the question of which faction to surrender to. Be a pity, Nith, if all our plans should come to naught in the moment of fruition, simply due to impetuosity on your part. By the way, where did you get the Yavac? I was informed that when my personal specially equipped model arrived it would be the only one in the entire Theater of Operations."

"It was only a little mistake, Your Superiority—that is, I was rushing to your assistance."

"So the scheme *is* common knowledge, since you knew I was here—supposed to be the second-best-kept secret of the whole campaign. Who spilled his guts, Nith? Speak up! When I know the identity of the spy, perhaps I can yet salvage something."

A dazed-looking Creepy emerged hesitantly from the

ruined shack, gave the Boss a casual salute, and crept off into the dust cloud.

"Gloob wasn't a bad chap, for a Crawlie," his former colleague commented glumly. "That blast took all the rank paint off his shins and, as you see, reduced him to a state of near-idiocy. As for poor Gith, he keeps muttering about his baggage checks. Perhaps I'd best see to him. You may wait here, Nith; I must destroy my files. I'll inspect your machine later." He reentered the hut, thrusting aside the broken door, which fell with a crash.

"It appears that hardship has addled His Superiority's wits," Nith breathed as soon as the Boss was out of earshot. "From his remarks, the coarse-minded might receive the impression that he himself was in charge of this nefarious operation, rather than a captive of these scoundrels."

"I have a *very* coarse mind, Mr. Ambassador," Retief replied coolly. "Which brings me to an elementary point of protocol. You, as Ambassador Extraordinary and Minister Plenipotentiary, accredited here as the personal representative of your Groacian Chief of State, outrank any fellow Groaci here, other than Chairman Shish himself. That being the case, how is it you take it so meekly when this Boss fellow orders you about like a flunky?"

"Ah, as to that," Nith began uncertainly, "one mustn't be too punctilious in demanding one's perquisites when the offending personage is of princely rank, chief of the armed forces, and actual head of the Foreign Service in which one holds one's commissions, rank, and these self-same perquisites. After all, one day one hopes to go home again."

"Sounds like a really big Big Shot," Retief commented. "In fact he sounds like a Chief of State, none other than Shish himself. Now what could bring Chairman Shish way out here without so much as an honor guard? This must be a bigger swindle than just taking over one backward planet."

" 'Undeveloped,' you mean, I assume, Retief," Nith corrected sharply.

"And now we know why Prince Blue was wandering around out in the brush," Retief went on. "He had a summit appointment with the head of Boge's traditional ally, Groac."

"Nonsense!" Nith sputtered. "You're raving, Retief! Boge, far from being an ally of the Groacian state, is an interplanetary rogue-world subsisting on warmongering! What possible commonality of interest could exist between such a band of pirates and peace-loving Groac?"

"Well," a gluey Furtheronian voice cut in, as its owner, a medium-sized Creepy in a splendid blue cloak, emerged from the collapsed hutment. "That's a fair question, bub, and you're pretty sharp to of ast it. So sharp, in fact, I guess I got to terminate relations here with what they call 'Extreme Prejudice.' That means the boys take you out back, or maybe out front, and knock you off. Let's go. And as fer you, pal," he added, addressing Retief. "Sure, I know, you're just a dumb guy which old five-eyes here he like dragooned ya to drive him into trouble. You stand fast until Gloob gets back and I get around to having you stuffed in a mortar and fired back to safe territory. Nobody can't say General Blug don't look out for the well bean of noncombatants and all, right? Now I got to see to my command." He swaggered off.

"Here, I heard that slur on the superior optical endowments of the Groacian people!" a breathy voice hissed faintly from the ruins, as the taller-than-average Groaci, now freshly arrayed in jeweled eye shields, silver inlaid greaves, and a gold-brocaded hip cloak, picked his way gingerly over fallen panels to pause by Nith, who, halfway through a leg salute, attempted to curtsy and fell heavily.

"As you were, Nith," Shish condescended. "We see what sort of chap this Blug fellow is beneath his protestations of undying amity. So much for the Groac-Boge Axis. Now we'd best clean up this misbegotten operation and get back to your Embassy to get off a hot despatch to the Department. I assume you have Shaped Wave Interference Front Transmission capability?"

"Well, sir," Nith replied hesitantly. "On paper we do, but somehow the field seems to have gotten bollixed up—some local interference of some kind that my tech boys haven't nailed down yet—so I don't know. A fast dodge out of the Sector on our dispatch boat might be the best bet."

Shish looked coldly at him. "Government handouts state quite clearly that our SWIFT gear is immune to jamming, as I'm sure you're aware. Ergo, your pitiful excuses are treasonable, and will, in due course, be dealt with as such."

"Never mind, Mr. Chairman," Retief said soothingly. "Right now we have the problem of getting all of us out of here intact—including a Terran diplomat, Mr. Magnan. So if you'll just make yourselves comfy in the aft lazaret, we can get going." He went to the looming Yavac and climbed inside. Without demur, Nith and his chief followed.

"Just show His Superiority to his quarters, if you please, Mr. Ambassador," Retief suggested. Nith complied silently, ignoring Shish's queries as to who was bossing whom.

3

Retief started up the engines, backed, came about, and headed the giant machine relentlessly toward the pithead, where the scattered troops had gathered in a ragged formation under General Blug. A single round, fired high, from the forward turret sufficed to disperse them.

Leaving a trail of pulverized rock, crushed packing crates, and collapsed hutments, the hundred-and-fifty-ton combat unit descended the slope leading to the yawning pit which was the center and focus of all activity in the Scary Place. As the shadows closed about them, Nith reappeared at Retief's side.

"Stop, mad Terran!" he croaked. "I've changed my mind on closer examination. As the slope steepens, we'll lose traction and slide into the horrid great black hole! Anyway, it's too small! We'll be stuck!"

"Headquarters seems to be down there, and that's where they've taken Mr. Magnan," Retief replied. "So that's where we need to go."

"See here, Retief," Nith protested. "A little loyalty to an old colleague is all very well, but this . . . To plunge us all to certain death will avail Ben naught . . ."

4

The great machine lunged forward, its sides grating against stone walls; then, with bone-wrenching deceleration, it slammed against some barrier which yielded reluctantly to let it roll forward on a level keel. The screens showed a narrow, dim-lit tunnel ahead.

"It seems the first part is the steepest," Retief commented. "Only two degrees' incline here." He switched on the forward searchlight; ahead, obscure forms scuttled for cover in a multitude of branching side passages.

"To go back," Nith shrilled, "while still we can. To escape this morbid catacomb ere we're wedged fast, or lose ourselves in its recesses!"

"You'd better go back into your coma, Nith," Retief suggested. "We've only started. Anyway, I'm leaving a dyemarker trail just in case we need to get out in a hurry."

"Such caution in one with a reputation for impetuosity is surprising," Nith replied more calmly. "And reassuring to some slight degree." He obediently slumped into his comatose state, snoring gently.

Blinding light flashed ahead, and an impact rocked the Yavac, causing the instrument lights to flicker. As the glare faded, Retief saw General Blug beating out smoldering patches on his cloak, while dazed artillerymen picked themselves up and attempted to right their fieldpiece, which lay on its side, its shielding collapsed.

"I guess the boys got the worst of that one," Retief said thoughtfully. "Blug should have known better, in this tight space." He passed the gun crew as the last of them withdrew into the cross passage. The gun made a mild *crunch* under the treads.

Nith roused long enough to jeer at the discomfited Blug as he fled for cover, the last to desert his post.

"I don't think we'll have any more trouble from that quarter," Retief said.

"That leaves only collapsed tunnels, pits, various inflammables, and maybe suicide crews with wiring diagrams and penetration charges to worry us," Nith answered wryly. Then, with a groan, he reentered coma.

Keeping to what appeared to be the main bore, Retief continued straight ahead for half an hour, until dead reckoning indicated they had passed under the crater rim. The dim light glowed ahead, and soon they entered a vast chamber, nearly filled with heavy machines, work rather than battle-scarred, Retief noticed. A conveyor belt carried what appeared to be ordinary rubble up from a side tunnel into shadows above. The light came from a bank of polyarcs, far across the big room. Uniformed personnel—Creepy, Crawlie, and a few officious Groaci—moved restlessly all across the wide floor space, engaged in obscure tasks. Retief brought the Yavac to a halt. Only then did the occupants of the vast cave appear to take notice of the new arrival. The lights dimmed briefly, then came up on a transformed scene. The raggedly parked machines—excavators, Retief saw—had been aligned smartly, and their crews, dusting uniforms and slicking back tangled tendrils, were just completing falling in, while the scattered Groaci had formed up in a ceremonial square and stood at attention, facing the Yavac.

"Better come to, Nith," Retief suggested. "It looks like your turn to earn your keep."

The Groaci's eye stalks snapped erect, tilted toward the screen, and abruptly Nith was galvanized, coming to the Groaci approximation of the Position of a Soldier, Sitting, Class One, All Personnel, for the Guidance of.

"Great Galloping Galaxies!" he hissed in awe. "That's General Gnish and a full Top-Class Honor Guard waiting out there. Even the privates outrank an ordinary full bird. I wonder . . . but they must be expecting—"

"Precisely," Retief cut in. "So let's not disappoint 'em. Go back and borrow His Superiority's fancy getup and prepare to inspect the Guard."

Nith protested faintly, but complied when Retief pointed out the alternative: to emerge just as he was, to explain why he was riding around in the Chairman's personal transport, disrupting operations, upsetting time tables, and making a jackass of the Commanding General and the Honor Guard. Retief escorted Nith to the aft personnel hatch, ignoring the vigorous pounding emanating from the locked storage compartment where the Groaci had reluctantly confined His Superiority. "It's *lèse-majesté* of the worst stripe!" Nith complained to Retief.

"Don't worry, Mr. Ambassador," Retief reassured the nervous diplomat. "After you've explained to him, back in the comfort of the VIP suite at the Embassy of Groac, that it was the only way you could save him from the torture pole, I'm sure he'll not only forgive you but bump you a couple of grades. You'll be in charge of the Furtheronian Desk back at Groac City in no time, and after that, who knows?"

"But in the meantime what's to keep *me* from the self-same torture pole?" Nith queried. "I shall never forget Ben's expression as he said his last farewells, inverted as he was." Nith shuddered, but braced his narrow shoulders; as the hatch cover swung out, he rode the ramp down and stepped off to confront the solid front rank of the unmoving Honor Guard.

He dithered and was about to detour to one side when Gnish's harsh voice barked, "Detail! Open ranks! Even squads right face! Odds left face! Do it!" This precisely executed maneuver opened a lane directly before Nith, two rigid rows of grim-faced Guards staring at each other across the aisle down which he proceeded hesitantly, as the commanding officer hurried up to fall in step on his left and slightly to the rear.

Retief watched on the high-resolution screen as Nith carried out the ritual, after which he was surrounded by lesser officers, including a number of Furtheronians in rich robes, plus a few unmistakable newshawks, and a lone Bogan, all striving to be first to salute the distinguished Groaci, until the Guards commander shooed them away. For a moment the commander stood in earnest conversation with the presumed Boss; then he turned and spoke curtly to an aide. Moments later the Guard had re-formed, this time all facing the exit port, blast rifles at port arms.

"All right, Terry spy," an amplified voice boomed out. "Come out with your hands up! Take it slowly; at any sudden move an automatic spotter gun in the east cornice will blast you to atoms! Now! Do it!"

Pausing only to detach an inconspicuous object from its bracket under the main panel, Retief stepped through the open port. Ranks of alert eye stalks canted toward him until the voice of command roared, "Eyes front!" at which they snapped back to a precise angle of forty-five degrees. The scowling Groaci commander, Nith hovering beside him, stood waiting at the end of the narrow alley through the rigid soldiers. Retief sauntered casually, his glance flicking over the immaculately uniformed troops, noting razor-edge creases, freshly whitened piping, gleaming brass, holstered small arms, glittering insignia of rank and unit, polished carapaces, plain GI eyeshields.

"To congratulate you, General," he remarked offhandedly as he by-passed the officer to pause before Nith.

"Well, Mr. Ambassador, it seems you were right after all," he said to Nith in a grim tone. "Headquarters has been penetrated in spite of all our precautions. So it seems we go to Plan B."

"What's this?" the general demanded hoarsely, confronting Nith. "You've given this Terry access to top sensitive information, in addition to the incredible breach of security in actually bringing him *here*, of all places? And what did he call Your Superiority? Ambassador? But that incompetent figurehead Nith is our AE and MP. Probably sitting in his office back in the city at this moment, totting up commissary breakage reports."

Nith stiffened. "Figurehead, you say? But Ambassador Nith is nonetheless the accredited Groacian envoy here. The protocols must be observed, my dear General. I must forbid you publicly to disparage a faithful public servant, who, after all, is acting in accordance with instructions from the top. As for Retief here, you must have misunderstood me: I wasn't denouncing him: his presence is an earnest of the new Groaci-Terra Accord, agreed to only hours ago. Clearly, nothing is to be said or done to jeopardize this newly achieved alliance. You're well aware of the inconveniences Groacian policy has suffered in the past due to the obstructionism of proud Terra. Now we have the opportunity to lay to rest for all time this threat to the fulfillment of our Groacian destiny!"

"Groac—and Terra—*allies*?" Gnish croaked. "Unheard of—and certainly I should have been the first to hear of it, Your Superiority! If I've loused up anything, it's because GHQ failed to brief me properly. But no harm is done. He's only a Terry, and none of them ever bothers to learn our mellifluous Groacian tongue, so as far as *he* knows he's been getting the glad hand, Class One, and we're congratulating each other on the new treaty." He beamed at Nith, then grabbed the Ambassador's hand and shook it enthusiastically. "But he *did* greet me in Groaci; top dialect, too," he went on hesitantly. "Probably just memorized it, eh, Your Superiority?"

"No doubt," Nith agreed hastily, "but just to complete the impression, hadn't we better hurry along with the rest of the formalities? Twenty-three guns, remember, for such an occasion. You may omit my personal twenty-one. These salutes give me a sharp pain in the auditory membranes." As Nith fell silent, Gnish signaled, and the ceremonial noise guns drawn up behind the troops boomed out twenty-three times, temporarily deafening all present, and driving the Creepy and Crawlie flunkies from the scene, sure that open hostilities had broken out between their allies. When the last echo of the din had reverberated into a silence broken only by the clatter of small stones falling from the ceiling high above, Retief turned to the general.

"These trifling exercises are all very well, General, but it seems you are holding a Terran diplomat here, under conditions which are at best perilous to any continued *détente* in Terra-Groaci relations."

The general's eye stalks quivered in a complex expression denoting Good Intentions Misinterpreted, coupled with Resolve to Fix Everything, but overlaid with an unmistakable I Smell an Ulsio. Nith spoke up hastily. "I'm certain, Retief, that I can assure you the General will quickly correct any unfortunate errors committed by his subordinates due to an excess of zeal in the absence of current information regarding the treaty negotiations; eh, my dear General?"

"Yeah, what he said," the officer agreed blurrily. "But you don't mean this little slip of I and my boys could blow the whole treaty?"

"That is precisely what I mean, sir," Nith replied coldly. "I suggest you take immediate action to counteract any unfortunate impression Mr. Magnan may have gained during his visit."

5

The general uttered curt commands; staff officers hurried off to attend to them. Then, with a hoarse yell, a Furtheronian aborigine in full war paint thrust through the clump of aides surrounding the VIPs to confront the general.

"Me hearum order let Terry criminal out cage!" he yelled. "Me gottum big payoff coming for bring Terry to you, and you better payum plenty chop-chop, whether you make big juju with Terry or not. My boys ready stickum spear in all Five-eyes in place, you no pay up!"

"Why, I fear you've got aholt of a wrong idear, Irving," the general replied in fluent Creepy. "I merely ordered the sacrificial victim brought here so as to complete his ceremonial dismemberment in the presence of the Terry spy!"

"Me no dummy, Gnish! Me see you and other Five-eyes chum up with this here Terry, not even hoist him on ceremonial torture pole! You figger to slip me the old double-cross, think me heap dumb savage!"

"By no means, Irving!" The general protested. "But

my Groacian guest here is an official of the highest
rank; he of course has his reasons for tolerating the
existence of this Terry; as for the prisoner, his demise
will demonstrate clearly to all that I am second to none
in carrying-out of long-established policy! I'll teach these
stuffed shirts at Supreme HQ to omit me from their
planning!" Gnish impatiently shook off Nith's attempt
to remonstrate.

Then the pole bearers arrived with a bustle, the fore-
man giving the general a sloppy spear salute which
nearly impaled the officer's neck.

"Skip the formalities, fellow," the general spluttered,
"and fall out for a ten-minute break, smoke if you got
'em." With that he turned to address Magnan, still
securely lashed to the pole, head down, his face level
with the five-foot Groaci.

"And are you quite comfortable, sir?" the general
inquired unctuously. "I trust you had a pleasant trip in,
via the special transport I laid in for your reception."

Magnan's mouth worked in his now almost purple
face, but no sound emerged. His bulging eyes were
fixed on Retief.

"Mr. Magnan would be more comfortable if he were
inverted," Retief pointed out.

"Eh, what's that, 'inverted'?" the general repeated in
puzzlement. "You mean to say this chap would enjoy
being turned upside-down? Demmed odd."

"He's already upside-down, General," Retief explained.

"Oh, I see; I *thought* he seemed to be arranged
differently somehow from your esteemed self. He's got
his sneaker on top, and that complicated purple part at
the bottom. The boys must have made a slip." He gave
the command, and the bearers clumsily turned the pole
point-up. Magnan drew a deep breath and sagged in his
bonds.

"He still looks different," the general stated. "The
noisy part at the top end—the face, I suppose one

should call it—is changing color: first it was deep purple, and now it's a shade of magenta, I should say, while yours is pinkish tan."

"Merely an expression of His Lordship's satisfaction at the treatment he's received, sir," Retief reassured the general. He went to Magnan and caught him as he sagged when the ropes were cut. Magnan's eyes fluttered, opened.

"Retief? Am I dreaming? Or am I actually here, in the Scary Place, the center of a mob of Creepies and Groaci, and right side up at last?"

"If it's a dream, we'd better stick with it a few minutes longer," Retief suggested. Magnan nodded and lapsed into unconsciousness.

The general, noticing, stepped forward to address the newly arrived Terran Special Envoy.

"My dear Terry," he intoned, conscious of History. "To express my most profound satisfaction, et cetera, on this occasion, symbolic as it is of our two nations' Triumph, and prelude to the final success of all our ventures! I salute you, sir—" at which he executed a faultless leg salute.

"I never could master that damned toe dance," Nith confided to Retief. "Gnish does it with such grace. No wonder he made three stars in record time."

"And now," the general went on, "I propose a toast"—he paused again to signal to an aide—"to the Groac-Terra Accord, a landmark in Galactic history!"

"Never!" Magnan spoke up groggily. "I admit the Service has been guilty of certain chicaneries in the past, but as men—or beings—of the world, we're all aware that a degree of expediency, not to say villainy, is essential to realistic diplomacy. But *this* proposal—that Terra join with Groac to connive in this—whatever dirty tricks you Groaci are up to here—that is too much even for the CDT. Secretary Smartfinger himself would blanch at such a proposal!"

"Ix-nay," Mr. Magnan," Retief said in a low but urgent tone. "Don't oh-blay the situation; it's still delicate."

"What's this?" the general demanded. "What's the idea of speaking that strange tongue? That's not Terran! Could they be impostors?" he inquired archly of Nith.

"By no means, sir," the Groaci hastily reassured the affronted officer. "That's merely the Lesser Obfuscese, originally a *bêche-de-mer* trade dialect, but now commonly used among diplomats—a sort of professional language, you might say."

"Of course," the general agreed, relaxing. "Actually, I caught a word or two: 'The situation's delicate,' he said, doubtless a reference to the precarious status of the Groac-Terra Accord."

"Quite," Nith agreed serenely.

"Hut's wappening?" Magnan inquired dazedly.

"We'd better stick to Standard, Mr. Magnan," Retief said. "I see you're still a bit dazed after the unexpected splendor of your reception here by our new allies."

"New allies?" Magnan burst out. "All I see is Creepies or maybe Crawlies, and Groaci—plus one or two Bogan adviser types standing around."

"Bogans? Fie upon them!" the Groaci general said, and spat. "I never *did* trust those self-serving opportunists! Which reminds me: all Bogan 'advisers' are to be placed under arrest at once."

"How about this one, General, sir?" a harassed-looking Creepy, recognizable by his charred uniform as General Blug, inquired, pushing through the attendant underlings with a bedraggled humanoid in tow. The latter abruptly threw off the restraints as his bloodshot eyes fixed on Nith. He stood erect, dusted at the matted dirt and leaf mold on his once-natty uniform, and demanded loudly:

"Hasn't this farce proceeded far enough, Mr. Ambassador? I don't know who this loud-mouthed chum of yours is," he said, indicating Gnish. "But I heard that crack about noble Boge! 'Arrest all Bogans' indeed! This incident, I fear, could bring to naught all our plans. Groac will have to look elsewhere, it seems, for the equipment to carry out her policies."

"Prince Blue!" Nith gasped. "Oh dear, to leap to no unfortunate conclusions, Your Imperial Highness—all can be explained satisfactorily. But for the moment it's necessary to ay-play along-hay. You see, General Gnish had not, due to an unfortunate administrative oversight, been fully apprised of the situation." He turned to the general with a 907-j (Being-of-the-Worldly Tolerance of the Failings of Lesser Mortals) amplified by a touch of 735-x (Perseverance in a Spirit of Mutual Comradely Trust Toward Great Ends, in Spite of Appearances), and embellished with just a hint of 316-b (You Know Me, Pal), resulting in a complex expression which earned a snort of contempt from Gnish. "To remind Your Superiority that this is not mating time among the pagans! No need to flutter your eye stalks at me in that unseemly fashion! I confess," he went on more moderately, "that my staff and I are somewhat confused as to the dynamics of the situation—Headquarters' fault, you understand. But it appears now that lordly Groac has entered into alliance not only with arrogant Terra but with vile Boge as well! Which makes Boge and Terra bedfellows of a sort, I suppose, a contretemps which one can scarcely envision, after all their hypocritical propaganda attacking each other. What's a simple soldier to do?" His tirade fading off into a moan, Gnish inclined his eye stalks in a dispirited salute to Nith. "I leave matters in the hands of Your Superiority's commands. I'll have my DCS Chicanery type up a formal document so stating for Your Superiority's signature."

"Stand fast, General!" Nith rasped. "It's clear the mischief's afoot here." He aimed two glaring eyes at

Prince Blue, transfixing the hapless Gnish with the other three.

"I knew this fellow as one General Snart, a freebooting brigand who menaced my person when we happened to meet in mid-jungle."

"Of course, Mr. Ambassador," Prince Blue agreed placatingly. "But that was at first. Afterward, you'll recall, we got to be good buddies aboard ship, whilst this opportunist Terry here was holding the aces. Glad to see you overpowered him and drug him here to GHQ for a reckoning—and there's that other Terry, too, the one I rescued from the cannibals. Some gratitude!"

"That's all by the way," said Nith, dismissing the Bogan's complaint. "But you misinterpreted Retief's role in affairs. It was not *he* who held the aces—and the power gun; I was at all times in full command. In fact, my dear Prince, it was precisely my rendezvous with your esteemed self which brought me here. In spite of certain difficulties in the way, I took delivery of my little go-car which you so kindly delivered—though I must point out that there were certain discrepancies for which deductions will be made before payment is tendered."

"Sure, no sweat. Like Your—uh—Excellency seen, I had a spot of bother there with them damn Creepies which I personally don't see why you Groaci wanna bother taking over this dump—but I was spose to meet—you must be—cripes, you're Premier Shish hisself. Par' me, Your Excellency, for not rendering the old royal salute and all."

"Never mind, my dear Blue. But I must point out that 'taking over this dump,' as you so inelegantly phrase it, is indeed far from the intentions of noble Groac. Let me refresh your memory: Furtheron being a benighted and backward world existing in a state of continual warfare, it is clearly Groac's duty, as the foremost civilized power, to uplift these savages—"

"Sure, by modernizing and all," Prince Blue put in eagerly. "Fixing 'em up with the latest Bogan armaments, so's they can get on with their war in a like more efficient manner and all."

"You put it rather crudely, Prince Blue," Nith replied tartly.

"Just call me 'Field Marshal,' Mr. Premier—and I hope Your Excellency'll overlook the boner, taking you for a mere Ambassador. But you *did* tell me that's who ya were, and I accorded ya all appropriate honors and all, remember."

"One employs a cover identity, Field Marshal—or General Snart, as you yourself were introduced, I seem to recall."

Prince Blue nodded. "Yeah, it's all part of the old interplanetary intrigue game," he conceded. "But what about these two Terries? Who're they supposed to be?"

"Mr. Retief is of course the Terran High Commissioner in the matter of the Groac-Terra Accord, while Mr. Magnan is a high official of the Terran Mission to Furtheron and a member of ITCH."

"Geeze," Prince Blue murmured, impressed. "If I would've known they was big in the treaty end, I wouldn't of like give 'em short shrift and all. Whyn't ya tell me?"

"What, and blow the entire operation?" Nith dismissed the criticism. "Pity you're not more experienced in field technique, Field Marshal."

"Here," General Gnish butted in. "Whilst you guys stood around and chewed the fat, H-hour has come and M-minute is getting close. I gotta go now and see to the last-minute details before the automatic countdown commences without me. Hang loose, and get ready for the Big One!" He dashed off, trailed by his staff, the Honor Guard bringing up the rear smartly.

"The Big One?" Nith echoed in dismay, then started after Gnish.

"One moment, General," he cried after the retreating officer. "I must order an indefinite hold until I know more of the latest developments! Come on, Ben," he added to Magnan, who was standing dazedly by. "Help me stop this wacky Groaci before he does something we can't negotiate!"

" 'Wacky Groaci,' " Magnan repeated. "That's very clever, Nith; I'm surprised I didn't think of it myself!"

"The expression is a cliché, I fear, Ben," Nith called over his shoulder. "Don't credit me for it. It is of course in no way a pejorative, but really the equivalent of your own succinct 'madman.' "

" 'Wacky Groaci,' " Magnan mused. "How well it fits some senior diplomats we've known, eh, Nith?"

"Alas," Nith conceded, hurrying Magnan along, "it can't be denied that from time to time some rather eccentric individuals have been appointed to high rank in the Groacian Foreign Service, but no system of selection is perfect. The CDT has harbored a number of kooks in its time, as I'm sure you'll be first to agree, Ben. Remember dear old Ambassador Shrinkfit, back at Boondock Beta?"

"An undiagnosed lobotomy case, without doubt, Nith," Magnan agreed. "But what of His Excellency Ambassador Tiss, at Brunt? He was right out of his tree!"

"While 'out of his tree' is not, perhaps, a term which I would employ, Ben, in reference to the head of one of Groac's noblest families, it is undoubtedly true that cerebral excitement did, as you suggest, exist in a marked degree. But enough of these pleasantries. Flawed though they are, professionals would never have allowed matters to deteriorate to their present condition. Imagine! Prince Blue meeting secretly with our Premier. Two chiefs of state! It's arrant summitry!"

"Premier Shish, *here*?" Magnan gasped. "And meeting with that Bogan robber baron the Prince of the Blue? Ghastly! No wonder I was suspended head-down, in violation of solemn interplanetary accord."

"Well, actually I'm an impostor, Ben," Nith declared. "That is, I *am* Nith, Ambassador Extraordinary and Minister Plenipotentiary of the Groacian Autonomy to benighted Furtheron: I'm just not Premier Shish, who is indisposed at the moment. As for Prince Blue, the notorious black sheep of Boge, he's genuine enough— though not quite precisely Chief of State unless his recent attempted coup was more successful than we've been led to believe."

"Even so, he's a dignitary of the top echelon," Magnan countered. "And why would two such dignitaries bother to meet here, in the hintermost hinterland?"

"Gold," Nith said impressively, "and uranium, plus all the other metals, hardly to mention corundum, gem-caliber crystals of unusual size and brilliance, and, of course, all the lesser minerals."

"Gold? Here on Furtheron?"

"Look for yourself." Nith pointed to a garish, brassy streak on the rough-hewn wall of the passage into which they had followed General Gnish.

"Someone's splashed gold paint on the rock, it appears," Magnan said, peering at the display, only half visible in the dim light.

"A vein over a hundred gruggs in length, and up to six pluds thick; minimum yield of this deposit alone is estimated at three zillion guck, I understand," Nith stated firmly. "But of course no one's bothered with it, with so much more interesting material to be excavated. Marvelous formations, Ben. You know something of the geology of Furtheron?"

"Only that the planet's supposed to be hollow," Magnan replied.

"Not precisely hollow, Ben, but honeycombed. It appears an uncommon amount of degassing occurred during the final stages of hardening of the planetary crust which quite whipped the magma up into foam. After it had cooled and hardened, gas pressure forced molten metallic and other elements up to fill the voids, creating veins of pure substances, not even requiring refining! The entire planet is a treasure house ripe for the harvesting!"

"But surely, Nith," Magnan croaked, "these minerals are the property of the autochthonous Furtheronian people!"

"What, these savages? I'm sure, Ben, if they'd been interested they'd have spent their time mining, rather than eternally warring on each other. Thus, by default the minerals are the property of whoever wishes to collect them, in this case selfless Groac, here to end the war."

"Pure sophistry, Nith!" Magnan cried.

"I've always intended to look that word up some day," Nith said. "Just what does it mean, Ben?"

"Why, as to that, it's used only in the context I've just employed. It's something you call the other fellow's argument to discredit it."

"Oh, I see, it's as I suspected. In Groaci we say 'Yivshish.' 'Pure yivshish!' we cry, crushing all opposition. Fine word. But 'sophistry' is not bad. Sound impressively accusatory, both terms, eh, Ben? And without committing oneself to any specific position."

CHAPTER SEVEN

As the two slightly built diplomats scurried off in pursuit of the irate General Gnish, Retief turned to Prince Blue and without formalities slammed a pile-driver right to the Bogan's short ribs, causing that nobleman to bend over, wheezing.

"Just wait till I get unfolded here, you whippersnapper," the Bogan warlord managed at last, "and I'll pound you down into a throw rug! What's the idear, anyways?" he demanded plaintively, rubbing his abdomen with both large-knuckled hands. "Didn't I treat you right back aboard my car, which now I guess I'll hafta report you stold it, wise guy! What'd ya hafta go and sock Our Majesty for, bub? We coulda worked something out, especially with old Shish and that other Terry off chasing Gnish!"

"That," Retief said, as Prince Blue regained his feet, "was for taking a powder after you'd pledged your word."

"Oh, you got one of *them* hangups. Well, I come back, didn't I?" Prince Blue/Snart demanded righteously.

Retief drove another stiff blow to the Bogan's midriff, this time a left. Snart collapsed, groaning.

"That was a good two inches low, chum," he gasped. "Help me up so's I can clobber you!"

Retief caught the big fellow's wrist and yanked him upright. Snart looked wildly about, appearing not to see Retief standing directly before him.

"Where'd he go?" he demanded, staggering off a few wobbly steps. "Wait'll I find you, you son of a one-legged joy-girl!" Then, abruptly, he set off at a remarkably steady run toward the parked Yavac. Retief took two quick steps and extended a foot to hook the fleeing Prince's ankle, bringing him down like a brain-shot dire-beast. Snart rolled over and fixed Retief with an accusatory glare.

"Oh, you came back, Sneaky. Next time I won't be so easy on you."

"Gosh, what a relief!" the Terran replied. "But I'm afraid all your plans are in for revision, General."

"How's that? Who, me? Look here, fellow, I happen to be—"

"—flat on your back and awaiting instructions," Retief finished for him. "Fun's over, Blue. Get up and let's get started undoing as much of your mischief as possible." He administered a light kick to the Bogan's formerly polished boot to urge him into motion.

"Kicking a fellow when he's down too, eh?" the Prince reproved. "And I heard you Terries was big on sportsmanship."

"Oh, I'm not a fanatic on the subject," Retief advised the Bogan.

"You know, Terry," Snart/Blue mused aloud, as he climbed to his feet, "maybe you and me could of got along, if ya wouldn't of socked me first." He rubbed his solar plexus gently.

"If I'd waited for you to sock me first," Retief pointed

out, "you being a practical sort of fellow, your hand would have had a knife in it."

"Nope, a little old Mark III Spattergun," Snart corrected, opening his hand to reveal the weapon he had slipped from his tunic and was now aiming at Retief. "Just you lay down on your belly, Terry, hands flat," he commanded coldly. "Then maybe I'll test out this year weepon on the back o' yer head-bone."

"No need, Blue," Retief said, and kicked him squarely in the sore spot. This time the big Bogan collapsed like a punctured air tent, breathing hoarsely. Retief retrieved the small handgun, snapped the butt open, and inserted one of the cylinders he had retrieved from Fliss's flight bag at the airport and had been carrying ever since.

"That one was for selling useless guns to your best customers, the Groaci Trade Mission," he said. "I'll bet you'd have held them up for plenty to deliver the power cells you've got stashed in the aft hold of your putt-putt over there." He nodded toward the untenanted Yavac parked at the end of a line of heavy excavating machines.

"Except that sharpy Nith glommed what the deal was, and latched onto a few boxes of detonators," Snart/Blue grieved, "and like to blowed the whole operation! He says you Terries got a like alliance with Groac now. Well, I'll clue you, Retief, on account of you got such a neat left hook: Watch them five-eyed slickers! What do ya say we kind of join forces and all, to outwit the scoundrels?" he started toward the Yavac. "Come on, we can start by cleaning up this here operation—"

"No deal, Blue," Retief cut him off both verbally and physically by stepping into his path.

Suddenly a shrill cry came from across the cavern, and a moment later Nith reappeared from the tunnel mouth into which he and Magnan had trailed Gnish.

"Help! Quick!" he called, avoiding a sluggish Creepy

sentry with an agile leap and heading straight toward Retief. "Retief—they're murdering Ben! They have him suspended over a slow fire and this time they mean business!" He was breathless; Retief supported him when he would have collapsed.

"OK, chum, I'm with you," Prince Blue put in eagerly. "Let's go get them Groaci double-crossers!"

"A moment, Highness," Nith demurred. "To confess I'm shocked at the prejudicial tone of your proposal! It's not *all* Groaci who are at fault, only General Gnish, an aberrant individual whose actions will doubtless be repudiated by the Groacian government as soon as is consistent with overall policy!"

"You mean you'll wait and milk all the advantage you can out of the little devil's tricks before ya give him the axe," Prince Blue clarified.

"Your Imperial Highness is imperiling the Groaci-Bogan Accord by these wild statements," Nith replied more calmly.

"Geeze," Blue said without heat, "I didn't mean to blow our deal; after all, I already made delivery, eh?"

"I should hardly call it 'delivery,' my dear Prince," Nith said coldly, "considering that the essential components are packed into unopenable containers in the locked lazaret of your conveyance yonder, itself under heavy guard by at least a battalion of Creepy troops, backed up by Gnish's turncoat brigade!"

"You were saying something about Mr. Magnan, I believe," Retief put in. "The diplomacy will have to wait until he's here. Let's go get him." He turned toward the big battle-scarred machine, urging the others ahead.

"But there's absolute masses of Crawlies in there, intent on roasting him alive," Nith protested. "The three of us—if one may count on the support of Prince Blue—can do nothing. In any case, he's over *that* way."

"You outsmarted yerself, Terry," Prince Blue said

harshly, "when you left the heap you stold unguarded. I stopped by it long enough to throw the main lock, and it'd take a factory expert six weeks to free her up without the combination which I'm the onney one knows it, and I'm not too sure I even remember it my own selft; I was in kind of a hurry."

Retief took from a side pocket the remote-controller unit he had detached from its bracket before leaving the machine. "It's a good thing you didn't try to start her up," Retief said. "With this out of its slot, you'd have melted down the reactor." He manipulated the levers on the small black box and, with a smooth whirr, the Yavac engines started up; the machine backed, turned, and advanced ponderously toward Retief. He halted it when the access hatch was opposite him, and invited Nith to enter first. When the overwrought Groaci declined, Retief went in, and a moment later his voice came quietly from the externally mounted PA speaker.

"Prince Blue, kindly get in and make yourself comfortable in your old quarters. Mr. Chairman, you may join me on the conn deck. It would be boring if you tried any comedy at this point. Do it."

The two complied sullenly. Inside, Nith took his place at Retief's side. Retief showed him the diagrams which explained the basic operation of the huge machine.

"That's just in case I need you to run it," he pointed out. "You'd better go back aft and reassure His Supremacy; when you explain how you enabled him to avoid all the bother you've just been through, he'll probably stop yelling and pounding on the bulkhead."

"To be sure," Nith agreed judiciously. "To hope His Supremacy will calm himself sufficiently to enable me to address him."

Retief was studying the scene on the big forward screen. Creepy and Groaci troops by the hundred had now collected in ragged formations all across the big cavern, dim-lit by shafts of dusty light from apertures far above. Across the hard-packed floor the openings of tunnels were deep black. The one from which Nith had emerged a few minutes earlier was approximately a hundred yards distant. A huddle of armed Groaci crowded its entrance.

"That looks a bit too small to get into with this thing," Nith observed tartly.

"Just what happened in there, Mr. Ambassador?" Retief asked. "Don't edit it, just give me the essentials."

"There's another room," Nith said. "Not as big a bubble as this one, of course; a sort of troop-marshaling area, it appeared. You were quite right about this place being an impact crater; it seems the strike heated the rock sufficiently to melt the metal veins all around, and the metal flowed out into the blast crater and solidified; after some centuries, the metal surface was covered over by sediment and consolidated into what is now the roof of this space. All the raw metal was mined long ago by the autochthons, assisted at the last by modern machinery shipped in by Groac. We're only beginning to exploit the smaller veins."

"What's the plan?" Retief demanded. "Groac keeps the war going as a diversion, and gets fat on Furtheronian minerals, while Boge gets the equipment business, eh?"

"I assure you, Retief, the orders we've placed with Boge are for heavy excavation equipment, not war machines."

"How about that load of detonators we've got aboard?" Retief inquired. "And the ones that fell out of your flight bag?"

"Purely for mining purposes," Nith stated flatly. "I had a few examples for testing."

"You boys have done a lot of work on your story," Retief conceded. "It almost hangs together. It's a very clever touch to admit to grabbing all the metals, to lend a touch of realism."

"Pah!" Nith croaked. "The metals are quite sufficient

rationale for all the trouble and expense to which self-less Groac has extended herself. Some fantastic alloys have turned up, quite by accident, formed when all those disparate metals mixed here in the vault. You'd be surprised at the properties of a correctly propor-tioned mixture of gold and aluminum, for example. We call it eka-bronze. Fantastic!"

"You were telling me what happened in there," Retief reminded the voluble diplomat, indicating the cave now just ahead.

"Gnish and his retinue were met by a disciplined body of Creepy troops, under a loudmouthed captain who seemed remarkably effective for a local. It appears that in the absence of orders, this Captain Tud ordered an automatic hold on whatever it is they've scheduled. Some sort of denial-to-the-enemy device, I shouldn't wonder. Time has run out, Retief. We have to get out now or never!"

"Keep cool, Mr. Ambassador," Retief soothed the little alien. "My assessment of the character of General Gnish suggests he'd be distinctly averse to suicide."

"Perhaps he has a private route to the surface," Nith suggested. "If so he's probably outside by now—breathing the pure outer air, basking in the sunlight!" Suddenly Retief thrust the Groaci aside, and turned in time to deal Prince Blue a terrific blow on the side of his massive jaw, causing him to stagger backward and drop the heavy wrench with which he had been about to skull Retief.

"Go on, Nith," Retief said, after binding up the Prince's arms with his own jewel-encrusted aiglettes. "You were just getting to the good part."

"To be sure," Nith replied dazedly. "You needn't have been so brutal, Retief," he grumped. "I believe you've broken the skin in three—no, four places."

"I'll put some red stuff on it," Retief offered.

"Does it hurt?" Nith demanded anxiously, eyeing the first-aid kit suspiciously.

"Not as bad as ceremonial sprog throttling," Retief reassured him. "His Supremacy is waiting."

"They saw us as soon as we emerged into the light," Nith resumed his narration. "We had no opportunity to retreat; troops posted around the periphery grabbed us—not gently, I assure you—and dragged us bodily before Gnish. The scoundrel then had the effrontery to offer me a deal—me, Chairman Shish as he believed, wielder of power of life or death over two million Groacians! He, a mere military figure, thought to dicker for immunity for himself on the grounds of the preservation of a united front in our deliberations with the Bogan representative. Naturally, I dismissed his feckless proposals, and assured him that in any case the Council would reject any such scheme as he had in mind. Clearly he's up to something on the side, in collusion with Prince Blue."

"That's swell, Nith," Retief said. "Only you're not Shish, so that leaves Groac in an equivocal position. What was Mr. Magnan doing while this was going on?"

"He was protesting vigorously at being suspended head-down over the fire. Gnish seemed determined to show him the courtesy of getting him right side up this time, but, alas, he was a trifle confused as to which end went where. As a result, poor Ben was coughing violently with his face in the smoke."

"What about S Second?" Retief demanded. "Did you find out what's going to happen?"

"I've no idea, Retief. Whatever it is it's doubtless beyond your poor power to add or detract. *Vamanos!*"

2

Retief gunned the engines and they rumbled toward the tunnel mouth, where the troops dithered, almost formed up a defensive line, then fled back into the shadows. At fifty feet from the opening, Retief halted the machine and adjusted the forward batteries for point-blank range. His first burst, directly along the axis of the narrow passage, elicited a brilliant flash of yellow light from the far end, silhouetting scuttling figures for an instant against boiling dust-and-smoke clouds. Next, Retief released a barricade mine, a bulky drum like a depth charge which rolled to the tunnel mouth, disappeared inside, and at once exploded with a blue-white flash, bringing down a cascade of rubble. Retief advanced over the broken ground, dozed aside major boulders, and entered the enlarged passage.

"How did you get out?" Retief demanded of Nith.

"It was while they were busy with Ben, adjusting the height, you know. I simply awaited my moment and walked briskly away. It's a trick I learned while on KP during my recruit service in the Groacian Army. Look as if you're busy and no one will bother you. Worked like a charm."

"Now it's my turn to look busy," Retief said. He gunned the engines, ramming the big machine forward with a squeal of metal against rock. The latter, being porous, crumbled away as the Yavac inched forward. Hard shots rattled off its impregnable bow armor. The inner end of the passage neared, merely a broadening of the vista of fire-lit smoke. Amid the fumes, at one side, Magnan's inverted form was visible intermittently writhing in bonds which wrapped him, mummylike, from toe to head.

"He's still wriggling with considerable vigor, if with little effect," Nith observed. "Perhaps he could still be saved."

"You know how to run this thing, Nith," Retief said. He had unstrapped from the command seat and stepped over Prince Blue, who was conscious again and rolling a baleful eye at him.

"This is as far as we go in comfort," Retief said. "I'm going in on foot to bring Mr. Magnan out. Don't do anything imaginative while I'm gone."

"You can't!" Nith protested. "They'll massacre you at first sight! And I could never maneuver this great ugly machine alone!"

"Maybe Prince Blue will help," Retief suggested. "Unless perhaps Your Highness would like to go with me," he addressed the bound Bogan.

"I'll take my chances here," Blue replied. "That Gnish would love to nail my hide to his door. And yours too, Terry. Why don't you give up this crazy idea? You tried, chum, and I'll be your witness, but you got too many decks stacked against you. Let's get out of here while they're busy with your pal."

3

Magnan had regained consciousness to find himself still—or again—inverted; a position, he found, to which he could not readily adapt. The headache, he estimated, was approximately three times as big as his head, and almost succeeded in distracting his attention from the burning sensation in his eyes, nose, and throat, accompanied by the penetrating reek of burning synthetics. His body ached in a milder, less compelling fashion, but failed to respond to his efforts to set it in rapid motion. After some moments of complete disorientation, he concluded that he was now strapped to a metal frame erected slightly to one side of a smudge pot, which in turn rested in the center of a showy conflagration whipped by a stiff breeze and fed by paper, some, he was able to glimpse through tears and smoke, bearing the heading: Ministry of Foreign Affairs—of what government he was unable to discern.

Reluctantly taking a breath, Magnan discovered to his surprise that at the level of his mouth, the draft unaccountably blowing across the floor supplied sufficient oxygen to enable him to sustain consciousness, a state of affairs of which he was not sure he entirely approved. He had a fragmentary recollection of something—a dream, no doubt—in which he had been freed, and turned right side up, and Retief had been there—but now that kindly delirium had passed and the flames below were real, if less voracious than they appeared. This time there really was no hope, Magnan admitted dismally. A pity, actually, when he had so much to report—but that, of course, was really why he was being done to death in this barbaric fashion: He Knew Too Much.

His dimming gaze fixed on a point of brilliant white light far beyond the veil of smoke—daylight! Then it was obscured by moving figures and massive machines. In the moment of clear viewing, Magnan had seen a smooth-walled bore, clearly of artificial origin. Why, in a mass of rock which was in itself a maze of tunnels, caverns, and fissures, would anyone be drilling holes . . . smooth as the bore of a cannon . . . ? His thoughts faded off into a confusion in which it seemed he felt a touch, heard a familiar voice.

"Hang in there, Mr. Magnan, another ten seconds. . ."

Then he was falling, falling: he grabbed for support, found nothing, and impacted with a force which, he was quite certain, had fractured every bone in his tormented body. To his astonishment, the pain of his multiple fractures failed to materialize, though his head was still aching abominably, and his eyes . . . like pockets of fire when he opened them . . .

Something moved: a face. Retief! Another hallucination. So this was death, the End. In a way, it wasn't so bad; better, that is, than the last bit of being alive. At least he could breathe now, and the throb of his pulse was fading from the reverberating *boom!* of pain to a more endurable stab of each heartbeat. But if his heart was beating, he couldn't be dead. He gave up the effort to grasp it all and went limp, but something seemed to be pulling at him, not letting him rest.

". . . if you can stand up. Wake up, Mr. Magnan, get your legs under you. This way, come on. If we can make it back to the Yavac before they get here—"

From somewhere Magnan summoned the strength to shout, "Retief, those tunnels—it all fits in with what Irving told me. The war—it's all a mistake! There's only one species here on Furtheron—one nation! When the meteorite hit and made these caverns—you see, the planet aggregated around an ice core, possibly a burned-out comet, and as the pressure increased and the temperature rose . . ." Magnan paused when he realized that only a feeble mumbling was passing his lips. He tried again: "Those frozen gases came boiling up, whipped the entire lithosphere into a froth; then the hardening crust sealed over, so that pressure built up."

"All right, Mr. Magnan," Retief's voice said clearly. Moments later, after a confused incident involving armed Crawlies, an excited Groaci officer, and the angry visage of General Gnish, Magnan realized that he was inside—somewhere—and at rest on his back, breathing clean air.

4

"I think we have all we need," the reedy voice of Ambassador Nith was saying. "Clearly it was really all Boge's fault. We Groaci were led down the garden path just as much as Terra was."

"Shall we hear what His Highness has to say?" Retief's voice came from somewhere above. Magnan winced as he opened his eyes. He was, he saw, in the crowded COC of some sort of military vehicle, whether air, space, or surface he was unsure. He uttered a groan. At once a five-eyed Groaci face appeared close to his own, eye stalks slightly crossed in expression of Sympathy, Inhibited by Inability to Help (71-c).

"Don't waste a 71-d on me, my dear chap," Magnan croaked. "There's no time for ritual courtesies. Where's Retief?"

"That was my 'c,' Ben," Nith explained. "Much less time consuming than the more elaborate degrees of the time-honored 71. He's right here."

"You've had a bad time, Mr. Magnan," Retief said, his face having replaced Nith's. "But you're safe now. I'm going to try to ram this thing back through to the surface."

After Retief explained to him the status of affairs, Magnan broke in eagerly, "Retief, I've discovered what this silly war is all about. Or rather, that it's about nothing. I overheard a Crawlie officer briefing General Gnish, the Groacian adviser. Sneaky, that," he added with a reproachful look at Nith, hovering behind Retief. "We at ITCH have been told nothing of a Groacian military presence here in the war zone."

"I myself was not informed," Nith whispered. "There are wheels within wheels, Ben. As you know, we Groaci are nothing if not sportsbeings—"

"As to that, Nith," Magnan interrupted, "I wouldn't call it fair play insinuating yourself into our councils in the Crawlie persona of Leroy, a shabby trick by any standard—especially when one considers that it was your own meddling which landed us all in this ridiculous situation to begin with. Whatever possessed you to hijack the ambassadorial limousine?"

"Oh, that was merely what one calls a target of

opportunity—and Captain Sprugg was not insistent; it was *his* idea, you know."

"Pass that," Retief said. "What is it you've discovered, Mr. Magnan?"

Before Magnan could reply, a tremendous impact rocked the armored vehicle. As all hands grabbed for support, it settled back to a stable position, only slightly tilted to port.

As the last echoes of the blast died away, a strange voice rasped from the hull plates: "That was only a sample, because I'm taking you more or less alive, for trade goods. Pop that hatch . . . now! Come out slow and easy, Prince Blue first. Any weapons in sight, or any tricky stuff, and I fire for effect and to hell with the negotiation! Do it!"

"It's a contact speaker, no doubt," Nith commented. "Once stuck to the hull, it will stick like a hide tick in the vroom fold."

"Good," Retief said, and manipulated a small control knob. A yell came in the same voice that had given the ultimatum: "All right, you clowns! That did it! Deal's off!"

"Whatever is he talking about?" Magnan queried.

"I fine-tuned the hot-hull field to send a few thousand zoules of inertiance back up the line," Retief explained. "Probably singed his boot soles, or maybe melted down the chair if he was sitting. So let's move out before he drops that next one on us." He slammed the big transmission control into Irresistible and fed eighty percent thrust to the drive train. With a lurch the great fighting machine responded, driving relentlessly through a resistance of over point nine on the Peabody scale.

"We seem to be buried in loose rubble," Retief commented, studying the gauges. The screens were uniformly an unrelieved black.

"Immolation!" Nith cried ecstatically. "The most sublime of all demises!"

"That's all very well for a life form that evolved from a burrowing-grublike ancestor," Magnan replied resentfully. "But we arboreal types feel differently."

"What I say is," Prince Blue spoke up, "why did the bum specify *me* first?"

The screens flashed suddenly into brilliance, showing a desolation of broken stone, heaped slag, and fragments of equipment scattered all across the now cracked and fissured floor.

"It appears we've survived the Big One," Retief said, as he swerved hard left to maneuver the Yavac along the narrow ridge between two major clefts, in the depths of which dim lights glowed.

"That Big One of old Gnish's was his special denial-to-the-enemy plan," Prince Blue said cheerfully. "Set up to do no real damage to the works, just kind of louse up the big bubble here, which it was only for show anyways. Figured to catch a big bunch of invading troops and seal off the real works at the same time. Old Gnish and his boys are all holed up in the tunnels outside the blast area, ready to jump out and say 'Boo!' "

"As I was saying, Retief," Magnan said, averting his blood-shot eyes from the screens, "the Furtheronians are a very argumentative people, little inclined to turn the other cheek."

"But they don't seem to be very serious about it," Retief pointed out. "They like to get all worked up and then just kind of wander off and forget about it. It's really a game to them."

"But," Nith spoke up, "the game can get out of hand, it seems, when it draws into its gambits such rogues as Prince Blue, and the renegade Gnish, to say nothing of luring the Groacian Premier himself to the scene. How fortunate that I was able to whisk His Excellency out of the focus of affairs before his presence was officially known. If he isn't properly grateful, I shall be, I confess, profoundly disappointed."

"To give it no further thought," a Groaci voice spoke up from behind him in his native tongue. "I realize now," it went on in Standard, "that I was most cleverly snookered by that archvillain His Imperial Highness the Prince of the Blue. Oh, there you are, Blue. Excuse me." Shish stepped over the still prone person of the Prince and continued: "Had it been revealed that I had entered into negotiations with the fellow, at the behest of General Gnish, I'd have been ruined, if not staked out on the sulphur pits at Yan."

"Your Excellency!" Nith gasped as the Premier came forward into the light from the shadows of the aisle.

"Just call me Shish," the Great One graciously commanded. "The blast sprung the door on my stateroom," he explained. "No complaint at the Spartan nature of my accommodations, Nith, gentlemen," he added hastily. "I owe you all a great deal—with the exception of you, Blue," he concluded, eyeing the trussed-up Bogan sourly. "But for your timely interruption, I might have found myself in a most unenviable position, strange-bedfellowswise." He tilted an ocular distastefully at Prince Blue, who spoke up with some heat.

"The trouble with you, Shish, is you're hopelessly small-time. Together, backing each other's play, we could of shaped up this end of the Arm. We still could, except now I'm mad." He glowered, demonstrating his ire.

"Mad, shmad," Shish murmured. "More to the point, Nith, how do you propose to extricate me from this present disaster?"

"Disaster, sir? But it's a triumph! We've penetrated the very sanctum sanctorum of the warmongers, driven them back in confusion, wrangling among themselves; and even destroyed their marshaling center."

"Um. And brought the latter down upon our heads. We're buried alive, a mile below the surface, surrounded by villains thirsting for our vascular fluids."

"Look there," Magnan put in, indicating the forward

screens, where a dusty Furtheronian had crept into view from a crevice half-covered by a fallen rock slab. The Creepy reared up, waving his stubby forelimbs in an agitated way.

"Take cover!" Nith hissed. "He's bent on mischief! I'll wager he has a bomb!"

"It's a trick," Magnan announced, "to distract our attention from that full platoon of Pink Bloomers moving up on the right."

"Perhaps he's only signaling," Shish hazarded.

"But he's one of Gnish's hired bounty hunters," Magnan protested.

"It's all right," Retief said. "It's Seymour, just a reserve private in the aboveground. He was with me when we picked up your trail, Mr. Magnan. Let's see what he wants." He halted close to Seymour, who scrambled eagerly forward to meet the big machine. Off to the right, the cautiously advancing commandos came hurrying forward at their best speed, concealment abandoned, some pausing to get off bursts of small-arms fire which kicked up dust devils around the frantically dodging Crawlie.

"Let him in, please, Mr. Magnan," Retief requested quietly. "Preferably before they get zeroed in."

Magnan went aft to comply. A moment later Seymour's breezy voice was heard commenting disparagingly on the Special Forces and adding perfectory thanks for the timely intervention.

"Hi there, Retief," he cried. "Glad to see you got clear OK. I couldn't talk plain before, with all them stoolies around. Last time I seen ya, before that, it didn't look good; them spooks had ya, I figgered, if the Security Patrol didn't. But why I come, I got a message fer ya, you know, from Mr. Pockenheimer, the big shot in the gang of Terries they're having like fun with right now, only Mr. P. made a break so's to get a chance to plant the message, which I wolumteered to deliver it."

Retief accepted the grubby scrap of paper on which was scrawled, in charcoal: LAST CHANST, OR MAYBE NOT EVEN THAT. COULD BE TOO LATE. MR. LACKLUSTER DON'T LOOK GOOD, AND EVEN HIS NIBS IS BEGINNING TO WILT. COME QUICK. LINE OF DUTY, SIGNED. F.

"Where's Fred now?" Retief asked.

"Well, since the roof fell in," Seymour replied, "a feller's sense o' direction gets kind of bollixed, ya know? Anyways, ya gotta go in the last part on foot, if the tunnel ain't fell in behind me; this big baby'd never make it. Come on, I'll lead yaz in—but I shichu not, I expect plenty of gucks in the old numbered account, eh? Let's maneuver in as close as we can get in this can first."

Following Seymour's laconic directions, Retief steered the mighty machine across rubble, fallen slabs of rock, past wrecked equipment, through disorganized clumps of Creepy and Groaci troops, who fired handguns at them as they passed.

"Looks like these boys are tryna beat us to it," Seymour commented. "The word must be out a bunch of Terries is up for grabs."

"Heavens," Magnan exclaimed. "Why should they all be so eager to lay grasping members on selfless Terran diplomats?"

"No wantum lay hands on 'em, chum," Seymour explained, lapsing into dialect. "More like lay a crowbar on 'em, or maybe a medium-bomber strike. Anyway, they got this idea Terries makeum roof fall in, louse up swell racket. No more new sneaker, ham sandwich for lunch, and all that."

A wider-than-average fissure in the cracked wall loomed ahead.

"In there," Seymour specified. Retief estimated the width of the opening, slowed, and fired two contact bombs. Light bloomed in the black depths, dust boiled out, shot through with hurtling rock fragments; then

Retief advanced into the now generous opening. The going was rough, but the massive treads ground rock to powder and passed on, delayed only momentarily when the hull creaked as the machine drove into the narrowest section, wedging itself, treads threshing; then it burst through. There was dim light ahead. Massive metal gates loomed up; they fell like *papier-mâché* theater props, and they were through into a spacious bubble with spongelike walls perforated by numerous apertures of all sizes, from tiny pores to great caverns, some of which were sealed by concrete. Seymour spoke up. "Right here is where I useta work, in the good old days," he said. "That there tunnel is the one you want." He indicated a hole not visibly different from all the others. "Over there," he went on, "is what boss callum 'active bore,' place where gas pressure build up, block off by rock fallum down into passage; afterwhile, big blow-off where rock givum way and next rock drop down, blockum gas again. Plenty rock, and after Seymour and other downtrodden working-class straighten passage, clear out obstruction, work like big peashooter. Run out rocks some day, maybe, if five-eye pal not keepum supply line open, pack plenty round rock over rim of little crater up topside. Rock boil around in high-pressure gas plenum, wear off smooth like pebble on seashore."

"Goodness!" Magnan cried. "It's a natural—almost— cannon, one might say. Trapped gases have pressurized the outlets which are blocked by constantly replenished rock falls, the expelled debris having cut a smooth bore over the ages. So that's why the bombardment is so haphazard and never lets up. Other such formations have kept a steady fire on random target areas all round this diabolical place, no doubt," he mused on. "No wonder the autochthons have been at war from the earliest times. Evolving in this curiously hostile environment, and being argumentive by nature, they of course ascribed the unending bombardment to some anonymous enemy, and retaliated as best they could. Poor creatures; they've never known a peaceful moment since the lithosphere hardened in this unusual fashion."

"Sure, no poor creature," Seymour protested. "Lucky fellow, Creepy, Crawlie have something exciting happen all time; never get bore. And Five-eye come along, organize regular government, give Lib Glip favor job, swap plenty obsolete tank, prop biplane, rubber-band gun under provision paragraph 91-2, all legal, make more fun get own finger in pie, only be careful finger not get cooked. Why Terry come along, try spoil fun? Crazy Terry, no want simple, unspoiled primitive have any kicks. But still, Terry do some good, too. Got to give Pouncetrifle his due."

"Oh, you mean the theater," Magnan spoke up," and the Yankee Stadium-type sports arena, and the whole Cultural Uplift and Sweetness Scheme!"

"Nope, CUSS program OK for egghead, maybe, but simple villager like bubble gum, old TV rerun—and car lot, billboard, fancy picture former Ambassador Straphanger, Crodfoller, hang up and throw dart at in pub."

"Gross!" Magnan declared. "The ingratitude of the lower classes is a phenomenon CUSS has never encountered in such crass form as here on Furtheron! And ITCH hasn't fared much better." He changed the subject abruptly. "Come, Retief, what are we to do? This great ugly monster will never pass through that tiny aperture, and if you go on enlarging routes in the same rude fashion as the last time, the entire complex will collapse about our heads."

"To be apparent," Shish spoke up, "that it will be necessary to send a rescue party in on foot. I myself would volunteer, if I hadn't a recurrence of an old gamesman's knee, brought on by my harsh confinement. Perhaps you, Nith, would like to cinch that next promo. . . ."

"On the other hand," Nith suggested, "why don't we just go home—if we can find the way out? No one can say we don't try, eh, Ben?"

"No problem get out," Seymour contributed, "just findum nearest active bore, and see daylight at end."

"What?" Magnan gasped. "Escape via the barrel of a giant cannon, about to fire at any moment?"

"Look here," Prince Blue spoke up, "in return for indemnity for any spurious charges brought against me by the coarse-minded, I myself will volunteer to go in there and snatch your friends to safety."

"No deal, Blue," Retief said. "But you can come with me, in case I encounter a need for a little extra muscle. Come on." He stepped over the fallen Prince and led the way aft.

"I better come too, boss," Seymour called, and followed.

5

Magnan uttered a feeble protest and subsided. Nith was humming a little tune. He looked at Magnan pityingly, an emotion he expressed by causing two pairs of eyes to stare intently into each other, while the fifth strained upward as if to see over the others.

"I think I'll just go catatonic again," the Groaci said. "Why don't you try it, Ben? Later, if all goes well, we'll awaken to find all the unpleasantness past, whereas if it doesn't—we shall never know."

"It's tempting," Magnan said, "but, unfortunately, the technique was not included in the curriculum at the Institute. We used to read the Manual instead," he ruminated on. "Capital notion!" he congratulated himself, recalling halcyon student days, and at once stepped back to the log cubicle for a copy of the Manual which he had noted among the standard references shelved there. "Some sections are better than others, of course," he explained, resuming his seat. "10-A is not bad, instructions for preparing the semiannual requisition, you know. But good old FSR-209-B-13-a," he mused on, "covering reciprocity in matters of protocol and precedence among underlings—that works like a charm." He had read only a few lines when his head lolled sideways and a gentle snore emanated from him.

"Fantastic!" Nith whispered. "Better than 5 cc. of drifton mainlined into the carotid. Pity I never learned to read Standard."

"It's just as well," Retief said behind him. "I need someone on the job here anyway. Better open up that aft personnel hatch now."

Nith had all five eyes fixed on the peek screen. "I can't!" he wailed. "That is, I mustn't! There's someone there! A brigand! He's ready and waiting to swarm in as soon as the hatch cracks!"

"Go ahead," Retief said. "We'll be on hand to welcome him." He returned aft. With a moan, Nith operated the complex interlocks, and the OPEN light winked on.

As the hatch cycled open the first inch, wisps of dust drifted in, accompanied by a faint sound, originating nearby, it seemed.

"To wonder," Nith remarked, as the hatch cycled slowly, "what that odd whining noise could be . . . ?" He drew back as a grubby human hand thrust in, gripped the hand hold, followed a moment later by a scratched and dusty face—that of Fred Pockenheimer. Retief helped him in. The chauffeur recoiled at sight of Seymour, then relaxed.

"Say, am I glad to see you, Mr. Retief," Fred gasped. "I just about decided old Seymour ducked out on me. Couldn't find him after the roof fell in. Then I seen this baby, and at first I thought—"

"Never mind, Fred," Retief calmed the man. "You're

OK now—at least as OK as the rest of us. Where are the others?"

"Oh, His Nibs—excuse me, Counselor Clutchplate and Old Pouncy, I mean—they're in the VIP cell, and the rest o' the boys are staked out in some kinda big tube, like a subway tunnel kind of. These here local Creepies talk awful rough, but the Pink Bloomers—Creepy Special Forces, you know—they been keeping 'em under control, waiting for orders from topside. Oh, hi, Mr. Ambassador," Fred concluded, glimpsing Nith in the background. "Kinda lucky ya happened along. You can tell Cap Swinth, he's head of the guard detail, to escort our fellows back up to the surface."

"I shall be pleased to do so," Nith replied grandly. "But how can we be sure the native levies won't dismember us at first sight?"

"We can't," Prince Blue supplied, and stepped out.

"Stand by, Mr. Magnan," Retief said into the talker beside the entry port. "Go on aboard, Fred. I'll close the hatch with the dead-man's switch. Watch us on number-two screen, and be ready to open up fast." He jumped down and assisted Nith to follow. When he turned, Prince Blue was waiting, with a fist-sized rock in his big-knuckled hand. Nith gasped.

"If you fellows wouldn't of took my side arm," Blue complained mildly, "it would of been handy now."

"That's all right, Snart," Retief said. "Let's just handle it bare-handed." He took a step toward the burly Bogan, who eyed him warily, dropped the rock, and said. "Yeah—some other time."

"Better get going, gents," Fred urged, "you maybe ain't got much time. I heard the captain say some kinda big gun goes off on the hour—and it's only three minutes till."

Seymour undulated down from the hatch, his head tendrils moving alertly. "Old Fred's right," he said. "This way, gents." He set off at a fast clip, his long body humping over the rubble-strewn rock floor at a rate the others were hard put to match. In a moment they were inside a narrow cleft with an upward-trending floor.

6

"This is where gettum sticky," Seymour said. "Me go first, givum guard big hello, like old-timer on nostalgia kick, come back see place where long ago guard kickum hell out of young fellow. While keep occupy, new chums do sneak across to Special Bore yonder." He pointed to a makeshift control booth set up beside a seemingly sealed-off tunnel mouth.

"Stand by, pretty soon me be there, show works, get inside before too late, maybe, get Terry out." Without awaiting confirmation, Seymour emerged boldly into the dim-lit cave, uttered glad cries as a squad of Crawlie turnkeys converged on him. Retief waited until they met, with a great slinging of arms and slapping of backs; then he led his ill-assorted party across, keeping to the shadows. The door opened to a hearty tug. Inside, in an odor of old garg and unwashed Furtheronians, heavy-duty blast controls loomed incongruously tidy in the disorder.

"Those are of Groacian manufacture," Nith supplied. "I think I know how to operate them."

"Not yet, Mr. Ambassador," Retief cautioned. "We'd better wait for Seymour."

Out in the center of the cavern, the group had broken up. Abruptly a uniformed Creepy rose into the air, propelled, Retief saw, by Seymour's hammer lock on his median limbs. As the chastened guard fell back among his fellows, Seymour stepped clear and, pausing only to dust his hands and call over his shoulder, advanced toward the control hut.

"Feelum good get sneaker on other pedal extremity,"

he muttered as he joined the aliens. "For minute there, lookum like bluff no go, but then Irving make slip: try to get tough, and all of sudden I see red, give Irv old heave-ho, and all get good yock, except maybe Irv, which I stepped on his face maybe a coupla times, helping him up, you know—no hard feelings, old pal, remember Good Old Days. Me ease out while all eyes full tears; no gottum time waste now, throw HOLD lever, get ten more seconds try save Terries." He turned, hesitated as he saw Nith grasp a red-painted lever and throw it home.

"Oh, five-eyes know about 'second-thought' switch," he said. "That OK that time, but better leave all control me, knowum all booby trap."

"Booby trap?" Nith shrieked and fell back, half-fainting. "To mean . . . that I . . . ? We could all have been blown to Kingdom Come!"

"No, just outskirts town," Seymour corrected blandly. "Now open last-man valve gain ingress Main Tube." He worked an inconspicuous lever and a vertical slot opened in the side wall. "Better hurry up, before next sched-uled shot," he said, and slithered into the narrow cleft; the rest followed.

CHAPTER EIGHT

"MR. RETIEF!" cried a fruity voice, which Retief recognized as that of counselor Clutchplate. Retief used his cigar lighter on wide-open beam to cast a dim, reddish glow on his surroundings, and made out a barred door to which clung both the counselor and his chief, Ajax Pouncetrifle, Terran AE and MP.

"Heads will roll," the portly diplomat boomed. "When I report this outrage back at Sector—"

"They'll never believe you, Ajax," Clutchplate reminded his senior, "officially, that is: inconvenient to have to go to all the bother of issuing ritual *aides mémoires* and all that. Better just save it to spice up your personal memoirs."

"Good advice, Clutchplate," Pouncetrifle conceded, "but if it's to be of any use, we'd best turn our thoughts to modes of return to my Mission."

"Sound thinking, Your Excellency," Clutchplate returned. "Why not just direct Fred to bring the car around? While he's here he can open these confounded cage doors."

"You forget, Clutchplate. Ben Magnan went mad and made off with the Official Vehicle at the concert, some days ago. As for Fred, he was trepanned along with the limousine, just before we ourselves were seized."

"To be sure; the trifle had escaped me," Clutchplate said, nodding solemnly.

"Mr. Ambassador, sir," Magnan yelped, leaping forward. "That's hardly fair, sir, considering I was taken away at gunpoint, protesting the while, at hazard of life and limb!"

"Oh," Pouncetrifle returned skeptically. "And just who do you allege committed this infernal piece of impudence?"

"A pair of ferocious dacoits, a Captain Sprugg and a low-caste Creepy called Leroy."

"I see. And have you placed these two pirates under close arrest?" He peered through the bars as if trying to see them over Magnan's shoulder.

"Well, not exactly, sir. You see, the captain was taken away by cannibals—"

"Serves the beggar right," Pouncetrifle interjected.

"—and as for Leroy, he doesn't exist—that is, he was in disguise—"

"Very convenient, Ben," the Ambassador said coldly. "Nonetheless, I shall hold in abeyance proceedings for grand theft and desertion until I'm back at my desk in my chancery."

"Oh," Magnan temporized, turning to Nith, "perhaps if you'd explain, Mr. Ambassador—"

"Nith!" Pouncetrifle barked. "What the devil—that is, I *thought* I'd find you mixed up in this somewhere! It's an outrage, a violation of every diplomatic convention since the Iranian Fiasco! Now tell your minions to release me at once—oh, and Clutchplate as well. I'm waiting, Mr. Ambassador!"

"You imply, Ajax, that *I*, Groac's legate, am implicated? Sir, Groac resents—"

Magnan unobtrusively withdrew from the line of fire between the battling titans.

"Retief! Whatever are we to do?" he wailed. "Even were we ourselves to find a path to the surface, *they're* still incarcerated behind bars, and time is short, remember?"

"You dare to accuse *me*, Ajax?" Nith demanded sternly, drawing close to the bars. "After I've suffered personal hardship in my determination to seek you out and right this grievous wrong? Besides, you can't prove a thing."

"Perhaps I was hasty, Excellency," Pouncetrifle recanted. "But you see, Clutchplate and I were placed here, precisely in the breech of some sort of giant cannon, I understand, set up to fire automatically at irregular intervals—and we'll be blown to a thin paste on the walls. Serves to lubricate the passage of the cannon ball. An ancient custom, they tell me."

"Right," Seymour spoke up. "Date back to week before last, maybe, time nosy Crawlie stick face in where not invite, get in here, hide, and *boom!*—record range on that shot. Creepy smart, supply grease all time now. And time short; cannon ball arrive any time now." He winced as a dull roar sounded, concluding with a *thump!* which shook the floor of living rock. The dim light was suddenly dimmer.

"OK, lock and load; buildum pressure now, gents. In a few more second, all eardrums pop, pretty soon all blood vessel rupture, pass out, kindly provision nature, not know next."

"Perhaps," Nith proposed, "we should be going." The crowded space seemed suddenly hot.

"Not without His Excellency!" Magnan protested. "And you, too, of course, Mr. Clutchplate," he amended, offering a fragile smile to the latter official, noting as he did that his breathing had become labored.

"In that case you'd best remove this obstruction,"

Pouncetrifle declared, giving the massive iron grill a feeble shake.

"That don't look so tough," the bass voice of Prince Blue interjected. He jostled his way forward, took a grip on the stout bars with his massive hands, set himself, and heaved until his ragged tunic split. A few flakes of rust fell as steel groaned against rock, but nothing yielded. Blue stepped back and dusted his horny palms. "Tougher'n it looks," he said. "Well, let's get moving, fellows. According to my briefing, which I got the word direct from Gnish, it only takes about two zips of a doodly-bug to build up to operating pressure."

Retief came forward, used his lighter on tight beam to cut through the two-inch locking bar, pocketed the device, and gripped the bars. With a slow, steady pressure he bent the panel outward.

"Better come out fast, while I hold it," he said between clenched teeth.

"But—suppose you slip?" Pouncetrifle warbled, drawing back from the narrow gap. "I'd be squashed!" With one arm, he waved Clutchplate back.

Prince Blue reached in, caught the distraught Ambassador's nearest arm, and hauled him out. His counselor followed quickly. Seymour stepped up to wedge a stone of appropriate size into the gap Retief was still holding open; he relaxed and turned—to see a larger-than-average Crawlie appear through the same aperture his own party had used. The newcomer came forward, his head tendrils writhing in expression of savage anticipation.

"Hi there, Seymour old kid!" he called genially. "I don't b'leeve I meetum all pal you, got no time for introduction now, zero second coming up fast. What you hangum around blast chamber for, get close view next shot?" He appeared to notice for the first time that the tiny barred cell was vacant. "Hey, what givum?" He demanded, leveling his blast gun. "You try make simian out old pal Irv?" he yelled. "Where prisoner go? Oh, there you are, gents. I guess I got a little excited, cause if you give slip, me gettum honor take place."

"Right!" Retief said, as he put a one-handed lock grip on the guard sergeant's arm and propelled his forequarters into the cell, at the same time lifting the weapon from his grip.

"Better get the rest in fast, Irv," he said. "When I take this rock out, it's going to snap hard." Irv complied frantically, turned to look mournfully out past the bars.

"Seymour," he moaned, "you old pal and all, takum side foreigner, let out while let old pal in, suffer dire fate reserve for vile criminal?"

"And for incompetents," Seymour pointed out. "Dumb play let Retief get close. Him tougher'n a mule worm's brisket."

"Now you tellum," Irv complained. "How I know all Terry not like silly old maid, jabber plenty, do nothing?"

"I guess you forgettum Section 3-b-7 Field Manual, *Know Your Victim*," Seymour suggested.

"Yeah, I guess I got it coming, Seymour, but Fred ain't going to like it."

"That's tough E-pores for Fred, which me no likum traitors, even on our side."

2

"No time to waste," Nith hissed. "The pressure is intolerable, and any time now it's going to blow." He motioned frantically, herding Pouncetrifle and Clutchplate along to the exit valve and out. Compressed air hissed as the valve cycled open briefly, then snapped shut. The rest followed, Retief last, after letting the barred door clang back into place. A few feet along the narrow passage, Seymour operated a lever to open a secret slitlike accessway, this one letting into a spacious circular tunnel, perfectly straight, with a disc of wan daylight at its far end.

"Good heavens, Seymour!" Magnan cried. "This is the barrel of the cannon! Out of the hot fat into the glowing embers, with a vengeance!"

"Sure, Terry right," Seymour agreed cheerfully. "Nice easy route to surface, but better gettum move on, not much space scrooch back let big rock go by."

Without further delay, the little party of refugees hurried off along the curving floor, Prince Blue hustling the Terran Ambassador and his equally disapproving Number Two, who seemed determined to hold a conference before retreating.

Halfway along the half-mile bore, Retief noticed a narrow fissure in the otherwise smooth wall. He paused long enough to stuff into it one of the small detonator cylinders which had fallen from the hand baggage of the newly arrived Groaci, Fliss, at the terminal, only a few days before. Here, close to daylight, the air was cooler.

The party emerged on a bleak rock slope affording a view of the outer crater wall and the deep green jungle below, the river tracing a silver serpentine in the middle distance. Far away a pall of dust hung over the patched roofs of the city. They had barely thrown themselves flat, at Seymour's behest, when the rock shook beneath them, a *Bang!* like a sonic boom seemed to shake the world, and a great cloud of rock fragments whistled from the yawning pit they had just vacated. Air hissed and moaned as the relieved gases found pressure equilibrium. Then, as if by afterthought, the tunnel collapsed, sending out a final spurt of dust and grit.

"Hot damn!" Seymour cried. "Never seeum *that* before! Big gun go off, then self-destruct! Neat! That servum bad Creepy right!" He made rude gestures at the Creepy troops who were emerging from shelter all around.

"Dear me," Counselor Clutchplate murmured. "More

complications; pity the tunnel collapsed; we could have gone back and gotten into our cage where we'd be out of the path of all this unseemly activity."

"Tell the beggars to sheer off there, Mr. Retief," Ambassador Pouncetrifle barked. "We're not to be intimidated by a mere gang of Creepies—er, Nether Furtheronians, that is."

"They don't intend to intimidate us, I suspect, Mr. Ambassador," Magnan corrected his superior. "Just kill and eat us." By now the soldiers were closed in, shaking their spears.

"Well, what about you, Nith?" Pouncetrifle demanded. "It's you people who've got the natives all stirred up—so do something!"

"You wrong me, Ajax," Nith replied loftily. "Selfless Groac's role here has been beyond reproach. Though we *did* wipe your eye by getting her first and stripping this cinder world of its useful minerals before you caught on. And peacefully, mind you."

"So that puts the bee on Boge, I guess," Prince Blue said heavily. "But it's just another bum rap. Sure, us Bogans sold maybe a few peashooters and heavy rubber-band guns to some o' these bums—but they was already beating each other's brains out. *We* din't start nothing. Get back, you!" the Prince put a large hand in the face of the nearest private and flipped him onto his back. His comrades paused, giving Blue resentful looks, and the Bogan eased back out of the line of verbal fire. Muttering started, swelled in volume. The tight cluster around the little band of foreigners was growing into a mob yelling for blood.

3

"Here, you fellows!" a commanding voice cut through the hubbub. "Knock that off and fall in, in a column of ducks!" The shouting diminished, faded into a faint muttering.

"Good afternoon, Colonel," Retief greeted the officer. "I'm glad to see you made it to rendezvous at M-minute. You can form up these spirited lads of yours and prepare to escort this party of VIPs back to their transport, which I assume has been fetched down from the treetops by now."

"Right, sir!" the colonel saluted smartly. "Would you care to inspect the troops first? I'll have 'em straightened out here in a minute."

"Pass that for now," Retief ordered. Counselor Clutchplate was plucking his sleeve. "See here, Mr. Retief," he said harshly, "if you're on friendly terms with these dacoits, it appears you're deeply involved in this skulduggery."

"Wrong gambit, Clutchplate," Pouncetrifle interceded. "Under the circumstances, we'd best wink at a trifle of collusion with the enemy—er, the locals, that is. As you were, Retief, just send these fellows packing."

"Your Excellency wishes to decline the services of my regiment?" Colonel Yan queried, taken aback. "I must caution Your Excellency that certain unruly elements lurking in the jungle yonder may attempt to impede your progress back to town."

"On second thought, my dear Colonel," Pouncetrifle conceded, "the idea of an armed escort has merit. I'll remember it at the inquiry, assuming we do indeed arrive safely, in time to greet the inspectors before they leave, bearing, perhaps, a less than favorable report as to the progress of ITCH in pacifying this madhouse. Come, Clutchplate, Ben." He paused as if struck by a sudden thought. "I seem to recall that my driver, Fred, was at the wheel at the time my car was taken. I wonder where he's got to?"

"Right here, chief." The chauffeur's distinctive voice

came cheerfully over the ranks. "I was just about to speak up when ya ast fer me."

"What in the world are you doing there, Fred, in the midst of a formation of native sepoys?" Clutchplate demanded. "Come here at once!"

"Sure, boss," Fred replied. "Just drifting with the tide, ya could say. But you better take it easy on the big shottery; these oy-bays got the idea someways that I'm the ig-bay oss-bay. They'd kind of resent you fellas ordering me around, like. The ituation-say is elicate-day like they say."

Amid a bustle of Creepy soldiers re-forming to open a lane, Fred appeared, lolling at his ease on an elaborate litter borne by four top sergeants. He waved genially, signaled to be put down, and dismissed his bearers.

"What happened," he stated in a tone of One Imparting Confidence (42-x), "is on account of I was at the wheel, the cannibals decided I was the Big Cheese. They give me special treatment, special transport tied to a kinda totem pole and all—"

"Upside-down?" Magnan inquired acidly.

"Sure—but ya gotta take the bitter with the sweet and all," Fred pointed out. "After a while they run into the government troops and worked out a swap. Seems like old Chief Barf is spose to get plenty guck for me, soon's the revolution's in power. I tole the Colonel here see'n I'm so valuable he better protect his investment by treating me right. I splained to him how excessive walking was bad for my bloof-organs—course I ain't got no bloof-organs, but *he* don't know that. And getting pushed around and not fed'll sprain a ulterior metacostal or something."

"You're a union man?" Clutchplate inquired sharply.

"All the way, pal, all the way," Fred confirmed. "And if my union knew what I'd went through in the line o' duty—well, I leave it to you gents to figger that one."

"To be sure," Pouncetrifle agreed. "One mustn't adopt any attitude which could give rise to irresponsible rumors conducive to labor unrest."

"Nix on that 'labor' tag, boss," Fred spoke up quickly. "The union—boss Greenblitch, I mean—decided that the word's pejorative: sounds too much like work, too. So nowadays we go by 'Creative Leisure,' kind of an unhandy term, ya gotta admit, so the boys usually say, 'See-ell.' Neat, huh? So we're eye to eye; we don't neither one of us want no CL unrest. Next item, a hike in the old pay packet, which I oughta be getting at least as much as old Charlie in the code room, which it ain't so hard to dope them machines anyways."

"Fred!" Pouncetrifle gasped. "You don't mean—there's been a breach of security!"

"Sure not," Fred confirmed. "I never told nobody. Security's tight as a hide tick in a Groaci's vroom fold. Let's get going, which the colonel is ready to do a escort number, and get us through all these here like hazards without ruffling a eyebrow."

"We mustn't be hasty, Fred," the Ambassador demured, "Eh, Clutchplate?"

"Bang on," Clutchplate agreed. Turning to Fred he inquired, "Just what faction does Colonel Yan represent?"

"Beats me, boss." Fred dismissed the question with a shake of his head. "What difference does it make? For the minute, he's ready to put away the skinning knives and be our bodyguard, so let's not shake a two-credit watch too hard, OK?"

"Fred," Pouncetrifle put in sternly, "as Chief of Mission of Terra, I can hardly appear to align myself with what may yet turn out to be a dissident element."

"Where's Captain Sprugg?" Magnan spoke up. "He seemed a candid sort of chap—we can ask him."

"Don't bother, Ben," Nith put in. "I can supply that information. You'll recall that in the persona of Private

Leroy, I pretended to assist the captain in the 'hijacking' of the official vehicle."

"What's this, Nith?" Pouncetrifle blustered. "*You*, an accredited ambassador of a Great Power, reduced to stealing used cars?"

"Not exactly, sir," Magnan contributed. "It seems it was Fred they were to convoy safely to his rendezvous with Prince Blue and another highly placed official," he concluded discreetly.

"Fred? That's insane. A mere lackey, when they could as easily have taken my own person? What for?"

"Fred, it seems, was the weak link in the solid Terran front," Nith explained patiently. "He harbored grudges due to low pay and status, and thus was found to be amenable when my agents approached him subtly. The prospect of early retirement with a ton of .999 fine gold tempted him beyond his ability to resist. I suggest he be dealt with leniently."

"Lenient, shmenient!" Fred sputtered. "I was on a like secret lay, which I figgered to con you and Blue here, and the turncoat colonel, and some Groac Big Shot all into a big meet, and then put an arm on the lot of them, and bring 'em in." With a sudden swift motion, Fred produced a heavy power gun from the recesses of the bulky bandage on his arm. "And it ain't too late to score the big coup," he went on. "Line up, the lot of you, backs against the rock, then we'll get started. All except you, wisey," he added, addressing Magnan. "For you and your big mouth I got special plans. Remember how you give me the horse laugh when I reported the black paint in my window squirts?"

"Fred," Colonel Yan spoke up. "Am I to understand that you propose to include me, your old confidant, in this act of insubordination or whatever it is?"

"Forget it, Sam," Fred said easily. "You're mixed up. It was the real Colonel Yan I figgered to hoist on his own petard, like they say. Since you taken over his outfit, you and me have got on swell. Now form up the boys and we'll make it to town before dark."

4

"As you were, Sam," Retief said coolly. "You will dispose your troops to guard every exit from the crater. Start by plugging this hole with rock; the next scheduled blast will backfire and send everyone inside to the nearest escape route on the double; just keep 'em inside. As for you, Fred," he went on, "that handgun you're so proud of lacks a detonator, so my little cigar lighter looks like top hand. Drop it." With his thumb Retief turned the beam control on his lighter up to the proper level to heat Fred's gun to a dull red, as it was already falling from the discomfited driver's scorched fingers. "I might've bought your Special Agent story if you hadn't overdone the act by having Mr. Magnan lashed to a torture pole as soon as you got your hands on him. And those tricky SOS messages helped."

"Me?" Fred objected as if astonished. "But it was Sol Dop and Beauregard who—I mean—what would *I* know about any torture pole?"

"Too much," Retief said. "The fake notes were a good idea, except that they told more than you intended."

"But how—?" Fred scratched at his scalp with a fingernail like a banjo pick, eliciting a loud rutching sound. Just then the rock trembled underfoot, and spurts of dust *whoof!*ed from the yawning but partially blocked mouth of the Special Bore. Small stones flew from a nearby cleft, and from another a helmeted Groaci head poked out and ducked back at sight of the waiting soldiers. Colonel Yan yelled orders, and more troops deployed all around the mile-wide rim of the Scary Place. In the distance, other special bores fired their boulders as usual, the troops rushing in at once to block them with debris.

"Mr. Ambassador," Retief said, "with the bombardment stopped, I think we'll find the locals more amenable to pacification. I suggest we get back on the job before the Groaci think up another angle. The limousine is only a mile or two away; we can reach it in half an hour."

"Precisely the order I was about to issue," Ajax Pouncetrifle, AE and MP, replied briskly. "And now that I've cleared up this tiresome affair, I hope to be back at my desk in time to forestall any ill-considered carping by the Inspection team. Let us go. By the way, Retief, I've been wondering about your own role in these matters; you were, I recall, aboard my car at the time it was stolen. I trust you have an adequate explanation for that curious circumstance."

"After all, Mr. Ambassador," Magnan volunteered, "Retief *was* sitting at the extreme rear. Small wonder he was last man out and noticed the approach of the thieves."

"Not thieves precisely, Ben," Nith objected. "It was clearly necessary for me to commandeer the vehicle in order to snare the wily Fred, thereby bringing to an end this disgraceful affair, in which he, alas, was prime mover."

"Not quite, Nith, or Shish, or whatever," Prince Blue spoke up. "I manipulated you Groaci so as to cause you to enlist Terry participation in our scheme. *Our* scheme, I emphasize, and a benign one, to provide harmless antique war toys to these primitives, to enable them to work off their aggressions without undue loss of life and property, while at the same time making Furtheronian minerals, like Fred's ton of gold, available to the Galactic economy. Now, gentlemen, I think it's time to go. I must be about dictating my memoirs whilst the events are still fresh in my mind." He moved off as if deep in thought.

"Ah, hold it there, Mr. Retief," a gluey Creepy voice cut in harshly. "You no forgettum big deal, plenty guck for deserving local boy for escort Terry spies back to town, me hopum."

"At ease, Corporal!" Colonel Yan barked. "You're outranked, and it appears the guck goes to your commander. Now you"—he turned to address Retief—"since the agreement was that you would remain behind as surety for payment, I'm sure you'll have no objection to just stepping to the rear of the formation, where my Chief Armorer, Sergeant Shipe, will fit you with a set of VIP manacles."

"Here—" Ambassador Pouncetrifle spoke up. "You have undertaken, Colonel, to escort me AND my staff back to my Embassy—so what's this talk of manacles?"

"A mere detail, Mr. Ambassador," Yan reassured the Great Man. "Unless Mr. Retief remains behind, what assurance have I that the payoff will proceed as agreed?"

"What payoff?" Pouncetrifle roared. "I assumed you were lending assistance out of sheer humanitarianism, and with an eye to favorable mention in my report."

"A little matter of forty billion guck, or maybe it was two million, or something. Anyway, lots more than a fellow would need to be set for life. Corporal Glop here has the details. "

"Outrageous!" the Terran AE and MP thundered. "You had the audacity to make this unconscionable demand when you imagined yourself in command of the situation? Poor planning on your part, Yan, thus to attempt to twist the tail of mighty Terra."

"Not me, chum," Yan demurred mildly. "It was Retief's idear. Us natives ain't sufficiently sophisticated to of come up with it. We'd of just had us a swell cook-out. But wunst he brang it up, we seen right away the scheme had like merit and all. So we went for it. Now let's form up and move out."

"Well," Pouncetrifle grumped, "since it was his own idea, I suppose . . ."

"It's all right, Mr. Ambassador," Retief said. "I'd just as soon take my chances here, just in case you don't have forty billion GUC in the safe."

CHAPTER NINE

As NONCOMS YELLED ORDERS, the troops gathered and
formed up, herding the aliens into a compact group in
midcolumn. Complaining, Fred was dumped from his
litter to join the escortees. Nith, evading a grab by a
private detailed to round up stragglers, ducked out of
sight in a cleft in the igneous rock. Retief casually
approached.

"I say, Retief," Nith spoke up, as soon as the Terran
was within range of his feeble Groaci voice, "I was just
wondering about His Supremacy, still incarcerated in
the Yavac down below, as I recall. Surely he's not to be
left to his fate?"

"Good thinking, Mr. Ambassador," Retief conceded.
"But someone else seems to have had the same idea. I
don't see Prince Blue."

"No, I saw the scamp sneaking off behind the boulders over *that* way." Nith pointed. "He's up to no good,
Retief. Probably he has some scheme of his own."

"Maybe we'd better go meet him," Retief suggested,

as Colonel Yan and his charges moved off into the jungle fringe below the crater's edge.

2

Leaving Nith posted as lookout at the rim of the bore, Retief climbed easily down the only-slightly-improved, near-vertical wall toward the bulk of the Yavac, a darker hulk in the darkness. Arriving amid a light clatter of falling pebbles, he went quickly to the nearest inspection hatch, lifted the hinged lid, and attached an induction pickup to the appropriate spot. He heard the clump of booted feet within, the wheezing of out-of-condition lungs, followed by a sharp rapping as of knuckles upon metal, then Prince Blue's unctuous voice:

"I say, Your Supremacy, are you there?"

"Where else would I be, you imperial idiot?" Chairman Shish's breathy voice responded at once. "How long have I been locked in this infernal broom closet this time?"

"Not long, old pal," Blue replied indifferently. "Just about long enough for me to get all the details of our plan ironed out. Ready to talk deal now?"

"*Our* plan indeed!" Shish retorted. "I remind you, sir, the insidious scheme was entirely yours from the beginning. I confess I was fool enough to listen—after all, you *are* a plausible scoundrel—but you promised there'd be no interference from hypocritical Terra, poking her nose in under the guise of uplift of the natives, to skim the cream off any arrangement we might have succeeded in making."

"Have no fears from that quarter," Blue reassured his colleague. "His Excellency the Terran Ambassador and his entire staff are at present under close arrest in the hands of a minion of mine, one Colonel Yan, to wit."

"Yan?" Shish hissed. "Aside from the fact that he's in

all probability the most inept blunderer uninstitution-alized in all of civilized space, he's *my* minion, de-puted to report faithfully on your every move."

"Oh, well, I kind of wondered why the old disguise didn't work out so good," Blue confided. "To think that lowly ex-corporal was crossing me, which I practically fished him outa the gutter, all the time I was keeping him and his Green Bloomers supplied with late-model Bogan equipment. But he did slip me a line on you and your boys from time to time, so it ain't a total loss. That's how I knew to step in and whisk like they say old Nith right outa the grasp of them Terries, Magnan and the big one."

"That's right! Ben Magnan *is* involved in this affair!" Shish wailed. "Perhaps it would be best after all if you simply left me here to meditate, rather than to spring me, only to be confronted by a phalanx of Terry nitpick-ers citing solemn interplanetary accords. Leave me, my dear Prince. And if your schemes should prosper, don't forget that it was I who spirited you out of the ambush laid for you by your fellow Bogans. Remember it was under the shield of my diplomatic immunity that you were slipped past the alert guard at the port, thereby wiping the eye of Ajax Pouncetrifle with a vengeance."

"Sure, I know all that jazz," Blue acknowledged. "But as Your Supremacy is doubtless aware, things went somewhat awry, and it was only by dint of super-Bogan effort I ever got you back outa the Scary Place, whence none is ever before reported to of escaped alive, except some o' them union labor, o' course, but they know better'n to blab anyways."

"Pah!" Shish dismissed the ploy. "It was my own personal envoy to Furtheron who so skillfully extricated me from that nest of conspirators. You, as I recall, were lying trussed in this very vehicle at the time. By the way, it was clever of you to regain your freedom. One day you must tell me just how you did it—after your trial and conviction, of course."

"You got it all wrong, Shish," Blue objected. "Look, we still got the situation well in hand. All we got to do is grab this here Mr. Magnan and the other one, and then get to the wire services with our story ahead o' the Terries."

"And just how are you going to work that?" Shish asked sarcastically. "After all, they are both with Colonel Yan."

"Maybe I could kinda work that out. I'm going to have a like look around and see how I should get us outa here," Blue replied in a patience-with-stupidity tone.

Retief disconnected his induction device and waited for Blue to put in an appearance. After a few minutes he heard the hatch scraping open. Two large-knuckled hands grasped the edge of the hatch; then the hard-looking bullet head of the Bogan gunrunner appeared; he glanced about in a perfunctory way, and climbed out.

When he was clear of the hatch, Retief spoke: "Halt and put your hands on top of your head. You're under citizen arrest."

"Retief!" Prince Blue exclaimed. "I knew I shoulda scragged you when I had the chanct. Whattaya mean 'citizen arrest'? You're no citizen of this dump, you're an alien interloper, just like me."

"Not quite like you, Blue," Retief demurred. "I've got the drop on you. Now back off and turn around with great care and I'll try to resist scragging *you* while I have the chance. Go on over the side, slowly, and start climbing."

The Prince peered dubiously over his shoulder and inquired: "Up, or down?"

"Down. And quietly."

"How do I know you even got a gun?" Blue demanded.

"Want to bet your life I don't?" Retief asked quietly.

"On the whole, I guess I better take the climb," Blue replied glumly. "But look, Retief, you and me could make a deal. You're not as tied up in red tape as most o' you Terry diplomats; you can see the sense in maybe stretching a reg here and there—not where anybody'd see you, o' course. I mean, I got a grasp of political reality after all. What say to a down-the-middle forty-sixty split on the gross take?"

"What good would your sixty do you in the VIP maximum security suite at Iceberg 9?" Retief inquired. "Anyway, I've already got mine. I know where the gold is hidden."

"Gold?" Blue came back quickly. "I admit I got a what-ya-might-say hangup on gold. Got it when I was just a kid, reading about ancient history and pirates' gold and all. Decided right then what I wanneda be when I grew up. What is it, objay darr, coins, ingots, dust, or what?"

"Just a vein of the pure stuff forty feet thick, a quarter-mile wide, and deeper than anybody's managed to dig," Retief explained. "But you can forget gold; what you've got coming is cold iron or hot lead."

"Don't get excited, I'm going, ain't I?" Prince Blue returned in a tone of One Who Suffers Injustice With Fortitude.

"Before you go, your Imperial Highness," Retief said, "What's the report on His Supremacy Premier Shish?"

"You mean that five-eyed little double-crosser really *is* the head Groaci?" the Bogan sounded regretful. "I guess maybe I blew it, Retief. This routine ain't going to go so good if we don't have the Groaci backing the play, too. Like it'd lack credibility, if you know what I mean."

"Maybe you'd better have another try," Retief ordered. "And this time remember you're dealing directly with a chief of state."

"Sure. Just gimme another crack at that sucker, I'll have him eating nid-nuts out of my hand in a trice—whatever a trice is. I always pictured it as a kind of a big diaper sort of sling. Right?"

"Close enough. Just be sure it's *his* haunches in the sling and not your own imperial hindquarters."

"OK if I go back in now?" Prince Blue inquired dubiously, edging toward the open hatch cover.

"The sooner the better—and remember the thing is wired for self-destruct and I've got the panic button," Retief reminded the fallen royalty.

"Don't do nothing hasty," Blue cautioned, and disappeared through the hatch.

3

Retief reattached his pickup and listened.

"Oh, Yer Supremacy," Blue's voice sounded unctuously, accompanied by a rap of horny knuckles against metal.

"Your Highness!" Shish's breathy voice returned at once, somewhat muffled by the thick panel behind which he was imprisoned. "You said you'd only be a moment—and it's been over ten minutes by most charitable estimate! Release me at once, as you agreed, and show me which way that Terran blackguard went!"

"Sure, sure, just take it easy, Mr. Premier," Blue soothed. "And it looks like our agreement needs a couple minor updates."

"Treachery!" Shish hissed. "Updates indeed! You entered into a solemn interplanetary pact to which I agreed only in its proper form."

"What form?" Blue snorted. "There's nothing on tape, remember? Anyways, the point is, we got to cut a Terry in—but he's got credentials."

"A vile Soft One?" The Groaci dignitary echoed stiffly.

"Have you, my dear Prince, taken leave of whatever rudimentary wits you formerly possessed?"

"Better hold the insults, Mr. Premier," Blue countered. "I'm still outside and you're still inside, remember?"

"See here, Blue," Shish came back in a more businesslike tone, "the essence of our scheme is simplicity itself: Whilst noble Groac completes her transferral of useful minerals from this cinder world, you of ruthless Boge will maintain the status quo—which preexisted Groacian discovery of the place, you'll recall, thus obviating mischievous charges of warmongering by my great nation—by the irreproachably equable device of supplying *both* factions with the necessary armaments, undeviatingly evenhandedly, except, of course, in those instances where the obstreperousness of the recipients themselves makes delivery awkward, if not impossible."

"Sure, Shish, all that part's OK," Blue interrupted the strident plea, "but now we got to figger a angle for old Retief. He can't hardly go back to his chief and tell him he let us cut him outa the action."

"True, one mustn't be greedy," Shish agreed, "so long as the principle of Groac's prior claim by right of discovery is in no way compromised."

4

Retief listened for another ten minutes to the wrangling of the two conspirators exchanging Yivshish before he entered the Q-chamber, paused to engage the manual lock on the outer hatch, and quietly advanced along the dim and cramped axial passage until he was directly behind the Bogan, crouched at the lazaret's ventilation grill.

"Tell His Supremacy he's got an appointment in town in about half an hour," Retief said, at which the Prince

uttered a yelp of alarm and leaped to his feet, causing
the overhead to ring like a bell as his horny skull
impacted it.

"Geeze, Retief, don't creep up on a guy like that," he
muttered. "If I wouldn't of had like nerves o' steel and
all, you coulda give me heart failure. Whattaya mean
'half a hour'?" It's a good two days like back to town,
even if you go in the right direction."

"Mr. Premier," Retief addressed the grill directly.
"Rescue is at hand. Please be prepared to explain Groac's
role in this affair as soon as we arrive at the Terran
chancery." Without awaiting a response, he returned to
the hatch and there fired a red flare. Nith arrived in
less than five seconds, accompanied by a hail of gravel.

"Where are they, Retief?" he demanded, going into a
traditional gunslinger's crouch, minus the gun.

"Relax, Mr. Ambassador," Retief urged. "If you'll
step inside and reassure His Supremacy that all is well,
we can get on with our planet saving."

"But *is* all indeed well?" Nith demanded uncertainly.
"After all, we're here, alone together, traditional antag-
onists, trapped in an underground maze, at the mercy
of all manner of brigand, dacoit, rebel, spook, and
native flesh eater—"

"True, and there's more," Retief agreed. "But that's
all the more reason to get on with it."

They returned to where the rogue prince and the
irate Groaci diplomat were wrangling noisily in the
cramped passage. Nith hurried forward to report to his
Chief of State, who replied hotly, "What's the meaning
of this outrage, Nith? By the way, aren't you my sister
Lish's husband's nephew or something?"

"Doubtless I would be, Supremacy," Nith conceded,
"were it not well known that nepotism does not exist in
our Groacian Foreign Service."

Ignoring the protests of the two, Retief herded them
along to the control deck, where he wedged them into

the navigation cubicle and took the operator's massive shock-mounted chair. After using the IR screens to scan the trap into which the big machine had blundered, he aimed the aft battery and fired a burst which caused the natural bore to collapse below him. Another burst fired forward blasted an aperture through which the great treads propelled the Yavac without difficulty.

"Your boys did a fair job of copying the Old Mark XV Bolo," Retief commented to Shish. "But if you'd used a Mark XX or later it would have had enough sense to blast its way out of here on its own."

"Our Groacian technical people regarded and still regard it as irresponsible in the extreme to delegate to a machine discretionary powers with regard to utilization of firepower," Shish retorted coldly. "Imagine, if you will, the contretemps which would result should such a device go rogue."

"I heard it happened once," Retief said, "not too long ago; but it worked out all right in the end, except for blowing a few minds by demonstrating what a disaster it would be if anybody ever lived up strictly to a campaign promise."

"Madness," Shish muttered. "After permitting myself to be decoyed here, largely at your own insistence, Nith," Shish railed, "I find myself assaulted, and imprisoned in a closet for an unconscionable period, only to be released by an interplanetary rascal of a fallen royalty with a price on his head, who urges devious schemes on me, supported, it appears, by haughty Terra with the assistance of none other than my own nephew-in-law, my chief diplomatic representative! It is not to be borne. . . ." He subsided, mumbling.

"Put that way, sir, it does sound bad," Nith conceded. "But look on the bright side: you're out of the broom closet, and we're on the move. We'll be back at the surface in a moment, and then we'll only be stranded in a wilderness full of cannibals and possibly the odd spook."

"Most comforting, I'm sure, Mr. Ambassador," Shish replied coldly. "I shall be sure to remember your cheerfulness under pressure at the Proceedings which will ensue so soon as I can convene a panel of reliable hanging judges."

"He's only joking, Retief," Nith explained. "Actually, he's grateful for the dramatic rescue effectuated by his loyal retainer's unswerving devotion to duty."

"He'd better be," Retief concurred. "After all, we're not clear yet, and accidents *do* happen."

"To be sure," Nith said crisply, as he offered his Premier a tissue to wipe away the tear which had appeared at the tip of that dignitary's eye stalk.

"Kneel, Nith, AE and MP," Shish said in a choked whisper. "Rise Sir Nith, Knight of the Order of the Legion of Winners, and to your bearings you may add as achievements the hook and crook or, plus a nice hike in the old pay packet. Now let's get the heck outa here."

5

As the battered but still potent Yavac ground its ponderous way across the last few yards of cracked stone at the lip of the bore, and watery dawn light gleamed dimly on the screens, a party of Creepy irregulars appeared, poking cautious eye stalks around protective rocks and screening brush. A few of the bolder ones brought up soot-stained tubes which belched blue, red, yellow, and green fire. When the machine failed to halt at this display, the troop dispersed, disappearing into near-invisible crevices, leaving their weapons scattered behind them. Retief retrieved and examined one. It was a Roman candle, made in Hong Kong.

It was a bumpy ten-minute ride to the clearing where Retief had concealed his borrowed Embassy car.

CHAPTER TEN

LESS THAN AN HOUR LATER, having settled the high-ranking official guests in comfortable quarters in the Embassy Officers' Club, Retief reported to the chancery, where Ambassador Pouncetrifle, bearing no more than a few nicely bandaged contusions, plus a slightly bruised eye, as evidence of his adventures, sat slumped behind his twelve-foot gold-trimmed desk, treasurewood, Chief of Mission, for the use of, glowering.

"Back so soon, Mr. Retief?" he grunted. "You'd have done well, my boy, to have remained among the cannibals; I've but now received a TWX via SWIFT that the Inspection Team is enroute, on their final leg; in fact they may well be in holding orbit even now. Spot of bother with the equipment; haven't yet talked personally with the Undersecretary, who, I understand, has sent one of his most valued deputies as Team Chief, the better to document my undoubted triumph as chief of ITCH, or so the TWX says." He crumpled the document and tossed it in the direction of the waste hopper.

"Odd about the SWIFT gear," he went on, as one willing to change the subject. "Seemed quite jammed; then, abruptly, it began disgorging socks, eye-stalk creams, dress greaves with jeweled sequins, some sort of brass cylinder things, well-worn classic paperbacks, and all that sort of stuff—as if someone had emptied a Groaci rubbish bin into the hopper."

"I suggest you look into the possibility of interference by the new baggage-handling system at the port, sir," Retief suggested. "And those cylinders will bear further study. But more to the point, the war is over."

Pouncetrifle nodded blandly. "Over, you say," he murmured, surreptitiously pushing a button under the edge of the desk. "No doubt, my boy, you've been under something of a strain—"

"At 9:00 A.M. sharp it will be," Retief amplified. "Then the annual war games begin, promptly at 9:01."

"War games!" Pouncetrifle yelled. "Ye gods, haven't these infernal Hithers and Nethers had enough of bombing and shooting and ambushing to satisfy them?"

"In a word, no," Retief supplied. "But there's a difference now that it's only a game. Instead of supplying their regular BANG line of live ammo, Boge has agreed to let their Acme Novelty Works handle the contract: lots of noise but no casualties."

"Splendid," Pouncetrifle purred. "Just as I planned; but does Boge know about this?"

"No less a personage than His Imperial Highness Lieutenant General the Prince of the Blue has sponsored the deal," Retief stated impressively.

"But I heard he'd been drummed out of the royal household!" Pouncetrifle yelped. "Disgraced! Exiled!"

"A base canard, my dear Ajax," an urbane voice cut in coolly, as Prince Blue, arrayed in full dress with medals and orders to the knee, strolled in from the anteroom.

"Ambassador Nith will never agree to this," Pouncetrifle wheezed. "He'll never agree, as deputy chairman of ITCH, to allow such a triumph to a Terran Chief of Mission."

"You're quite wrong, Ajax," Nith's breathy voice contradicted the Terran Ambassador's pronouncement. "Actually, I myself was instrumental in a small way in bringing about this most ingenious solution to our joint problems. Let the credit go to ITCH!"

"Done, Nith," Prouncetrifle cried and clasped hands with his rival. "But will your government accept it as a *fait accompli*?"

"Assuredly, Ajax. I'm dispatching a special envoy to Groac at once—via a distressed Groacian national whom I encountered in the jungle, as it happens. Chap named Shish, who'll be so grateful for repatriation that he'll represent our achievement in the most glowing terms to the Groacian press, eh, fellow?" He turned for confirmation to the bedraggled Groaci who had trailed him into the room.

"Quite, my dear Mr. Ambassador," Shish confirmed. "And I do hope to depart on the afternoon packet boat."

"Am I wrong, or has the shelling already diminished somewhat?" Pouncetrifle inquired rhetorically. "Oh, Mr. Retief, perhaps you'd best conduct a discreet reconnaissance among the former belligerents, just to insure that all parties have gotten the glad tidings of peace."

2

Retief withdrew, went to the Embassy garage, and commandeered the fast armed air car nominally assigned to the military attaché. He took off in an almost eerie stillness, climbed rapidly to cruise altitude, took a minute to tune the tightbeam finder to the personal code of the Hither Furtheronian Chief of State, and opened her up to full gate velocity.

Rocketing along at fifteen hundred feet, Retief had a superb view of the diminishing fireworks below. The Nether Furtheronian position in the hills north of town had apparently been expanded into a wide curve of armored units poised ready for the dusk assault that was to sweep the capital clear. To the west, Crawlie columns were massing for the couterstrike. At the point of juncture of the proposed assault lines, the lights of the Terran Embassy glowed forlornly.

Retief corrected course a degree and a half, still climbing rapidly, watching the quivering needles of the seek-and-find beam. The emerald-and-ruby glow of a set of navigation lights appeared a mile ahead, moving erratically at an angle to his course. He boosted the small flier to match altitudes, swung in on the other craft's tail. Close now, he could discern the bright-doped fabric-covered wings, the taut rigging wires, the brilliant orange blazon of the Hither Furtheronian national colors on the fuselage, above the ornate personal emblem of Air Chief Marshal Lib Glip. He could even make out the goggled features of the warrior Premier gleaming faintly in the greenish light from the instrument faces, his satsumatoned scarf streaming bravely behind him.

Retief maneuvered until he was directly above the unsuspecting radarless craft, then peeled off and hurtled past it on the left close enough to rock the light airplane violently in the buffeting slipstream. He came around in a hairpin turn, shot above the biplane as it banked right, did an abrupt left to pass under it, and saw a row of stars appear across the plastic canopy beside his head as the Crawlie ace made an inside turn, catching him with a burst from his machine guns.

Retief put the nose of the flier down, dived clear of the stream of lead, swung back and up in a tight curve, rolled out on the airplane's tail. Lib Glip, no mean pilot, put his ship through a series of vertical eights, snaprolls, Immelmanns, and falling leaves, to no avail. Retief held the courier boat glued to his tail almost close enough to brush the wildly wigwagging control surfaces.

After fifteen minutes of frantic evasive tactics, the Crawlie ship settled down to a straight speed run. Retief loafed alongside, pacing the desperate flier. When Lib Glip looked across at him, Retief made a downward motion of his hand and pointed at the ground. Then he eased over, placed himself directly above the bright-painted plane, and edged downward.

Below, he could see Lib Glip's face, staring upward through the cutout in the top wing; Retief lowered the boat another foot. The embattled Premier angled his plane downward. Retief stayed with him, forcing him down until the craft was racing along barely above the tops of the celery-shaped trees. A clearing appeared ahead. Retief dropped until his keel almost scraped the fuel tank atop Lib Glip's upper wing. The Crawlie, accepting the inevitable, throttled back, settled his ship in to a bumpy landing, and rolled to a stop just short of a rocky ridge. Retief dropped in and skidded to a halt beside him.

The enraged Premier was already out of his cockpit, waving a large clip-fed handgun, as Retief popped the hatch of the boat.

"What's the meaning of this?" the Crawlie yelled. "Who are you! How . . ." He broke off. "Hey, aren't you What's-His-Name, from the Terry Embassy?"

"Correct." Retief nodded. "I congratulate Your Excellency on your acute memory."

"What's the idea of this piece of unparalleled audacity?" the Crawlie leader barked. "Don't you know there's a war on? I was in the middle of leading a victorious air assault on those Creepy blue-bellies—"

"Really? I had the impression your squadrons were several miles to the north, tangling with an impressive armada of Creepy bombers and what seemed to be a pretty active fighter cover."

"Well, naturally I have to stand off at a reasonable distance in order to get the Big Picture," Lib Glip explained. "That still doesn't tell me why a Terry diplomat had the unvarnished gall to interfere with my movements! I've got a good mind to blast you full of holes and leave the explanations to my Chief of Propaganda!"

"I wouldn't try it," Retief suggested. "This little thing in my hand is a tight-beam blaster—not that there's any need for such implements among friendly associates."

"Armed diplomacy?" Lib Glip choked. "I've never heard of such a thing!"

"Oh, I'm off duty," Retief said. "This is just a personal call. There's a little favor I'd like to ask of you."

"A . . . favor? What is it?"

"Knock off this amateur war of yours."

"*Mine?*" Lib Glip looked astonished, an effect achieved by erecting the few head tendrils that had escaped from under his cap, while allowing all three eyes to droop. "I know you're new here," he acknowledged, "but even a greenhorn should know the war has been raging since antiquity, over a month ago. It's our great cultural heritage. Stop indeed! What reason would I have then for maintaining my stable of Spads, Nieuports, and Fokker Dr. I.'s?"

"Sport," Retief supplied. "A big planet-wide competition—minus the live ammunition."

"Even if I agreed, which is unthinkable," the Premier countered, "that rascal Barf would never agree. And who'd be left in possession of our glorious fatherland?"

"I'm sure those details could be worked out. By the way, with whom were you on the way to rendezvous?"

"Rondy-what?" Lib Glip's eye stems snapped upright in an expression of shocked indignation, while his head tendrils went slack. He brushed aside a few of the latter which had fallen over his low, seamed forehead. "You suggest that I, Premier and War Minister of all Hither Furtheron, would sneak out on a battle to parley with the enemy?"

"Not a bad idea," Retief commented. "But this really isn't the time for gossip. Let's go. Your ship or mine?"

"Go where, Terry interloper? Do you mean to compound your felonies by kidnapping me?"

"Sure, why not?" Retief reassured the agitated statesman. "Just a short trip out to the foothills."

"Terry, are you mad? The foothills are aswarm with cannibals, enemy troops, and all manner of spooks. No one has ever penetrated there and returned to tale the tell—tell the tale, I mean."

"I have," Retief said quietly. "Maybe you'd like me to show you."

"That tears it, Retief," Lib Glip announced in tones of doom. "Why not just let me go up and tear the wings off in a 9-G?"

"Because," Retief informed him, "somebody's being a little too tricky to suit me. And I still have a few ideas I want to check out."

"Look, Terry," the Premier said desperately, "we got a swell war going here. We *like* it; it's our traditional pastime. Besides, if we stop now, we'll never know who would've won, Barf or me."

"You might give some consideration to the Furtheronian population," Retief suggested. "While you're having fun flying this crate, they're getting the overkill from the bombardment."

"So what?" Lib Glip demanded. "All I'm concerned about is having a good time personally."

"I congratulate you on your candor, Mr. Premier. But how long will the fun go on after your alien bosses have got what they want?"

My bosses? It is to laugh. You forget *I'm* Premier here."

"Unless Barf slips a swifty over on you," Retief corrected. "But stop and think—who was it who set you up in business in the first place, told you who the enemy was; and all that?"

"If you're suggesting that my dear friend and adviser, Siss, the GSO at the Groaci Embassy, was in some way influencing me, you're quite wrong. All he ever did was offer suggestions."

"And any time you didn't follow 'em, supplies started to run short, eh?"

"Well, there were a few occasions—but this is bootless talk, Retief. It's that warmonger Barf who's causing me all the trouble. In any case, you didn't follow me here simply to gossip, I assume?"

"There *is* something else," Retief conceded.

Lib Glip eyed him warily. "And what, may I inquire, might that be?"

"I'd like a ride in your airplane," Retief stated bluntly.

"You mean you forced me to the ground just to . . . to . . ."

"Right. And there's not much time, so I think we'd better be going."

"I've heard of airplane fanciers, but this is fantastic! Still, now that you're here, I may as well point out to you that she has a sixteen-cylinder V-head mill, swinging a twenty-four-lamination sword-wood prop, synchronized 9 mm. lead spitters, twin spotlights, low-pressure tires *with* brakes, foamrubber seats, steerable tail wheel, real instruments—no idiot lights—and a ten-coat handrubbed lacquer job. Sharp, eh? And wait till you see the built-in bar."

"A magnificent craft, Your Excellency." Retief admired the machine. "I'll take the rear cockpit and tell you which way to steer."

"You'll tell *me*—"

"I have the blaster, remember?"

Lib Glip grunted and climbed into his seat. Retief strapped in behind him. The Premier started up, taxied to the far end of the field, gunned the engine, and lifted off into the tracer-streaked sky.

3

"That's him." Retief pointed to a lone vehicle perched on a hilltop above a lively fire-fight, clearly visible now against a landscape bathed in the bluish light of the newly risen crescent of Moon Five, whose lower curve was at the horizon, the upper halfway to Zenith.

"See here, this is dangerous," Lib Glip called over the whine of air thrumming the rigging wires as the plane glided down in a wide spiral. "That car packs plenty of firepower, and—" He broke off and banked sharply as vivid flashes of blue light stuttered suddenly from below. The brilliant light of a laser finder beam glinted from the armored car's elevated guns as they tracked the descending craft.

"Put a short burst across his bow," Retief said. "But be careful not to damage him."

"Why, that's Barf's personal car!" the Crawlie burst out. "I can't fire on him, or he might—that is, we have a sort of gentlemen's agreement—"

"Better do it," Retief said, watching the stream of tracers from below arc closer as Barf found the range. "Apparently he feels that at this range, the agreement's not in effect."

Lib Glip angled the nose of the craft toward the car and activated the twin lead spitters. A row of pockmarks appeared in the turf close beside the car as the plane swooped low over it.

"That'll teach him to shoot without looking," Lib Glip commented.

"Circle back and land," Retief called. The Premier grumbled but complied. The plane came to a halt a hundred feet from the armored car, which turned to pin the craft down in the beams of its headlights. Lib Glip rose, holding both hands overhead, and jumped down.

"I hope you realize what you're doing, Retief," he said bitterly. "Forcing me to place myself in the hands of this barbarian is flagrant interference in Furtheronian internal affairs! See here, if he's been crooked enough to offer you a bribe, I give you my word as a statesman that I'm crookeder: I'll up his offer—"

"Now, now, Your Excellency, this is merely a friendly get-together," Retief said reassuringly. "Let's go over and relieve the general's curiosity before he decides to clear his guns again."

As Retief and the Crawlie came up, a hatch opened at the top of the heavy car and one ocular stalk of the Creepy generalissimo emerged cautiously, followed in a moment by the other two. The three eyes looked over the situation; then the medal-hung rib cage of the officer appeared.

"Here, what's all this shooting?" he inquired in an irritated tone. "Is that you, Glip? Come out to arrange surrender terms, I suppose. Could have gotten yourself hurt—"

"Surrender my maternal great-aunt Bunny!" the Crawlie shrilled. "I was abducted by armed force and brought here at gunpoint!"

"Eh?" Barf peered at Retief. "I thought you'd brought Retief along as an impartial witness to the very liberal amnesty terms I'm prepared to offer—"

"Gentlemen, if you'll suspend hostilities for just a moment or two," Retief put in, "I believe I can explain the purpose of this meeting. I confess the delivery of invitations may have been a trifle informal, but when you hear the news, I'm sure you'll agree it was well worth the effort."

"What news?" both combatants echoed.

Retief drew a heavy, fan-shaped paper from an inner pocket. "The war news," he said crisply. "I happened to be rummaging through some old papers and came across a full account of the story behind the present conflict. I'm going to give it to the press first thing in the morning, but I felt you gentlebeings should get the word first, so that you can realign your war aims accordingly."

"Realign?" Barf said cautiously.

"Story?" Lib Glip queried.

"I assume, of course, that you're aware of the facts of history?" Retief paused, paper in hand.

"Why, ah, as a matter of fact . . . ," Barf said.

"I don't believe I actually, er . . . ," the Crawlie Premier harrumphed.

"But, of course, us Creepies don't need to delve into the past to find cause for the present crusade for restoration of national honor," Barf pointed out.

"Hither Furtheron has plenty of up-to-date reasons for her determination to drive the invaders from the fair soil of her homeland," Lib Glip snorted.

"Of course—but this will inspire the troops," Retief pointed out. "Imagine how morale will zoom, Mr. Premier," he went on, addressing the Crawlie, "when it becomes known that the original Crawlies were a group of government employees from Boondock, en route to the new penal colony here on Furtheron."

"Government employees, eh?" Lib Glip frowned. "I suppose they were high-ranking civil servants, that sort of thing?"

"No," Retief demured. "As a matter of fact, they were prison guards, with the rank of GB 19."

"Prison guards? GB 19?" Barf growled. "Why, that

was the lowest rank in the entire ancient government payroll!"

"Certainly there can be no charge of snobbery there," Retief said in tones of warm congratulation.

A choking sound issued from Lib Glip's speaking aperture. "Pardon my mirth," he gasped. "But after all the tripe we've heard—eek—eek—about the glorious past of Nether Furtheron— "

"And that brings us to the Crawlies," Retief put in smoothly. "They, it appears, were traveling on the same vessel at the time of the outbreak—or should I say break-out."

"Same vessel?"

Retief nodded. "After all, the guards had to have something to guard."

"You mean . . . ?"

"That's right," Retief said cheerfully. "The Crawlie founding fathers were a consignment of criminals sentenced to transportation for life. They revolted and took refuge in the caves."

General Barf uttered a loud screech of amusement and slapped himself on the thigh.

"I don't know why I didn't guess that intuitively!" he chortled. "How right you were, Retief, to dig out this charming intelligence!"

"See here!" Lib Glip shrilled. "You can't publish defamatory information of that sort! I'll take it to court—"

"And give the whole Galaxy a good laugh over the breakfast trough," Barf agreed. "A capital suggestion, my dear Glip!"

"Anyway, I don't believe it! Is a tissue of lies! A bunch of malarky! A dirty, lousy falsehood and a base canard!"

"Look for yourself," Retief offered the documents. Lib Glip fingered the heavy parchment, peered at the complicated characters.

"It seems to be printed in Old Crawlie," he grumbled. "I'm afraid I never went in for dead languages."

"General?" Retief handed over the papers. Barf glanced at them and handed them back, still chuckling. "No, sorry, I'll have to take your word for it. And I do."

"Fine, then," Retief said. "There's just one other little point. You gentlemen have been invading and counterinvading now for upward of two centuries, standard reckoning. Naturally, in that length of time the records have grown a trifle confused. However, I believe both sides are in agreement that the original home areas have changed hands, and that the Crawlies are occupying Creepy territory, while the Creepies have taken over the original Crawlie home territory."

Both belligerents nodded, one smiling, one glum.

"That's nearly correct," Retief said, "with just one minor correction. It isn't the land areas that have changed hands; it's the identities of the participants in the war."

"Eh?"

"What did you say?"

"It's true, gentlemen," Retief said solemnly. "You and your troops, General, are descendants of the original Crawlies; and your people"—he inclined his head to the Crawlie Premier—"inherit the mantle of Creepyship."

"But this is ghastly," General Barf groaned. "I've devoted half a lifetime to instilling a correct attitude toward Crawlies in my chaps. How can I face them now?"

"Me, a Creepy?" Lib Glip shuddered. "Still," he said as if to himself, "we *were* the guards, not the prisoners. I suppose on the whole we'll be able to console ourselves with the thought that we aren't representatives of the criminal class—"

"Criminal class!" Barf snorted. "By Pud, sir, I'd rather trace my descent from an honest victim of the venal lackeys of a totalitarian regime than claim kinship with a pack of hireling turnkeys!"

"Lackeys, eh? I suppose that's what a pack of sticky-fingered pickpockets would think of a decent servant of law and order!"

"Now, gentlemen, I'm sure these trifling differences can be settled peaceably—" Retief interceded.

"Ah-hah, so *that's* it!" Barf crowed. "You've dug the family skeletons out of the closet in the mistaken belief it would force us to suspend hostilities!"

"By no means, General," Retief said blandly. "Naturally, you'll want to exchange supplies of propaganda leaflets and go right on with the crusade. But of course you'll have to swap homelands too."

"How's that?"

"Certainly. The CDT can't stand by and see the entire populations of two homelands condemned to live on in exile on foreign soil. I'm sure I can arrange for a cadre of Corps beadles to supervise the transfer of population—"

"Just a minute," Lib Glip cut in. "You mean you're going to repatriate all us, uh, Creepies to Nether Furtheron, and give Hither Furtheron to these rascally, ah, Crawlies?"

"Minus the slanted adjectives, a very succinct statement of affairs."

"Now, just a minute," Barf put in. "You don't expect me to actually settle down on this dust-ridden surface full time, do you? With *my* sinus condition?"

"Me, live down there in some damp cave?" Lib Glip hooked a thumb groundward. "Why, my asthma would kill me in three weeks! That's why I've always stuck to lightning raids instead of long-drawn-out operations!"

"Well, gentlemen, the CDT certainly doesn't wish to be instrumental in undermining the health of two such cooperative statesmen . . ."

"Ah . . . how do you mean cooperative?" Barf voiced the question cautiously.

"You know how it is, General," Retief said. "When one has impatient superiors breathing down one's neck, it's a little hard to achieve really full rapport with even the most laudable aspirations of others. However, if Ambassador Pouncetrifle were in a position to show the inspectors a peaceful planet by this afternoon, it might very well influence him to defer the evacuation until further study of the question."

"But . . . my two-pronged panzer thrust," the general flattered. "The crowning achievement of my military career . . ."

"My magnificently coordinated one-two counterstrike . . ." Lib Glip wailed. "It cost me two months' golf to work out those logistics!"

"I might even go so far as to hazard a guess," Retief pressed on, "that in the excitement of the announcement of the armistice, I might even forget to publish my historical findings."

"Hmmm," Barf eyed his colleague. "It might be a trifle tricky, at that, to flog up the correct degree of anti-Creepy enthusiasm on such short notice."

"Yes, I can foresee a certain amount of residual sympathy for Crawlie institutions lingering on for quite some time," Lib Glip agreed.

"I'd still have the use of my car, of course," the general mused. "As well as my personal submarine, my plushed-up transport, and my various copters, unicycles, hoppers, and sedan chairs for use on rough terrain."

"And, of course," Retief put in, "it would be your duty to keep the armed forces at the peak of condition with annual War Games."

Lib Glip nodded and glanced at the general. "In fact, we might even work out some sort of scheme for joint maneuvers, eh, Barf, just to keep the recruits sharpened up."

"Not a bad idea, Glip. I might try for the single-engine pursuit trophy myself."

"Ha! Nothing you've got can touch my little beauty here when it comes to close-in combat work."

"I'm sure we can work out the details later, gentlemen," Retief said. "I must be getting back to the Embassy now. I hope your formal joint announcement will be along well before press time."

"Well . . ." Barf looked at Lib Glip. "Under the circumstances . . ."

"I suppose we can work out something," the latter assented glumly.

"I'll give you a lift back in my car, Retief," General Barf offered. "Just wait till you see how she handles on flat ground, my boy . . ."

4

In the pink light of dawn, Ambassador Pouncetrifle and his staff waited on the breeze-swept ramp to greet the party of portly officials descending from the Corps lighter.

"Well, Ajax," the senior member of the inspection team commented, looking around the immaculate environs of the port. "Seems we didn't need to delay landing after all. It looks as though perhaps some of those rumors we heard about a snag in the disarmament talks were a trifle exaggerated."

Pouncetrifle smiled blandly. "A purely routine affair. It was merely necessary for me to drop a few words in certain auditory organs, and the rest followed naturally. There aren't many of these local chieftains who can stand up to the veiled hint of a Pouncetrifle."

"Actually, I think it's time we began considering you for a more substantive post, Ajax," the Chief Inspector confided. "I've had my eye on you for quite some time . . ." The great men moved away, fencing cautiously.

Beside Retief, a tiny, elderly local in striped robes shook his head sadly.

"That was a dirty trick, Retief, getting yourself a pardon directly from young Lib Glip. I don't get much excitement over there in the stacks, you know."

"Things will be better from now on," Retief assured the oldster. "I think you can expect to see the library opened to the public in the near future."

"Oh, boy," the curator exclaimed. "Just what I've been wishing for, for years now! Plenty of snazzy young coeds coming in, eager to butter an old fellow up in return for a guaranteed crib sheet! Thanks, lad! I can see brighter days acoming!" He hurried away.

"Retief—" Magnan plucked at his sleeve. "I've heard a number of fragmentary rumors regarding events leading up to the truce; I trust your absence from the group for an hour or two early this evening was in no way connected with the various kidnappings, thefts, trespasses, assaults, blackmailings, breakings and enterings, and other breaches of diplomatic usage said to have occurred."

"Mr. Magnan, what a suggestion." Retief took out a fan-folded paper and began tearing it into strips.

"Sorry, Retief. I should have known better. By the way, isn't that an Old Creepy manuscript you're destroying?"

"This? Why, no, it's an old Chinese menu I came across tucked in the classified despatch binder." He dropped the scraps in a refuse bin.

"Oh. Well, why don't you join me in a quick bite before tonight's briefing for the inspectors? The Ambassador plans to give them his standard five-hour introductory chat, followed by a quick run-through of the voucher files—"

"No thanks. I have an appointment with Lib Glip to check out one of his new-model pursuit ships. It's the red one over there, fresh from the factory."

"Well, I suppose you have to humor him, inasmuch as he's Premier." Magnan cocked an eye at Retief. "I confess I don't understand how it is you get on such familiar terms with these bigwigs, restricted as your official duties are to preparation of reports in quintuplicate."

"I think it's merely a sort of informal manner I adopt in meeting them," Retief said. He waved and headed across the runway to where the little ship waited, sparkling in the morning sun.